The Lilac Bouquet

Center Point
Large Print

Also by Carolyn Brown and available from
Center Point Large Print:

The Wedding Pearls
The Lullaby Sky
The Barefoot Summer

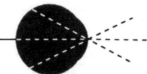

**This Large Print Book carries the
Seal of Approval of N.A.V.H.**

The Lilac Bouquet

CAROLYN BROWN

CENTER POINT LARGE PRINT
THORNDIKE, MAINE

This Center Point Large Print edition
is published in the year 2017 by arrangement with
Amazon Publishing, www.apub.com.

Orignially published in the United States by
Amazon Publishing, 2017.

The text of this Large Print edition is unabridged.
In other aspects, this book may vary
from the original edition.
Printed in the United States of America
on permanent paper.
Set in 16-point Times New Roman type.

ISBN: 978-1-68324-566-7

Library of Congress Cataloging-in-Publication Data

Names: Brown, Carolyn, 1948- author.
Title: The lilac bouquet / Carolyn Brown.
Description: Large print edition. | Thorndike, Maine :
    Center Point Large Print, 2017.
Identifiers: LCCN 2017035562 | ISBN 9781683245667
    (hardcover : alk. paper)
Subjects: LCSH: Large type books. | GSAFD: Love stories.
Classification: LCC PS3552.R685275 L545 2017 | DDC 813/.54—dc23
LC record available at https://lccn.loc.gov/2017035562

This book is for my husband
and my best friend, Charles C.
for sharing life and love with me
for more than fifty years.

CHAPTER ONE

There were no secrets in Hickory, Texas—except for whatever was between Seth Thomas, Jesse Grady, and Tandy Massey. And since they were now in their early eighties, it might be that they'd take that secret to the grave with them. Usually Emmy Jo Massey's grandmother, Tandy, laughed off rumors, but that night she was doing a tap dance on her soapbox.

"Over my damn dead body." Tandy shook a wooden spoon at her great-granddaughter. "You are not going to work for Seth Thomas in any form or fashion, and I mean it. And you damn sure are not going to live in that house."

"It's good money, Granny, and it's only for two months. I don't have to do any actual nursing work. I've been hired as his assistant. That means I drive him wherever he needs to go, fetch and get for him, make phone calls, write letters—that kind of thing. The money will pay for my dream wedding," Emmy Jo said.

Tandy went back to stirring the brownie batter. "I said no and I mean it."

In her heyday Tandy had black hair and snapping green eyes. Now her hair had mostly gone gray and her eyes had faded, but then she was past eighty. Anyone in town could testify, and would be glad to do so, about Tandy's rough living up until about twenty years ago, when she'd found Jesus.

To Emmy Jo, her grandmother was ten feet tall and bulletproof, but she was also meaner than a junkyard dog when she got mad. Once Tandy made up her mind, no power—not God, Jesus, the Holy Spirit, or Lucifer—could make her change it.

There weren't many times that Tandy had gotten that look in her eyes. The first was when Emmy Jo was thirteen. Tandy had sat her down at the kitchen table and told her that if she ever got pregnant, she was on her own, because Tandy was not raising another child. Icy-cold shivers had run down Emmy Jo's backbone at the time, even worse than when she watched scary movies with her friend Diana. The tone in Tandy's voice left no doubt that she was speaking the pure, unadulterated truth.

So far, so good—Emmy Jo had not gotten pregnant.

It didn't take a degree in psychology to understand why Tandy was adamant about the baby business. Her daughter, Rose, had gotten pregnant out of wedlock, had the baby, and then before her child, Crystal, was a year old, had been killed by a drunk driver, leaving her child for Tandy to raise. Then Crystal had gotten pregnant. She had planned to marry the now-gone father of her baby, but three days after Emmy Jo was born, she died when a blood clot lodged in her heart. And Tandy had another baby to raise.

The second time Tandy went into that mode was when Emmy Jo started dating Logan Grady. That night she'd thrown a hissy fit that would have scared the horns off the devil. It was the first time and wouldn't be the last time that Tandy danced on the soapbox on that issue. She also hated Logan's grandpa, Jesse Grady, with a red-hot passion. She wouldn't say why. When Emmy Jo badgered her for a legitimate reason, Tandy usually glared at her and cussed loud enough to blister the paint on the kitchen cabinets.

This was the third time that they'd butted heads. Emmy Jo was not backing down. She leaned across the kitchen bar until her nose was only inches from Tandy's. "I'm twenty-one years old. I can work for him if I want to."

The spoon stayed in the batter, but Tandy's finger shot out like a bullet. "You know how I feel about Seth Thomas. Why in the hell did you agree to work for him?"

Emmy Jo backed up a couple of feet. "Because I work at the Hickory Health Care Company and I'll lose my job if I don't hold up my end of the bargain. And because I need the money for my wedding. There's two reasons—are you happy?"

Tandy's old eyes narrowed in a bed of wrinkles.

"Why can't you just go to the courthouse and get married?"

"A church wedding is the real deal. It says that . . ." She paused.

"It don't say jack squat. You only need a marriage license and someone to say the words," Tandy said with a coldness that sank into Emmy Jo's bones.

"It means more than that to me, Granny. It means that my kids will really be legitimate, that no one in school can ever whisper the word *bastard* and giggle behind their hand. It means the whole world to me that everyone knows for a fact that Logan and I are married and that there is no doubt."

"Why would there be a doubt?" Tandy asked.

"There'd always be questions about whether Logan and I were really married if we went to the courthouse. If I have my dream wedding, then by golly, everyone will be there to see the preacher say the words, and those that aren't can sure enough go hear all the other folks in town talk about how pretty it was," Emmy Jo argued. "Why do you hate Seth Thomas so much, anyway?"

"That is my business, not yours." Tandy's gaze shot daggers toward Emmy Jo.

"Why?" Emmy Jo wrapped her arms around her body in an effort to steel herself.

"Don't intend to explain or talk about it any

more. Why do you have to marry Jesse Grady's grandson, anyway? You know I don't like that family," Tandy said with her characteristic bluntness.

"Because I love him, and you are changing the subject like you always do. I signed a contract to work as Seth's assistant for two months and I will honor it."

Tandy poured the batter into a pan and slid it into the oven. "Tell Seth's sister, Nora, that you changed your mind. She's a good person. She'll understand. You haven't started the job, so the contract can be shredded. Someone else can be his assistant."

"How do you know Nora? Did y'all go to school together or something?" Emmy Jo tried again as she licked the spoon Tandy had used to stir the brownies.

"Wash that bowl when you get finished, and don't test me," Tandy barked. "I'm going to bingo at the church tonight. Take them brownies out when the timer goes off. You going to be here when I get home?"

Emmy Jo shrugged. "I'll be here until the brownies get done."

"Turn off the oven when they're finished. House burns down, it'll be your fault." Tandy shuffled toward her bedroom to change into her red knit pants and lucky floral shirt to go to bingo.

Emmy Jo flopped down on the worn sofa,

leaned her head back, and shut her eyes. Lord, what a mess! No one—not even Diana—could talk her out of starting the job tomorrow. Her eyes opened to scan the place that had been her home her entire life. Tandy had bought the small trailer forty years ago after she'd won a big bingo pot one night. Emmy Jo's mother was just a baby at the time, so it had seen her raised and then Emmy Jo.

Once a bright blue on the outside, it had sun bleached to almost white, but it was the best-kept trailer in the whole place. Not a weed grew anywhere near Tandy's place. The bloodred roses beside the porch and the flower beds were so pretty that they could have been featured in a magazine. Once a year the porch got a fresh coat of paint, and Tandy did her spring cleaning religiously. Dust and mold had no more place in Tandy's heart than Seth Thomas or Jesse Grady.

"What is it about those two old guys that sets her off so bad?" Emmy Jo wondered out loud. "Maybe I can figure it out while I'm working for Seth."

She headed past the utility room to the other end of the trailer, where her bedroom was located. Opening the only suitcase that she owned, she threw in as much clothing as she could and still shut the lid. Then she got the box of trash bags from the kitchen and proceeded to fill one to the brim, tossing in all her bridal magazines and her wedding book at the end.

"I'm leaving now," Tandy yelled. "Don't forget them brownies." The door shut, and the engine of Tandy's fifteen-year-old Ford rattled into life.

Not wanting another lecture or ultimatum, Emmy Jo waited until she couldn't hear the car and hauled her possessions to her ten-year-old Chevy, crammed part of them into the trunk, and the rest into the backseat. Her best friend, Diana, would let her crash there for one night. Emmy Jo sure didn't want to stay in the trailer tonight and put up with her granny's cussing and arguing. She stiffened her quivering upper lip. Maybe in a few days, or a week at the most, Tandy would start to miss Emmy Jo and things could go back to normal.

And if she doesn't? that nagging voice in her head asked.

She always comes around, Emmy Jo argued.

She pulled her phone from her purse and hit "Speed Dial" to call her fiancé, Logan Grady, but it went straight to voice mail. Sometimes the reception wasn't real good outside the trailer, so she tried twice more before she gave up and tossed the phone over on the passenger seat. She was backing out of the narrow drive when she remembered the brownies. She braked and hurried back inside just as the timer went off.

Allowing time for hitting the single traffic light on Main Street, and maybe having to actually

13

come to a full stop at the four-way, it took five minutes to travel from the trailer court to Diana's place. That evening the town's single night policeman decided to fall in behind her.

"Dammit!" She slapped the steering wheel as she kept the speed at twenty-five miles an hour. No doubt about it, Tandy had called her best friend, Henry Clary, who worked as a reserve police officer, and the old coot would report back to Tandy. He'd probably even seen her loading her things into the car.

Emmy Jo got out of her car and waved at Henry Clary as he drove past in the only squad car the Hickory Police Department owned. Seething and wanting to get inside to tell Diana what had happened, she rang the doorbell, but no one answered—not even after she leaned on the thing six times.

The lights were on and she could hear the television. Picturing Diana with earbuds in her ears and the music turned up, Emmy Jo reached for her phone and then realized it was in the car. She shivered as she ran down the porch steps and slid into the driver's seat. She hit Diana's "Speed Dial." No answer, but a flutter behind the living room curtains said that someone was home. She dialed the number again, and Diana answered on the second ring.

"You cannot stay here, Emmy Jo, not even one night."

"Well, hello, how are you doing, what's going on in your world, too?" Emmy Jo said.

"Don't be a smart-ass. I've stood up for you for years. I even got you the job at Hickory Health, remember?" Strange, but Diana's voice sounded a lot like Tandy's.

"And I've done the same for you. That's what friends do."

The whole world had gone crazy. Her best friend had never turned her away.

"Friends also tell you when you are about to make a huge mistake," Diana said.

"So if I go through with this job, I'm not welcome in your house anymore?" Emmy Jo asked.

"I didn't say that."

Emmy Jo had her hand on the "End" button, but she couldn't push it. "What are you saying, then?"

"That I'm not going to make this easy for you. You can't stay here tonight. I don't agree with you doing this job. Two whole months up in that place, living there . . ." Diana paused. "Don't do it. He's an old recluse, and my mama says that he's always been—"

"Been what?" Emmy Jo asked.

"Smart but a little odd. There's just something strange, and I don't think you should be around him," Diana said. "So if you are going to be stubborn, then you can't stay here."

"Tough love?" Emmy Jo snapped.

"Call it what you want. Drive over to Graham and get a hotel for tonight if you are determined to do this thing. Or be smart and go home and call it off," Diana said.

"You got any idea why this is such a big thing? It's only a two-month position, not a contract to work in a mental institution for the criminally insane."

"You know what they say about Seth Thomas's mama."

"I also know what they say about my granny," Emmy Jo said. "There's got to be something a lot deeper, maybe something that even the best gossip hounds in Hickory don't know about. Logan's grandpa and Seth are the only folks I know of that Granny despises. Maybe I'll figure out why while I'm working up there."

"Whatever it is, it don't need to be dug up. 'Bye now."

The steering wheel took a pounding. And the words that came from Emmy Jo's mouth were so hot they came close to fogging the windows. *Dammit!* This was not fair.

She had been sure she could sweet-talk her way into the house and that Diana would let her stay. Now she'd have to go to the hotel after all. That would take money from her wedding fund.

She sighed and checked for any phone messages, hoping that Diana had told her to park around back and sneak in through the garage door. Her hopes soared when she saw there were three messages but plummeted when she saw they were all from Logan.

"Well, crap!" She gazed up at the twinkling stars. "That's not even nice. I'm sorry, God. I love Logan and I'm glad that he sent messages, but I don't want to drive to Graham tonight."

The first message said that Logan and Jack had gone fishing but caught nothing. The second one said he loved her and was on his way back into town. The third asked her to call him as soon as she could.

"So that's why he didn't answer when I called. There's no reception on the creek." She groaned as she pulled over to the side of the road and hit his number.

"Where are you? Jack just talked to Diana and—"

She butted in when he paused. "I'm not giving up this job."

"Let's just go to the courthouse tomorrow and get married. We're both over twenty-one and we don't need a big wedding. I love you, Emmy Jo, and I'm worried about you," Logan begged.

"I love you, too, but I'm having my wedding. These two months of work will bring in enough that I can buy everything we'd like. Since it's a twenty-four-hour job, five days a week, Ruth is paying me the same as if I'd worked three shifts

17

a day. Do you even realize how much money that is? It's the equivalent of six months' paychecks in only two, and I won't pay for rent or food. This whole town will be invited to our wedding to see we are doing things right." Saying no to Logan had never been easy, but this time her heels were set.

"You are one stubborn redhead," he chuckled. "Want to meet at the park?"

"Sounds good. We can see if that might be a good place for a June wedding. Give me ten minutes to get turned around and drive back to town." She'd have to be strong, or else he'd wear her down with his deep Texas drawl.

"They've got peanut parfaits half price tonight. We could sit at the picnic table and eat while we talk venues for the wedding."

Not even an oversize sundae was going to make her change her mind. He'd have a better chance if they shared the hotel room that night than ice cream.

She parked beside his truck, checked her reflection in the rearview to reapply lipstick, and then got out of the car and headed toward the picnic bench. He waved, and her pulse kicked up a notch. After all this time, she still got butterflies in her stomach when she saw him. Six feet tall, dark haired and green eyed, Logan didn't look a thing like the men in his family. They were all blonds, neither short nor tall, and built.

• • •

"I'm going to miss seeing you every night." Logan's mouth went dry at the sight of her.

"It's only for two months, and I get Tuesdays and Thursdays off from eight in the morning until five in the afternoon." She walked into his open arms and wrapped her arms around his neck. His heart skipped a beat and then raced ahead. He hugged her tightly and then stepped back just enough that he could tip up her chin with a fist. Her long lashes fluttered, and her tongue flicked out to moisten her lips. Time stopped, and like always, when their lips met in a passionate kiss, he felt as if they were in a vacuum—completely alone and secluded. When the string of kisses ended, he groaned and pulled her toward the old wooden picnic bench.

"I'd rather make out all night," he said, "but we'd better start eating or it's going to melt. You know it's a sin to waste ice cream, and, Emmy Jo, I'm only off every other Saturday afternoon and Sunday. How are we ever going to see each other if you take the job?"

"You get half a day through the week when you work Saturday morning, right? Take it on Tuesday or Thursday and we can have that time together, plus on those two days I'll meet you for lunch," she said.

"Evenings are going to be long. What if you let me help pay for the wedding and didn't have to work the full two months?"

19

"That's not proper. The bride's family pays for the wedding." She sat down at the table and dug down deep into the sundae. "Mmm, this is so cold, you might need to kiss me some more to keep me from freezing."

"Oh, honey, we can't let that happen." He cupped her cheeks in his hands and kissed her again, tasting ice cream and the sweetness that was just naturally Emmy Jo. "Think that will do it?" he whispered.

"I'm not sure. Brain freeze might be setting in." She smiled against his lips.

"Well, we'll have to take care of that." He pushed her hair back and lowered his mouth to hers again. "I could do this all night."

"We should take this to the hotel," she panted.

He shook his head. "I can't tonight, darlin'. Wish I could, but it's not possible."

"Tough love?" she asked.

He cocked his head to one side. "What?"

"Diana won't let me stay at her place, and now you are turning down a night with me at the hotel. Are you playin' the tough-love card, too?"

"No, I have to spend the evening with Grandpa," he said. "Besides, tomorrow is my morning to work the drive-through window, and it opens an hour earlier than the bank. And if I go to the hotel with you, neither of us will get any sleep. But I really don't want you to work for Seth. Please change your mind. My grandpa says

Seth is strange, and I worry about you being up there."

"You are the second person tonight that's said that about him."

"Was the other one Tandy?" That mean old gal probably hated Logan even worse than she did Seth and Jesse combined. That his relationship with Emmy Jo had survived had certainly been in spite of Tandy Massey. She'd tried every way in the books to break them up.

"No, she says things a lot stronger about him and your grandpa." Emmy Jo laughed.

"So?"

"What?" she asked as she took a small bite of ice cream.

"Who said that Seth was strange? We all really did think that place was haunted when we were kids."

"Diana told me," she answered. "And she won't let me stay with her tonight unless I give up the job. I'm not doing that. I'd shovel crap out of his horse barn for the money I'd make. It's going to give us a fabulous wedding. And I promise, if I see a ghost, I'm out of there."

Logan chuckled and then laughed out loud. Emmy Jo could always turn a situation into something humorous. Poor old Seth might be getting more than he wanted when she arrived at his mansion up there on the hill overlooking Hickory.

"Does he have a horse barn? Maybe the ghosts are hiding in there," Logan teased.

"You know rattling chains would scare the horses, but if they do I'll scoot right on home to Tandy and listen to her tell me that she was right eighty times a day," she answered.

He brushed a soft kiss across her lips. "One more time and then I won't mention it again tonight. Will you please not do this?"

"Logan, I would die for you. I would fight a forest fire for you or face down a tornado to save your life, but I am going up there on the hill tomorrow morning and I'm going to do the job. This wedding is important to me, and not even you can talk me out of getting that money."

"You work with a dozen women who'd jump at the chance to make that much money in such a short time," he said in a last-ditch effort to convince her that this was a bad idea.

Her pretty red ponytail flipped back and forth when she shook her head. "When Mr. Thomas's sister called to make the offer, my boss asked everyone in the place, starting with the most senior. I was the last one on the list. There is no one else. Now it's become as much about principle as the money." She stopped long enough to eat two bites of ice cream before she went on. "Why the big fuss? He's an old man who's broken his hip and needs a helper. If it was Henry Clary, they'd give me medals instead of grief, so what's the big deal?"

"I will support your decision, but I don't agree with it," he said.

She covered his hand with hers. "Darlin', we have been through far worse than this—your parents don't like me, my granny doesn't like you. It's like Romeo and Juliet, though those two knew why their families were at war, at least. We don't even get that much. But we are strong as steel, and don't you forget it. Even if Seth is an oddball and strange, I can endure it for two months."

"I wish I could take you home with me." He mentally kicked himself for not moving into the trailer with his friend Jack when they came back to Hickory. If he'd only done that rather than moving into the church's garage apartment, there would be no problem with her spending the night with him.

She rolled her big round eyes toward the stars. "That would go over about as well as prom night."

Logan shivered at the memory of when Tandy caught him kissing Emmy Jo good-night after his senior prom. He'd thought she might really fire that sawed-off shotgun she'd waved around when she flipped on the porch light.

"It was not pretty," Emmy Jo said. "But back to the job issue. Nora said I'll have a room on the second floor with my own bathroom. Mr.

Thomas never goes up there, and with a broken hip, I don't see how he could, anyway."

"Will you promise me that if you feel threatened or weird, you'll throw in the towel and leave?"

"I promise, and if there are ghosts or if my hair starts going gray or if I gain forty pounds the first week, I'll get out so fast it'll give everyone in town something else to talk about." She smiled and kissed his cheek.

He resisted his desire to pull her in for a deeper kiss in favor of the subject at hand. "Don't tease. No one knows a thing about that house and very little about Seth. He's been a recluse for more than twenty years."

"The only person who has been in the house in all these years is Oma Lynn Smith, and Granny says that no one has ever been able to get a word out of her." Emmy Jo lowered her voice. "But then, no one will get one out of me, either, with that nondisclosure we all had to sign at Hickory Health Care. Speaking of privacy, you sure you can't follow me to the motel? I could sure use a night in your arms before a two-month dry spell."

He ran a thumb down her cheek. "I can't tonight. I promised Gramps that I'd watch a movie with him. He's been such an old bear lately that I'm hoping this might soften his mood toward us."

"I liked it better when you were in college," she

said. "No one there cared about us or even knew there was a Hickory, Texas. Will you meet me at Libby's for coffee before work?"

"Be there at six thirty. I'll have doughnuts and coffee on the table." Logan planted a kiss on the tip of her nose. "But remember, we can be at the courthouse on Monday morning if you change your mind."

"My job will end on the last day of May, and I want my wedding to take place the next week. So let's plan on June 10," she said.

"We have a definite date, then?" He grinned.

"We do. I've always wanted to get married in the summer, and I can plan the wedding and get things done in the evenings." She slapped a mosquito from her arm. "That ends this place as a venue for sure. I don't want my guests to spend the whole evening swatting mosquitoes."

"Guess that means we should get out of here. I'll plan on lunch on Tuesday with you." He drew her into his arms for a long good-night kiss. He'd never get tired of the way her body felt next to his, the heat between them, or the way nothing else mattered when they were together. It had been like that since they were sixteen and eighteen and had only intensified through the next five years. Now they were twenty-one and twenty-three, and he hoped that when they were ninety-one and ninety-three they'd still feel the same way.

"We can text and call every evening." She

panted as she slipped her hand into his and pulled him up with her. "I love you, Logan."

He gently squeezed her hand. "Love you, too, Emmy Jo."

When they reached her car, Emmy Jo rolled up on her tiptoes and wrapped her arms around Logan's neck, pulling his face to hers for a final kiss. He thought she was stubborn and bullheaded, but so was he. He was supposed to go into the ministry like his grandfather and father, but he'd wanted to study finance, not the Bible. It had caused so many arguments in his house that he'd told her he was glad to get away from his family and go to college.

Her heart melted when she looked into his green eyes. If he'd asked her right then to meet him at the courthouse on Monday morning, she might have changed her mind. But he hugged her tightly one more time and then got into his truck.

Half an hour later she had checked into the motel in Graham and was lying on the bed, staring at the ceiling. "I will have my wedding, and the whole county will know about it."

Her children would have a father listed on their birth certificates and everyone would know that she was legitimately married at least nine months before the first one was born.

CHAPTER TWO

Most days Seth Thomas loved his sister, Nora. What he liked best was that she lived more than two hundred miles away. But on his birthdays, when she sent useless presents and pried into his business, he wasn't too fond of the old gal. That year she called two days early, just before he left the hospital after hip surgery, to tell him that she'd hired him an assistant. He yelled and grumbled and griped, none of which did a bit of good. Nora had already signed the contract and paid half the money, and the lady would arrive that very morning.

He did not need a distraction in his routine, especially when he was healing from the surgery. What was Nora thinking? Just because the doctor wouldn't give him a release to drive his car was no reason for Nora to pay good money for someone who would only have one job a week—to drive him to the cemetery on Sunday afternoons to put lilacs on his mother's grave.

His housekeeper, Oma Lynn, had been taking care of the cleaning and cooking for the past twenty years. He could have given her fifty bucks to do that extra bit and not had to endure another person in his house every day.

Nora's birthday was at the end of May, and he had a whole month to think about payback. Maybe he'd have a truckload of cow manure dumped on the front lawn of her big house in Amarillo.

The phone beside the table rang, and he grabbed it. The short cord didn't reach quite far enough, leaving the heavy base dangling. "Hello," he growled as he got a hold on the thing and set it beside him on the chaise lounge.

"Happy birthday, brother." Nora's voice came through loud and clear. "You must have been expecting my call, because Oma Lynn didn't have to take the phone from the office to the patio for you."

"I'm not deaf. You don't have to yell." Of course he expected her call. She always harassed him on his birthday in one way or another. This year she was doing double time.

"Still grumpy as ever, I see. Should I come to Hickory and cheer you up?"

"You've already done enough to ruin my day." *Dammit!* Just thinking of having a perfect stranger coming to his house every day and getting in the way of his routine was enough to aggravate Jesus himself.

Nora giggled. "Oh, don't get comfortable, because I'm about to tell you all about the rest of your present."

"You've done enough, thank you," Seth said.

"Please, Nora, I'll pay you back the money you'll lose if you break that contract. It's not too late to cancel this thing."

"I will not," she declared. "There's more. She is going to live in the house. That way someone is there all the time until you are free to drive."

"Please tell me this is an April Fool's joke," he whispered. *Un-damn-believable! What was Nora thinking—telling a stranger that she could live in my house?*

"It is not. I'm too old to come to Hickory and take care of you. I tried to hire Oma Lynn to stay with you twenty-four hours a day, and she wouldn't do it. So you will have an assistant."

"You might do well to remember that you have a birthday and I will get even," Seth said.

"Oh, boy! Send me one of them male dancers. The ladies here in the assisted living center will love him." Nora giggled.

"You are pure evil," he fussed.

"I am watching after my brother the best way I know how. He's all I got left in the way of siblings, and I don't want him dead just yet," she said seriously.

"Today he wishes you didn't even remember you had a brother."

"You'll get over it. And Seth, get a cordless phone or I'll send you one for Christmas."

"Damn technology and sisters both," he muttered.

"I love you, too. Have a lovely birthday," Nora said.

Emmy Jo sat at Libby's Diner through three coffee refills, weighing all the pros and cons of the job that morning. She even pulled a pen from her purse and made a list. When it was time to leave, the pros side was full and the only things on the cons side were two names: Logan and Tandy.

"It's time," Libby, Diana's mother, yelled from behind the counter. "If you are really going to do this, don't be late on your first day."

Emmy Jo had spent many hours at Diana's house when she was growing up. Tall, dark haired, and brown eyed, Libby had been named for her grandmother, the original Libby. Granny Anna Libby had passed the diner down to her daughter, Ellen, who in turn gave it to her daughter, Libby. Confusing as it might be to outsiders, everyone in Hickory knew the history.

Diana's dad, Phillip, and her mother ran the place with the help of a couple of part-time waitresses during the lunch rush. Libby did the waitress work and the bookkeeping. Phillip did most of the cooking and helped with busing.

Emmy Jo scooted across the booth seat, took a deep breath, and waved. "Wish me luck."

"You know I do." Libby waved back at her.

She'd only been close to the mansion on the hill when she and Diana drove past it one night. Diana had dared her one Halloween to ring the doorbell. She drove right to the house, but she'd been too scared to actually walk up those steps.

Now she parked at the foot of the stairs leading up to the front door and waited until five minutes to eight to get out of her car.

With each step of the twenty-five leading to the Thomas mansion, her feet got heavier and her knees weaker, until by the time she reached the top, it was only pure stubbornness that kept her from turning around and going home.

The house looked more like a fairy-tale castle than a modern-day mansion with the cut stone and cedar work on the outside, but the grounds were a different story. Last year's leaves covered the stairs and crunched underfoot. There wasn't a flower or even a shrub in sight. It needed someone like Tandy to plant flowers to make the place look inviting. Maybe a few rosebushes and some marigolds and petunias would give it some warmth.

She sucked in a lungful of air, reached out, and pushed the doorbell. That the house might be haunted did not frighten her one bit. She didn't believe in ghosts or spirits. She didn't even believe in fate. Her theory was that when a person died, their soul went to either heaven or

31

hell. It sure didn't hang around Earth to pester the people left behind. And the choices a person made created the consequences that they had to live with when it came time for the decision about pretty white clouds or a big, eternal bonfire. Fate had nothing to do with any part of life.

Likewise, Seth Thomas did not frighten her, either. She'd only seen him one time before in her life, and that was at the cemetery when she and Tandy went to put flowers on Tandy's mama's grave. He'd sat in a lawn chair, his eyes glued on the tombstone in front of him that always had beautiful lilacs in the fancy vase attached. She'd asked her granny who he was, but she'd hurried them out of the cemetery without answering her.

A short, round woman with a tight little gray knot of hair on top of her head opened the door. "You must be the new assistant. I think Nora has lost her mind." Between the woman's nasal voice and her sour expression, Emmy Jo suspected if she smiled, her face might crack wide open. "But come on in. You won't last through today, much less until the end of May. There ain't no television in this house and only one radio. All he listens to is the old country station." She stood to one side and motioned for Emmy Jo to enter the house. "Follow me. From now on you will drive around back and park in the garage and come in by the back door."

Emmy Jo had never backed down from a dare, and she wasn't starting that day.

Come on, the aggravating voice in her head said, *that was not a dare. She was only stating facts.*

I don't see it the same way, Emmy Jo argued. *She's thrown down a challenge by saying that I won't stay through the day, and I intend to show her that I will be here until the last minute on the contract that I signed—May 31 at five o'clock.*

She took a step through the dark, heavy door and followed the lady across an enormous living room, through a dining room, and out onto a patio. She recognized the old guy with a mop of gray hair curling to his shirt collar and a thick mustache to match. With steely-blue eyes set in a chiseled face, he glared at her.

"I hate red." His voice sounded like that actor Tandy swooned over every time she saw him— Sam Elliott, that was his name.

Emmy Jo looked down at her dark-red scrubs. "Well, I hate orange. Now that we've got that out of the way, you mind if I sit down?"

"You could just say *April Fools* and leave."

"I don't care if it's Christmas. Your sister hired me and I'm here to stay, so get used to it." Emmy Jo figured if she let him intimidate her in the first five minutes, she'd never earn his respect. "Again, may I sit or am I supposed to stand for eight hours?"

A flicker of amusement crossed his face. "Suit yourself, but don't expect me to entertain you. What's your name?"

"Emmy Jo Massey." She eased down into a chair beside him. "And happy birthday to you."

All the color drained from his face, turning it the same color as his hair and mustache. She thought for a minute he might faint dead away, but then he picked up one of the half dozen newspapers from the table separating them, shook it out, and started to read, hiding his face behind it.

She wasn't sure what to do, so she stared out over the panoramic view from the top of the hill down to where the little town of Hickory was laid out. Straight ahead, almost dead center in the view, the steeple of Logan's father's church rose up from the trees. Minty-green leaves had just begun to spread a hint of spring across Hickory. A bright-red cardinal hopped up on the patio wall and cocked his head at them. *How could anyone not like red when God made something as beautiful as a cardinal?*

She leaned forward slightly and squinted.

"What are you trying to see?" Seth asked.

"I can see the church steeple, but I was trying to visualize where the bank is located," she answered without taking her eyes from the scene before her.

Seth went back to reading his paper.

"Are you going to read all of those?" she asked.

"Yes. I'm finished with this one." He handed it to her. "You read it now."

"What if I don't want to read the *Dallas Morning News*?" She loved novels and her bridal magazines, but newspapers bored her to tears. All that stuff about murder and mayhem and those crazy advice columns would depress a saint.

"You have been hired as my assistant, so you do what I say. Your first job is to read this newspaper," he said.

"Will there be a test later?" she smarted off.

"No, but reading current events won't kill you," he shot right back in the same tone.

Nora had said to do whatever he wanted, whether it was listening to music with him or taking him for a drive in his car, so she took the newspaper and flipped back to the social pages.

When he finished the second one, he handed it to her and she laid it in her lap while she read the last bit of the advice column in the first paper. She was drawn to advice columns in magazines but always figured people had to be out of their minds to write such personal things to a public forum. It was like that old television show her granny watched when she was a kid. What was it called? A tall guy always had folks on his show that told about crazy problems in their lives. *Jerry Springer*, that was it! She smiled when she remembered.

Hey, wait a minute. She glanced over at Seth. *Maybe if I got him and Granny and Jesse Grady all in the same spot at the same time, I'd figure out what started this thing between them. But that show went off television years ago. Maybe I should write a letter to an advice column, even an online one.* Her eyes went back to the paper. *Dear whoever, my granny and my fiancé's grandfather have not spoken in more than sixty years. How do we get them to come clean about the past?*

If she could clear up the past, the present problems could be understood a little better. Like why Tandy was so against her getting married to Logan. And why his parents blamed her for him not following in his grandpa's and his daddy's footsteps and becoming a preacher.

They went through four newspapers by midmorning without another word. She pored over the lifestyle and cartoon sections, and he read every word of the front-page news, the sports pages, and, as near as she could figure, all the real estate ads. At ten o'clock Oma Lynn brought a tray with two cups of black coffee, a bottle of water, and two muffins to the patio.

"Thank you," Seth said.

Oma Lynn nodded and glanced at Emmy Jo. "I didn't know if you liked coffee or not."

Emmy Jo smiled. "Yes, I do, and thank you."

"Midmorning snack at ten. Lunch at twelve.

36

Afternoon snack at three. Supper at five, and on Saturday from noon and all day Sunday you will be responsible for taking care of that job," Oma Lynn told her. "Think you can handle that?"

"Yes, ma'am," Emmy Jo said.

Seth picked up a muffin in one hand and a cup of coffee in the other. "Now this is coffee. That stuff they gave me in the hospital couldn't be classified as anything more than murdered water, and young lady, you get it black in this house or you drink water."

"I hope it's strong." She followed his lead. "I hate weak coffee. To put sugar and cream in good coffee should be counted as a major sin." That old coot was not going to get the best of her. But despite her words, the first sip of that thick black liquid almost gagged her.

"You are Tandy Massey's granddaughter, aren't you? You don't look a thing like her." Seth finished his cranberry muffin and sipped at the mug of coffee.

"Great-granddaughter. They say I look like my father. Rose was my grandmother and Crystal was my mother. I never knew either of them." She nodded. "You know my granny?"

"I did a long time ago."

"How did you know her? Did y'all go to school together or what?" She frowned.

"It's not important. I'm not talking about your grandmother. Young lady, I don't want you here.

Go on back home, and I'll call Nora and tell her that you didn't like the job."

"I'm not going away, Mr. Thomas. I can run errands for you. Drive you wherever you want to go. Sit right here and read these papers all day or twiddle my thumbs, but I'm not leaving." She'd overcome the first hurdle that morning when she rang the doorbell; all the others were nothing in comparison.

"Sassy piece of baggage, aren't you?" Seth said. "That much is exactly like Tandy."

She'd been called worse. "I suppose her determination did rub off on me."

Seth reached for his walker. "I feel sorry for the man you're engaged to."

She rushed to his side and held the walker steady while he slowly pulled himself up. "Most people do."

He grimaced, and his veined hands shook slightly as he gripped the walker tightly. "What's his name?"

"Logan Grady."

"That would be Jesse Grady's grandson?" Seth moved slowly toward the sliding doors leading into the house.

"It is." She followed him as he slowly made his way across the patio.

"You are my assistant whether I like it or not, so get around here in front of me and open this door. And I'm tired of talking. Oma Lynn, we are going to the office," he called out. "We'll have our lunch in there at noon."

Rumor had it that Seth Thomas built the house because of a woman. He'd met her out in Amarillo when he went to visit his family and fallen in love with her. Once the house was finished, the wedding was going to be held in the backyard. A week before the big ceremony, she'd called it off, and he'd lived in the big house all alone ever since. Parties had not been thrown there. Christmas lights weren't put up. It had never had an ounce of life in it, even though Seth had lived there for more than fifty years.

A wave of pity washed over Emmy Jo as she followed him into the office, a cozy room with full bookcases flanking a rock fireplace. To have all this at his fingertips and yet have nothing but sameness day after day would be downright depressing. Tears welled up in her eyes, but she kept them at bay. She crossed the floor to the marble mantel and stared at the two pictures there. One was an old black-and-white picture in an antique frame of a tall lady holding a baby, with a light-haired man beside her. The woman had dark hair and light eyes and her smile said that she was happy. The way the man beside her looked at her, Emmy Jo could easily imagine him adoring her.

The other picture, framed to match the first one, was a small oil painting, maybe eight by ten, matted in pale blue to match the sky behind a huge two-story, white-frame house with lilacs in full bloom.

"Your mother?" she asked.

"The baby is my mother." He parked his walker at the end of a buttery-soft leather sofa and winced when he sat down. "Folks are not supposed to outlive their bones. You see that rack of records over there beside the player?"

She glanced toward them.

"I want you to play them one at a time. When the first one ends, turn it over and play the back side, then put it back into the cover and play the next one," he said.

"What are we going to do while we listen to them?" If this was going to be an everyday occurrence, then she'd bring her bridal magazines tomorrow.

"Enjoy the music," he answered.

After almost two hours of music from the fifties, Emmy Jo was glad to see Oma Lynn bring lunch into the room at noon. The first tray held bowls of steaming-hot potato soup and bacon-and-cheese sandwiches cut diagonally. Two thick pieces of chocolate cake and two glasses of milk were on the second.

Oma Lynn quickly set up a small folding table in front of Seth and put his part of the food on it. "You can use the desk," she told Emmy Jo.

"Is this birthday cake?" Emmy Jo asked.

"Sent special from Nora. Arrived yesterday. She sends one every year from some fancy place out there in Amarillo. Has it shipped here on ice so the chocolate icing don't get soft," Oma Lynn answered.

"Shall we sing?" Emmy Jo sucked up a lungful of air to begin the song.

Seth nearly skewered her with his pointer finger. "You do and I'll shoot you."

"After this morning's music appreciation lesson, I thought you liked singing," Emmy Jo said. She liked country music, but two hours of that old stuff had come close to boring her to death. Maybe that's what he had in mind—kill her graveyard dead with boredom.

"Don't you get sassy with me, girl," Seth growled.

"You can't fire me, and I'd bet your sister won't. You could shoot me, but then you'd have to make your own food on the weekend. Looks like we're stuck with each other. Sassy and grumpy. We could be some of the seven dwarfs if you weren't so tall," she answered.

"I might have to endure it, but I don't have to like it. And you can wipe that smile off your face, Oma Lynn," Seth said.

"Why? She called it right. You are grumpy," Oma Lynn said as she left the room. "I'll see y'all on Monday morning in time to make breakfast. I hope you know how to make chicken and dumplings, missy. That's what's on the Sunday dinner menu every week, and he likes them made fresh on Sunday."

"I can do a fair job," Emmy Jo answered, glad that Tandy had made her learn to cook. "What's for supper on Saturday nights?"

"The month's menu is on the refrigerator door. You'll find what you need to fix it. If she leaves before Monday, there are frozen dinners in the freezer, Seth."

"I'd gladly eat them if that miracle would happen," he growled.

After they'd finished, she carried the dishes to the kitchen and studied the menu. Tonight she was supposed to make spaghetti with meat sauce, hot rolls, and salad. A bright-pink note was stuck to the fridge that said there was a rising of bread on the cabinet for the hot rolls. Emmy Jo checked under the towel-covered bowl and figured that there was plenty to make rolls for supper and also a loaf for dinner tomorrow.

When she returned to the office, Seth had stretched out on the sofa, a pillow under his head and a throw draped over his body. "I take a nap from one to two thirty. After that I like my afternoon snack."

"What are my orders during this time?" she asked.

"You can either leave or unload your things

into the room that Oma Lynn has fixed for you. It's the one with the open door."

"I'll see you at three, then." Her heart kicked in an extra beat at having some time to unpack and actually see the room where she'd be staying the next several weeks.

"I hope not." Seth shut his eyes.

Emmy Jo raced back to the kitchen and checked the menu. Afternoon snack on Saturday was a peanut butter and jelly sandwich, an apple that had been peeled and quartered, and a glass of milk. She could throw that together in ten minutes; she had plenty of time to explore her new room.

What she figured was the pantry door was ajar. She started to close it, but then thought she'd go ahead and get out the peanut butter and apples. When she threw it open, a set of fairly steep stairs led from there down into a basement garage. She found a light switch and flipped it on, then made her way to the bottom of the steps.

She wasn't surprised to see an older-model pickup truck or the brand-new Cadillac, but that shiny black vintage convertible made her big blue eyes pop wide open. There was plenty of room for her car, so she abandoned her idea to get out the peanut butter and apples and opened the garage door to get her car in.

Once her vehicle was parked and the door shut, she carried the first load of her belongings up the stairs to the kitchen and then the second set to the floor where her room was located. Panting with the exertion of getting a plastic garbage bag from the basement to the second floor, she left them outside the door and sat down on the top step to catch her breath.

She hit the "Speed Dial" button to call Logan, launching right into conversation as he answered. "This room better be worth it, but I'm not looking at it until I get the last suitcase up here."

"What better be worth what?" he asked. "Do I need to come rescue you? Did you hear chains rattling in the attic?"

"Don't tease me," she quipped. "I was talking to myself. I'm getting my things up two flights of stairs to my room while Seth has his nap. I just wanted to check in with you because I knew you'd be worried."

"You are so right. I've thought about you all morning," he said. "So how is it going?"

His drawl made her whole body hum with desire. "I want you so bad right now that I'd almost throw all my stuff back down the stairs and leave for one long, hot kiss."

"I can promise more than that if you'll do it," he said.

She shut her eyes and visualized him behind his desk at the bank. He wore dark dress slacks, a pin-striped shirt, and a little tie tack with his engraved initials holding down his tie. She'd given him the tiny piece of jewelry for his high school graduation gift. He'd smother her with kisses and they'd go to the courthouse and get married.

And no one in town would believe that you were really married, because they didn't see the ceremony. They'd all say that you were just shacking up with him.

Her eyes popped wide open. "Darlin', it's only two months. Eight short weeks and then we'll be married properly. Mr. Grumpy takes his afternoon nap at this time every day, so we can talk if you'll manage to take your break right after two," she said.

"Mr. Grumpy?" He chuckled.

"That's his nickname. He's worse than Tandy when she loses at bingo. And I have a whole new appreciation for old country music." She went on to give him a play-by-play of her day.

"So is this going to be the daily routine?" Logan asked.

"I really think he's trying to make me leave by way of boredom. But I'm as stubborn as he is. I'd better not keep you any longer. I've got to get my moving-in done by three so I can take his afternoon snack to him. I'm responsible for the cooking only Saturday afternoon and Sunday. Oma Lynn does it all the rest of the time," she answered.

"I love you," he whispered. "If I shut my eyes, I can imagine you in my arms."

"Oh, Logan!" She groaned. "It's going to be a long two months, but we will live."

"I hope so, because I'm planning an amazing honeymoon," he said. "Got to go, sweetheart. Talk to you tomorrow at this same time."

She brought up the rest of her things and pushed the heavy door the rest of the way open. Twice or maybe even three times the size of her bedroom in the trailer, the room had a queen-size four-poster bed, nightstands with crystal lamps, a six-drawer chest, and a ten-drawer dresser with a mirror above it. All of the drawers were empty except for two in the chest—one held extra sheets and the other a quilt. An overstuffed rocking chair sat in front of french doors that opened out onto a balcony that overlooked the patio. From there, she could see the church steeple even better as it rose up out of the trees. A door to her left led into a walk-in closet and one to the right into a private bathroom with a huge claw-foot tub and a mirror half the size of Texas hanging above a pretty vanity.

She plopped down into the rocking chair and blinked several times, but nothing changed. It could be a fancy vacation or a prison. It was up to her to decide whether the whole experience would be positive or not.

Her phone rang, and she smiled when she saw

that it was Tandy. "Hey, Granny. Did you win last night?"

"A little," Tandy answered. "Have you proved your point? Are you ready to come on home?"

"No, ma'am. I'm sticking it out until the end. I've got a lovely room with a balcony."

"Bullshit! You're just telling me that so you will win this fight."

Emmy Jo chuckled. "Nope, Granny, it's the God's honest truth. Why don't you come on up here and see for yourself? Just tell Oma Lynn you are here to see me."

"Humph." Tandy snorted. "It ain't got that cold in hell. I don't reckon it will any time soon. I imagine you'll be home in a week at the most."

"Want to bet?" Emmy Jo asked.

"Wouldn't want to take your money. Got to go now. My program is on television."

"See you on Tuesday? That's my day off," Emmy Jo said.

"I might still be mad at you," she said tersely.

"And I might still be mad at you, but we can visit. I wanted to talk to you about borrowing your pearls for the wedding."

"Not if you marry that boy, you ain't. You're not wearing my pearls," Tandy said. "We'll talk before Tuesday and see if I'm over my spell enough to talk to you."

"Granny, you are talking to me now," Emmy Jo said.

"Yeah, but I can fix that," she said and hung up.

Emmy Jo shoved the phone back into her pocket. "I'll show you! Before this is all done, you'll be sorry you are being so stubborn. I'm not backing down."

She'd glanced at the clock and saw that it was past two thirty. Unpacking would have to wait. It was time to get the snack ready and then start supper. Thankful for something to do other than read papers or listen to music, she made her way down to the kitchen and fixed peanut butter sandwiches and apples. After she'd poured two glasses of milk, she put it all on the tray and started for the office. Seth was already pushing his walker down the length of the foyer and out onto the patio, so she turned and headed that way.

Hardwood floors so shiny that she could see the reflection of her red scrubs in them, rich paneling halfway up on the walls, and above that a soft winter-white paint without a scratch or smudge on it—everything to suggest warmth and love, and yet there was none of that in the big house.

When she was a little girl, she'd fantasized about living in a big house with a staircase and double doors opening out onto a patio. A prince would ride up on a pretty white horse and call out her name, and she'd ride away with him just like in the storybooks. But in real life, things didn't work that way at all. She wasn't the princess but an old man's assistant, and she was being very careful not to fall on the slick floors as she carried the tray outside. And Logan might be her prince, but he'd never be an actual prince, because they'd have to work hard for everything they ever got out of life. Besides he didn't even own a white horse.

"Did you have a good nap?" she asked as she backed out the door and held it for him.

"I did until I woke up and found you still here," he grouched.

"You can bitch and moan every waking hour, but that won't change. What do you usually do after your nap?" It wasn't disrespectful—not when he started it.

"I have my snack and read until supper time."

"What do you read?" She put the tray on the table between his lounge and her chair and dreaded reading through more newspapers.

He narrowed his eyes at her. "If I say you have to read *Moby-Dick* to me each evening, will that scare you off?"

"If you can stand to listen to that boring crap, I will read every single word of it to you," she answered. "I'll even read all those whale details twice."

Seth picked up his sandwich and bit into it. "I hate to be read to. It makes me sleepy. Did you move your car to the garage and get your stuff to your room?"

"I did." She said a silent prayer of thankfulness that he'd turned down her offer. She hated to read out loud.

"Did Oma Lynn show you where the elevator is?" he asked.

"She did not!" Emmy Jo gasped.

Seth smiled for the first time. "Well, bully for her."

"Paybacks are a bitch, Mr. Thomas," she said.

"Tell that to my sister. Her birthday is the month after mine, which means I've got a whole month to figure out what I'm going to do to get her back for this stunt. And if you are going to stay here, you can call me Seth."

"Okay, then, Seth it is. Are you the oldest or is Nora?" Emmy Jo asked.

"I am by thirteen months, but we graduated high school the same year. She was one of those smart kids who finished a year early," he said.

"How did she wind up in Amarillo?" Emmy Jo asked, just to keep him talking more than out of actual interest.

"Married a man from there."

"You aren't much of a conversationalist, are you?" she asked.

"You ask too damn many questions," he answered.

He finished his sandwich and apple, drank his milk, and picked up a book. She was glad to see that it was a Louis L'Amour. She gathered up the dirty dishes and carried them to the kitchen. Supper at five after a snack like that was pushing it for her, but she'd adjust. From now on she'd eat less at mealtimes if she was going to have snacks twice a day, or else she'd have to buy a wedding dress four sizes bigger. How Seth Thomas stayed so slim was a mystery for sure.

So his sister, Nora, graduated at the same time as Seth and probably Tandy and Jesse. How much more could she discover in two whole months? So many questions with no answers, but the fact that she'd gotten him to talk even a little bit that first day put a smile on her face.

The house lapsed into eerie stillness that evening after she'd washed the supper dishes and put a chicken into the slow cooker to stew all night. By tomorrow morning the meat would fall off the bones and the broth would make wonderful dumplings. She unpacked the rest of her things and took a long soaking bath in the tub, and yet it was still only eight o'clock.

She would love to call Diana and talk for a couple of hours, but Saturday night was her and Jack Ramsey's date night. No way would Emmy Jo intrude on their time together. She stepped out onto the balcony and inhaled the clean night air. From the patio below her, she heard voices, but when she peeked over the edge of the railing, it was only Seth listening to the Grand Ole Opry on his radio. He must have one powerful radio or a connection with the angels to get that station to come in all the way from Nashville. She soon found herself tapping her foot to the tunes. When her phone rang, she rushed back into the room, saw Logan's picture, and hit the button to answer.

"I'm so glad you called. The only thing going on up here is country music on Seth's radio. I'm tired of listening to music and my new romance novel isn't holding my attention, so talk to me," she said all in a breath before she stopped to inhale.

"You could watch reruns of something on television," Logan said.

"No television," she said.

"You are kiddin' me. Gramps told me that Seth was strange, but no television? Good Lord!"

"Eccentric, not strange. And maybe just a little bit OCD. He likes things done on time. But let's talk about us, not Seth."

"I'm sitting at the foot of the hill on the tailgate of my truck. I can see one little light shining up there in the dark house. Is that where you are?" he asked.

"I'm sure it is." She walked out on the balcony. The moon was bright and the stars twinkled, but they didn't provide enough light to see a pickup parked half a mile away on a country road. "I can't see you, but knowing you're there makes me happy. This isn't a bad job, darlin'. It's easier than any of the others that I've had; the only downside is that we're apart every night."

"That's a pretty big downside, isn't it?"

His sexy voice made it easy to imagine him right next to her. A delicious little shiver chased down her spine.

She squinted, but she still could not see even the glitter of moonlight flashing off his truck. "Tomorrow afternoon I will be in the cemetery about one thirty. If you should happen to be in the vicinity, I might catch a glimpse of you. That would hold me until Tuesday."

"If you are going to be there, I'll be parked a little ways down from Mary Thomas's grave. That is where he goes, isn't it?" he asked.

"It sure is, and if he doesn't want me to stick around, I might even get to steal a kiss or two from you," Emmy Jo said.

The music stopping interrupted her call. She looked out over the balcony, and there Seth was, pushing his walker toward the doors, going inside and wobbling his head from side to side as he hummed a country tune.

"He's not all bad," she said.

She smiled at his bravado, even if ninety percent of it was bluff. At a time in his life when giving up and going to bed would have been easy, she respected his determination to work through the pain and get well. Any octogenarian who had

Seth Thomas's wit and willpower simply had to have some good hiding down in his heart.

"I'm glad to hear that," Logan said. "Good night, darlin'. I wish you were in my arms."

"Me, too. 'Night."

She left the balcony doors open so the night air could continue to flow through the room and set the alarm for six thirty so she'd have plenty of time to get breakfast ready by seven. The menu said that on Sunday morning he ate one hard-boiled egg and one thick slice of toast browned in an iron skillet, strawberry jam, and a cup of black coffee. His ten o'clock snack was to be a bowl of fresh fruit—which Oma Lynn had left in a covered container—a cup of coffee, and a bottle of water. The noon meal was chicken and dumplings with slices of homemade bread or rolls and a salad. They would have chocolate cake for dessert. Supper was to be leftovers of the same thing.

"I'm declaring a mission," she whispered into the darkness. "I'm going to make him like me."

CHAPTER THREE

Seth pushed his walker to one side of the elevator and pushed the button. "I told you that I hate red."

"Well, red scrubs are what I work in," she answered.

"Wear something else."

"Is that an order?"

"You are my assistant, not my nurse. From now on wear plain clothes, not that ugly thing," he said.

"Yes, sir. No red of any kind, or just not this shade?" Why would he despise an uplifting color so much? It didn't make a bit of sense, but then she'd never liked orange. Although she did have a good reason—in elementary school a little girl had told her that she looked horrid in an orange shirt she was wearing that day. "You look like what I puked up after I ate too many oranges," the kid had said. Emmy Jo had blacked her eye and had to pick up trash from the playground for two days, but it was worth it. She wondered if something similar had happened to Seth.

"Anything is fine as long as it isn't red," he answered. "And pick up one of those boxes over there in the corner that has my name on it. Put it in the trunk with my walker. And don't *sir* me. I tell you to do something, just do it."

"Jeans all right?" she asked.

"If that's what you want," he said.

Curiosity almost got the best of her, but before she could peek inside, he'd gotten situated in the passenger seat and left his walker to be folded and put into the trunk with a lawn chair and a tattered old quilt.

When she got into the driver's seat, he handed her the keys. "We're going to the cemetery. Go through the side gate, not the front one. The grave is the second one on the left. Park beside the road, and then you can go do whatever you want and come back in one hour."

"You are going to trust me to drive this car for an hour?" she asked.

"I am not," he said. "You can walk to wherever you want, or call your fiancé to come and get you as long as you are back in one hour. I just don't want you sitting beside me or smothering me to death."

Nora had said she wasn't to let him out of her sight. Emmy Jo understood the reasoning, because he could fall or need help, but how far did that go? Not so far that she couldn't visually see him. He sure wasn't going to get away from her traveling at a snail's pace with that walker.

She decided that if Logan wasn't parked close enough that she could see Seth, then she'd ask him to move the truck closer. Just thinking about being close to Logan made her want to floor the gas pedal so they could get there faster. But there was no way she was driving recklessly with Seth in the car. That would give Nora a really good reason to fire her. She stayed a mile below the speed limit and hummed one of those old country tunes he'd been listening to the day before. Something called "My Everything," with a slow beat that used up every love phrase in the universe but said it all when it came to how she felt about Logan.

"What makes you so happy?" Seth asked. "That's an old Eddy Arnold tune you are humming. I didn't know you smarty-pants kids even listened to his music."

"Never heard of him until yesterday, but it reminds me of Logan. I get to see him today."

"You really love that boy, don't you?"

"Yes, I do. I wouldn't be marrying him if I didn't," she answered.

"Humph!" Seth snorted and looked out the side window.

From house to cemetery meant driving down a winding road to the bottom of the hill, through Hickory's two blocks of Main Street, turning right at the traffic light, and going a mile to the side gate. It took all of seven minutes. By the time Seth eased out of the car, she had his walker unfolded and was standing in front of him.

"Do you want the quilt or just the box?"

"Both," he said. "The box and then the chair and the quilt, in that order."

She carried the cardboard box and followed behind him. When he reached the grave site, he nodded toward her. "Open it for me."

She carefully pulled the tape from the top and slid out a beautiful purple silk lilac bouquet exactly like the faded one in the vase beside the tombstone. He reached out, and she put it in his hands. Although he flinched with the pain of bending, he removed the old blooms, handed them to her, and put the new ones in the vase. "I'm sorry that your flowers faded, Mama. I couldn't get here for the past two weeks." He straightened up and turned to Emmy Jo. "Now I need the chair and the quilt. And I see a black truck parked down there." He pointed. "If that's your feller, then that's a good distance."

She tossed the old flowers into the empty box and put it into the trunk. After she'd set the chair up and he'd gotten as comfortable as possible in it, she handed him the quilt. He laid it on his lap and waved her away.

Everyone in Hickory had heard of Mary Thomas. Even when Emmy Jo was a young child, Tandy had usually whispered Mary's name when she spoke of her. Mary had a horrible reputation, and folks said that marriages could have been ruined if wives found out where their husbands went at night.

But no one ever talked about the two people buried beside her. Those small granite stones rested flat on the ground. One said "Mother of Mary." The other said "Father of Mary." So those two people right there on the other side of Mary were the young couple in the photograph. Why weren't their names engraved?

Mary's pale-pink granite stone sat about knee high. Engraved on the front were the dates October 1, 1917, and May 23, 1953. And below that in lovely script lettering were the words *Beloved Mother*. Emmy Jo couldn't stop staring at the dates. Mary was only thirty-five years old when she died. Was it an accident, or had she had some incurable disease?

She wanted to sit down on the grass and ask questions, but Logan awaited.

"Well?" Seth said tersely.

She checked the time on her phone. "One hour, right?"

"Yes, two o'clock exactly," he said. "And you need a watch. That thing could die or get lost. A watch around your wrist won't."

She pulled up the sleeve of her bright-red hoodie and showed him a wristwatch. "For pulse readings and all that kind of thing, but since I'm an assistant and not a nurse's aide today, I can use my phone for the time. I will be back at two on the dot."

"Sassy girl's got an answer for everything,"

he grumbled as he waved her away with a flick of the wrist. When she was about halfway to Logan's truck, she glanced over her shoulder. She could see that his lips were moving, but she couldn't hear a word. Did he talk to his mother out loud every week?

Logan waited in the backseat of his club-cab truck, and she crawled into his lap, wrapped her arms around his neck, and kissed him—long, lingering, and passionately. He stared into her blue eyes long after the kiss ended. "I miss seeing you every night. You look sad."

She never could hide her emotions from Logan. She laid her head on his shoulder and sighed. "I am a little bit. Look at him. He's a sad old guy who has no one to talk except his mother. He has no children, and his sister lives more than two hundred miles away."

"And the house?" Logan asked.

"What's that got to do with anything?" She frowned.

"Is it a depressing place?"

She nodded, thinking of the contrast it made to her trailer with Tandy. "Yes, it is. All those lovely rooms. Four bedrooms with a bathroom each on the second floor, and there's an attic that I haven't even seen. There's no life in there. I can't imagine living in that place forever. It needs laughter and stories and kids sliding down the staircase and . . ."

He ran his hand down her bare arm and then laced his fingers in hers. "Our house is going to be filled with happiness."

"Of course it is." She gave his hand a squeeze. "We are in love and we're going to work at making it amazing."

"That's what marriage is—teamwork." He grinned. "At least that's what Gramps preaches at weddings he officiates at," Logan said. "Have you found out more about the fight between those three?"

"No, but I found out in the first three seconds that he hates red. Like, really hates it. I'm going to find out why. Now tell me about your weekend."

"I worked half a day yesterday and then Gramps and I went fishing last night. Saw Diana at church this morning, and she said to tell you to call her this evening. She's missing you."

"Diana and I argued. She didn't want me to work for Seth," she said.

"I know," he said softly.

"I hate it when we fight. She's been my best friend my whole life." She and Diana had not come down on opposing sides like this since they were little.

"I know that, too. And I don't think I've ever known you two to argue about anything," he said.

"We did once when we were kids. It was a silly

little girls' fight when I thought she was throwing me away for another friend. She said she could have two best friends, and I disagreed."

"What happened?"

"The other little girl moved away the next week, and we were both miserable until we made up."

Emmy Jo remembered the way her stomach hurt that week and how she couldn't eat. Tandy had threatened to take her to the doctor if she didn't straighten up. This time she didn't have trouble eating, but there was an emptiness in her life when she couldn't see and talk to her best friend every day.

"Call her and straighten it out. Even best friends don't always agree," he said.

"Sometimes engaged people don't, either," she said.

"But they compromise and work it out like we do." He toyed with her promise ring, a tiny diamond in the middle of connecting hearts. "I wish you would let me buy you an engagement ring."

She held up the ring to let the sunlight dance on the little stone. She loved that ring and relived the excitement of the night when he'd put it on her finger every time she looked at it. A bigger diamond couldn't possibly bring her more happiness. "This promise ring will do until I can have a wide gold band."

· · ·

"I'm in a bit of a pickle here, Mama," Seth said. "Nora has made a big mess of things. She thinks she's helping, but she's not, and I can't explain it to her without going all the way back to the beginning. She and Walter did good, helping to finish raising Matt. He did better out where nobody knew anything about the Thomas family."

He paused and watched a robin fly down and peck at the ground not five feet from him. "This is a tough time of year for me. I like to think that Matt is with you and it's a comfort. But now it's just me and Nora left. You know that, but this year is double bad. Lord, what was Nora thinking? She wasn't thinking, is the answer. She was so wrapped up in her own love life with Walter our senior year in high school that she was oblivious to anything else. She might have known Tandy at school, but she had no idea that Tandy and I were more than just class-mates."

He grimaced. *I've always wondered if Tandy was telling me the truth that horrible night when we all graduated.*

He caught a movement in his peripheral vision and checked his watch. It was exactly two o'clock. *Where had the time gone? The hour had never passed so quickly.*

"You ready?" Emmy Jo asked.

"I hoped you'd drive off with that kid in the truck and never look back," he said.

He eyed her carefully. Not a single thing looked like her great-grandmother. Red hair, blue eyes, short—nothing at all like the tall, dark-haired, green-eyed girl he'd known more than six decades ago. Even after all this time, thinking about the way she laughed when they were together and how her hand felt in his put a little extra thump in his heart.

"In your dreams." She laughed. "Where to now?"

"To the Dairy Queen. I have a soft vanilla ice-cream cone for my afternoon snack on Sunday afternoons after I visit the cemetery. I suppose you could have one, too, if you like." He handed her the quilt and rose slowly to his feet.

She took the chair and the quilt to the car, put them into the trunk, and got out his walker. "I like a peanut parfait occasionally, but a plain old vanilla is the best ever."

"Don't patronize me," he growled. "I'm not going to be your friend, and you are not going to make me like you."

"I don't mollycoddle anyone. And I'm tellin' the truth. I like vanilla ice cream," she shot back at him.

He put his hands on the walker and grimaced. He'd hoped to be better than this after the surgery a week ago. The doctor really wanted him to go to a physical therapy place for six weeks now that the staples were out. But Seth would have been ready for a mental institution if he'd had to endure other people that long, so the doctor said walking was the next best thing he could do. He'd gotten out of the hospital two days ago and he'd expected to get better hourly. So far that wasn't happening.

"So vanilla is really your favorite?" He slowly made his way to the car.

"Only thing better than Dairy Queen is homemade in one of those old crank freezers. Granny used to let me turn hers when I was a little girl. And the only thing better than that is snow ice cream." She opened the passenger door for him and waited for him to get settled before she folded the walker and took it to the trunk.

She hummed the whole time she worked and was still at it when she got into the driver's seat and started the engine. It shouldn't annoy him but it did, maybe even more than that ugly red outfit she was wearing. He set his jaw and stared straight ahead. By midsummer, he'd be back in his routine, driving himself to the cemetery, and that damned walker was going straight to the trash bin.

"Home after we get ice cream?" she asked as she drove back to town and lined up behind two cars at the Dairy Queen drive-through.

"No, we are going to the cabin, the house where I was raised. I'll sit on the porch for an hour or two while I eat my ice cream and then we'll go home. We should get there about four thirty, and at five you can heat up leftover dumplings for our supper," he answered.

He'd never taken anyone to the cabin, not even when he was a kid. He'd learned early on that mamas didn't let their children go to *that place*. Would it be strange to have Emmy Jo there? Maybe he should have changed his routine and not visited the cabin again until she was gone.

"Why do you keep to such a strict schedule?" she asked.

"Because I want to," he said bluntly. "I'll want a large ice cream in a cup."

The lady at the window keyed his order into the register and then looked at Emmy Jo, who ordered a small cone.

"You should get it in a cup. It'll melt while you drive to the cabin." If she was going to bug him about his schedule, he would boss her about her order.

"I can eat and drive, too. I like a cone," she argued.

He shrugged. "Have it your way, but don't ask me to help you."

"Five dollars and nineteen cents," the lady in the window answered.

He took a five and a one from his shirt pocket

and handed it to Emmy Jo. "Tell her to keep the change."

They were pulling back out onto Main Street when he pointed to the right. "Go to the traffic light and then two more blocks. Turn left and keep going until the road ends and make a right. The place is right there on the corner. Just park in the front yard."

His hands got a little clammy. It was just a run-down shack, but it had been the only place he'd known peace for years. If she ruined that for him that day, he wouldn't come back until he could drive himself.

"This it?" she asked as she made the last turn. Her tone and the way her eyes bugged out told him that she was comparing this place to the house he now lived in. Seeing it through her eyes, he noticed how shabby the little house looked. A few bits of paint hanging on the place were the only signs that it had ever been white. The yard was a fright, and last year's leaves were stacked up in the corners of the porch.

He nodded. "This is the place."

"It don't look like a cabin." She grabbed her head with her free hand.

"Brain freeze?" he asked.

"Yes, and if I don't eat fast, my ice cream will be running down my arm," she said. "Where was I? Oh, yes, I was expecting a log cabin, I guess. This just looks like a house."

"It's what it is."

Since he'd been there last, the wisteria and forsythia were both in bloom and the magnolia tree in the front yard was about to outgrow the tire around it. His mother had planted it there the first year she was married to Sam Thomas. Another year and he'd have to remove the tire.

"Here, hold this." Emmy Jo shoved the rest of her ice-cream cone at him.

"You should have gotten it in a cup. I'm not helping you."

"Either take it or I'll set it in your lap," she said.

He held it between his thumb and forefinger.

"It's not a snake and I don't have germs," she told him.

"If it drips, it's going out the window." He raised his voice.

"How you going to roll it down with both your hands full?" she hollered back at him as she crawled out of the car and jogged around the front to open his door.

Sassy piece of baggage. So much of Tandy in her. A vision of Tandy with all that gorgeous dark hair and those big eyes with mischief in them appeared in Seth's mind, but he quickly shook it away.

And that's what makes you so angry, isn't it? The voice in his head sounded a hell of a lot like Nora's.

No, she's got a right to act like Tandy. I kind

of like that in her. Sparring with her is fun. It's those blue eyes that upset me, and that damn red outfit.

The door swung open, and his walker was already set up and waiting. "Give me my cone and your cup so you'll have both hands to get out. You really are doing better than most patients out of the hospital such a short time."

He winced when his feet hit the ground, but he bit back the groan. He was doing good, she said. Maybe by the time they came to the cabin next Sunday, he'd be able to walk without that damned contraption.

Nothing changed. Serenity surrounded him like a warm blanket when his feet hit the ground. He was home, and for a little while, all would be right in the world.

"You want anything from the trunk? The quilt or your folding chair?"

He shook his head and made a slow beeline for the porch, where an old wooden rocking chair sat. "That will do just fine. You can give me back my ice cream when I get there."

"Think you can manipulate those two steps?" she asked.

He frowned, his snow-white brows knitting together in a solid line. "I will, or else I'll crawl up there."

"No need for that. I'm trained in how to get you into that rocking chair."

"Little bitty thing like you is going to carry me up onto the porch." He snorted.

"No, I am not. Park your walker to one side. Now, I'm going to the first step and you will hug me like I'm a big teddy bear. I will put my arms around your waist and you will step up with your good leg first. Then we'll repeat the process and you will hold onto the porch post for support while I bring up the walker."

"If I get to the porch, I can use the railing for support," he said.

"If? Come on, Seth, give me a little credit. I've been working in home health for three years," she said.

"I'm a foot taller than you are, girl, and I outweigh you by seventy pounds."

"I may be short, but I'm strong. Now wrap those long arms around me and hold on." She set his cup on the porch railing and held her cone out widely so she wouldn't get ice cream on him. "Now hurry up or my ice cream will start to run and get all over both of us."

The girl was insane. She couldn't possibly support his weight, and if he fell and the staples broke loose, he could wind up back in the hospital.

"Come on. Don't be shy. It's a business hug," she said.

"If I fall—"

She held up a palm. "Hush and do what I say."

He had not hugged anyone in decades, but he opened up his arms and she walked into them.

"Now use your good leg and step up."

One step and then the next, and she stepped out of the embrace and he grabbed the porch post. *By damn, it worked.* Using the railing, he inched his way to the rocker and eased down into it.

He was eating his ice cream and enjoying the spring breeze on his face when he heard humming again. Seth glanced over to see that she'd finished eating her cone and was meandering about the yard, smelling the blooms on the flowering bushes. Her movements were like a happy little girl's, not at all like Tandy's had been back when she was young. Tandy had a sway to her walk and a way of lowering those dark lashes and cutting her eyes around to wink at him.

"Did you grow up here?" she asked as she made her way back to sit on the top step and prop her feet on the next one down.

"I was born here," he said.

"No kiddin'! How old is this place?" she asked.

"About ninety years, near as I can figure. My daddy won it in a poker game the year before I was born. Lost his family farm the same night in the same game." *Dammit!* He hadn't meant to tell her anything. That's what happened when someone invaded his perfect hermit world.

"So your mama wasn't born here? That woman

who's a baby in the picture on the mantel?" Emmy Jo asked.

"No, she wasn't."

"Was she born here in Hickory?"

He shook his head.

"What do you do for a whole hour while you are here?"

"I'm going to ignore your nosiness, for a start," he said.

Dratted girl. She was going to interfere with his quiet time at the cabin with her incessant questions and talk. Couldn't she simply sit there or even pick a bouquet? He wouldn't mind either one if she'd leave him alone.

She giggled. "I thought I was sassy."

"You can be both."

"Tell me about your mother. She died too young."

"Yes, she did." The pain in his hip grew worse as his whole body tensed. "It was the night I graduated from high school."

"Don't tell me about that time. Tell me about when she was a baby in that picture with your grandparents. They looked so happy," Emmy Jo said.

His body relaxed, and the pain lessened. She wasn't going to hush, so he might as well tell her something, but next week he might change his schedule. "I never knew them, but then neither did she. They died when she was a baby, not even a year old. The whole story didn't come out until I was past fifty and my uncle visited from Virginia. He was on the same mission that I was."

"Mission?" Emmy Jo's big blue eyes locked with his.

"Look, if you'll promise me you'll never wear red again, I will tell you about my grandparents." If he had to talk, then she could give a little something for the story.

"Deal," she said with a big smile.

"My grandmother was Delia Anderson, and she was born and raised on a fancy horse farm in Virginia. My grandfather was Adam Findley, and he was born and brought up in the same area. He worked for Delia's father as a trainer."

"And?"

"I told you about them. That's who they are." Just telling that much put a knot in his gut.

"And if I'm going to give up my red scrubs, you really should give me a little more than that," she said.

He had all the information tucked away in a safe in his office, and he'd never even had his grandparents' names put on their tombstones. What had happened was no one's business, but that nosy girl wasn't going to be happy until he told her more. Yes, sir, next week he would sacrifice his visit to the cabin for sure.

"Is your uncle your mother's brother? Or your father's?"

73

He inhaled and let it out in a huff. "Okay, okay. It's like this. Delia and Adam fell in love, but there was no way her father was ever going to let his only daughter marry a poor man. She'd been raised with the finest that money could buy, and Adam, well, he was the son of a woman whose husband had been killed in a coal mining accident before Adam was born. His mama moved from Kentucky to Virginia to be near her sister and took in laundry and sewing to make ends meet. They did all right with what Adam made at the horse ranch, but it sure wouldn't support Delia in the style that she'd been raised." Seth finished off his ice cream.

Dang the girl anyway. The last three bites were nothing but cold frothy milk.

"So they got married anyway and had your mother, right?"

He nodded, amazed that the knot in his gut was gone. He'd figured that it would grow and suffocate him plumb to death if he ever talked about his past, but it was kind of therapeutic. Not that he'd ever tell Nora that—she'd been after him for years to see a therapist.

"He told his mama he was going to join the army, since there was a war going on, and left on a Sunday morning. She thought he'd gotten captured and died overseas, because she never heard from him again. She passed away still denying that he and Delia ran away together. But

Delia's daddy knew what had happened and he disowned her, I later found out. Anyway, after his death, her older brother, Robert Anderson, set about to find out what happened to her—between the two of us we pieced it together."

He'd never told anyone, not even Nora, about the massive amount of money he'd spent finding out about his mother's heritage. His sister would only fuss at him, and she'd never cared about digging into old ashes like he did. But then she hadn't suffered what he had or caused the trouble he had, either.

"They ran away and came to Texas?" Emmy Jo asked.

"I don't know that I want to go further about this. This is not Hickory gossip—"

Emmy Jo held up her palm. "All our home health aides sign a paper about privacy. I can't repeat anything any of my patients say or they can fire me. I will keep your secrets, Seth."

He thought about that for a few moments before he went on. "They boarded a train and rode to Kentucky, where one of his friends was working on another horse ranch. Adam was hired on and they lived there a couple of months, then moved with the friend out to West Texas, near the New Mexico border. My mother, Mary, was born there on a cattle ranch. Delia and the wife of the owner struck up a friendship, and when the woman died, Delia wasn't happy there. And about that same

75

time, this area was entering the oil boom, so they packed up their belongings and came this way in a covered wagon."

"They had cars then," Emmy Jo said, "didn't they?"

"Rich folks did, but not the working population. Even two years after they'd run away they were still looking over their shoulder, so they didn't carry anything that said who they were except for that picture on my mantel. Out in West Texas they were known as Doris and Andy, but when they had their accident in Hickory no one knew their names, because they didn't carry identification. That's why their tombstones are labeled the way they are. They were just a young married couple."

"Is that how they died—an accident? What happened?"

"That's enough," he said.

"I did bring five red scrub outfits with me." She raised an eyebrow, reminding him of Nora more than Tandy. When Tandy was trying to get her way, she'd set her mouth in a cute little way that he could never refuse.

"I'll only tell you more if you give all five of them to Oma Lynn to hide until you leave. That way you can't blackmail me anymore," he said.

"I'll put them in a paper bag and deliver them to her in the morning," Emmy Jo agreed.

Seth went on. "The horses were spooked and the wagon overturned. A piece of the wagon wheel broke and pierced Delia's leg. The doctor's report said that she died of blood loss in only a few minutes. Adam's neck was broken. The baby was unharmed."

"What happened to the baby?" Emmy Jo asked.

"You asked about my grandparents. That's enough history."

She motioned toward the door. "Okay, then, can we go inside?"

"Not today. I only go in the house on the first Sunday of every month to make sure everything is all right." He checked his watch. "We've got fifteen more minutes. I want to just sit in quietness and not talk."

He wasn't sure if he'd opened a can of worms, but he felt better than he had since the surgery. It almost seemed like his mother's spirit was there beside him.

The rocker creaked like it always had when Mary sat in it at the close of day. A nice little breeze kicked up, blowing the aroma of the wisteria his way. It had been a good day, even if he did have to endure the presence of Tandy Massey's granddaughter.

Chapter Four

Emmy Jo paced to the top of the staircase at the top of the wide upstairs hallway, back to her room and to the balcony, only to start all over again several times before she finally plopped down in the wing-back chair out in the hall. The story that Seth told her kept playing through her mind. She'd never had a superstitious bone in her body, but that night she felt as if Seth's grandmother Delia was calling out to her to tell her story. Not just the chronological events, but the way she felt when she left her home to be with the man of her dreams and the thoughts she had those last moments before she died.

"But I didn't know you, so how do I know how you felt?" Emmy Jo whispered.

She stared out the open balcony doors at the stars twinkling around a quarter moon. Had Delia seen that same moon and stars from the wagon as she traveled through Hickory? Was she thinking of her little daughter when that accident happened?

"I should write this down. What if something happens to Seth and the story dies with him?" She brought out her laptop from the closet, opened it, and the words began to flow as she felt the urgency in Delia to run away with Adam.

Raw emotion wrapped itself around Emmy Jo as she wrote about Delia tucking that little painting of her home into her satchel that evening when she left everything else behind. She would have wanted something to remind her of the good times that she'd shared with her brother and family when she was growing up. At two in the morning, Emmy Jo stopped typing and went to bed.

With only a few hours sleep, she bailed out of bed when her alarm went off, brushed her teeth, pulled her hair up into a ponytail, and grabbed a set of scrubs.

"No, not those," she reminded herself and dressed in a pair of jeans and a bright-yellow T-shirt. She folded four sets of scrubs and carried them down the stairs. Seth wouldn't be able to keep his issue with red a secret for two whole months.

When she reached the kitchen, Oma Lynn looked up from the stove with something that passed for a smile. "So you are still here?"

"I am." Emmy Jo got a paper bag from the pantry and shoved the scrubs down into it, picked up a Magic Marker from a jar filled with pencils and pens, and wrote on the outside:

IOU one red scrub as soon as the laundry is done.

She folded down the top and handed it to Oma Lynn. Then she poured herself a cup of coffee. "What can I do to help?"

"You are Seth's assistant, not kitchen help. And what is this?"

"It's payment. I'll collect them to take home with me the last day I'm here. Seth and I made a deal. He talked about his family, and I agreed not to wear red while I'm here," Emmy Jo said. "I'm not going to sit down and let you wait on me, Oma Lynn. Tell me what to do."

Oma Lynn set the bag on the cabinet with a smile, and her face didn't even crack.

"Get another plate down and put it on the table. I didn't know if you were here, so I only set it for two. I'm making pancakes and sausage. You can get the syrup out of the pantry when you get that done."

"Which syrup? I see at least four kinds," Emmy Jo yelled from the pantry.

"All of them. I never know which one Mr. Seth will want," Oma Lynn said.

Well, butter my fanny and call me a biscuit, Emmy Jo thought. So he wasn't so OCD that he was stuck on the exact same thing every day.

The saying made her think of Tandy, and a pang of homesickness hit her right in the heart. She'd heard those words come out of Tandy's mouth too many times to count when something amazed her.

It had only been two days since she'd seen her, but it was always tough when they were arguing.

"Who makes up that menu on the fridge?" Emmy Jo asked.

"Mr. Seth does that the last week of the month. Sunday dinner never changes. Sometimes the rest of it stays the same. Sometimes he shifts it around a little."

"Why does Sunday never change?"

She shrugged. "You'll have to ask him."

"How did you manage chicken and dumplings and his Saturday night supper before his hip surgery?" Emmy Jo asked.

"I made it up beforehand and left a note on the top about heating it in the microwave," she answered.

"Did you know his mama?" Emmy Jo asked.

Oma Lynn shot her a dirty look. "I'm twenty-five years younger than he is and his mama died when he was only eighteen. You do the math."

Seth was already sitting at the end of the table when Emmy Jo carried the syrup to the dining room. His thick gray hair was combed back, and she caught a whiff of his shaving lotion. He'd dressed in a light-blue shirt and dark slacks, and his walker was right beside his chair.

"Happy Monday," she said cheerfully.

"Not for me. You're still here."

"Coffee?" she asked.

"Oma Lynn brings it with the breakfast," he answered with a sharp tone.

Mr. Grumpy was back in full force.

Seth had slept better than he had in years. There had been no Sunday-night nightmares about his mother's death. He'd awakened with a song in his mind. One that talked about opening a Bible and seeing his mama's teardrops on every line and then finding a faded blue ribbon and the remnants of a lilac bouquet. It had been years since he'd heard the old hymn, but he made a mental note to get out that record and listen to it that very day.

He hadn't been very old when he realized that lilacs were his mother's favorite flower. Many times he'd taken her a bouquet, and many days he'd seen his mother sitting on the porch with her Bible lying in her lap. She'd swipe at the tears, but the drops on the pages left no doubt that she had been crying.

Remembering her that morning with the song in his head brought a good feeling. She'd loved purple, and when the wisteria and the lilac bushes bloomed, the two-room cabin had been filled with the sweet aroma of the bouquets in fruit jars. Years ago he'd thought about having the weathered old place painted, but he couldn't make himself change a thing about it. Someday it would fall completely down, yet so far the roof was still shedding water and the foundation hadn't started to rot. Hopefully it would last until he was dead and buried, because it was the only place where he was at peace—at least on the porch. Inside the house was a different story.

They ate in silence and then he went to the patio to read the newspapers. That Oma Lynn motioned for Emmy Jo to follow him didn't escape his notice. He'd hoped that maybe the two women would strike up a friendship and leave him alone, but it didn't look as if that was going to happen.

"I suppose we're going to read the newspapers this morning," she said. "It's a little chilly out here this morning. Do you want a throw for your legs?"

"If I do, I'll tell you." He picked up the *Dallas Morning News* and flipped it open.

"Well, I'm going to get myself one, because that breeze is cold." She went back into the house. "I might have another cup of coffee, too."

He ignored her and read about the new president settling into the White House. With a frown, he mumbled, "If they ain't crooked before they go into that place, they will be when they come out of it."

"What are you fussin' about now?" Emmy Jo put a cup of coffee on the table beside him and flipped a throw over his walker so he could get to it.

"Politics!" He ignored the throw until he finished the front page, then dragged it over his legs. He took a sip of the coffee before turning the page. When he glanced over, he saw her head bobbing and her shoulders wiggling and wires going from a small thing on her lap to her ears.

"What are you listening to?" he asked.

She pulled a purple plug from her ear and raised an eyebrow. "You're ready for me to read that paper?"

"No, I asked what you are listening to?"

"Josh Turner and Randy Travis doing duets," she answered.

"Who is that?"

"They sing country music. Here, listen." She reached over and put the tiny device close to his ear.

They were singing something about digging up bones. Not bad voices, and at least it wasn't that horrible stuff that Nora's grandkids listened to the last time he was in Amarillo. Mercy, that had to be ten years ago.

He pushed her hand away. "That's enough. You can start reading from the bottom of the stack of newspapers instead of waiting on me to finish this one. Just put it back where you get it. I read them in order."

He expected her to ask him why he did, but she simply slipped the bottom one out and flipped it open.

Logan awoke that Monday morning to his phone ringing. He grabbed it from the nightstand without opening his eyes and drawled a deep hello.

"Good morning, son," his mother said. "We'll be sitting down to breakfast in ten minutes. Come on down and join us."

"I need to shave and get dressed before I leave. Don't wait for me," he said.

Fifteen minutes had passed by the time he got ready and went down the steps to the parsonage located next door. "Good morning," he called out as he opened the back door into the utility room and stepped inside to the aroma of bacon and coffee.

"Hello, grandson." Jesse smiled from the table.

"Gramps." Logan nodded.

"Get a cup of coffee and refill mine. We can visit while your mama finishes breakfast. Your dad is in the study preparing for the Wednesday-night sermon." Jesse's voice had turned raspy over the years, but then he had turned eighty-two years old just a few weeks ago. He hadn't preached in years, leaving it to his son, Wyatt, every Sunday morning.

Logan kissed his mother, Paula, on the cheek and filled a mug. Then he carried the pot to the table, where he topped off his grandfather's cup. "It sure smells good in here," he said.

"So Emmy Jo is up at Seth Thomas's place, right?" Jesse asked.

Logan didn't need a road map to see that this was an ambush. "She is, and the job is going well. I talked to her yesterday."

"At the cemetery for an hour while that crazy old fool sat in front of his mama's grave." Jesse's light-gray eyes had narrowed to mere slits in his round face. His hair had fallen out so long ago that Logan didn't remember him with anything other than a reddish-blond rim around his head. And when he drew his brows down into a frown, everyone knew that a storm was brewing.

Logan met him head-on. "That's right. And what is it that you have against Seth Thomas? You never told me why you two hate each other."

"And I never will," Jesse answered through clenched teeth. "I'm not going to talk about the past, grandson. I want to talk about your future. You like this banking job, right? And you don't intend to change your mind about me paying for you to go to seminary?"

"I love my job, and we've been over this a dozen times." Logan rubbed his eyes and tried to figure out a way to make his escape.

"It's that girl. She'd make a horrible preacher's wife and you know it. So this career choice is for her, isn't it?" He glared at Logan. "And she won't do much better as a banker's wife." Jesse sighed.

"God blessed me with a good son. I prayed he'd do the same for your father."

"I'm going to marry Emmy Jo. I'm sorry that you feel like this about her and about me, Gramps," Logan said.

Paula set a platter of hash-browned potatoes and scrambled eggs on the table. "God *did* bless us with a good son, and things could have been worse." She went back to the kitchen and returned with a second platter of bacon and waffles.

"I don't see how," Jesse growled.

"Good morning," Wyatt said as he took his place at the head of the table and bowed his head. "Dad, say grace for us before this fantastic breakfast gets cold."

Jesse's gruff voice always softened when he talked to God. Evidently he and the Lord had a better relationship than he had with his only grandchild. That Monday morning, Logan wished that instead of his dad being an only child, his grandparents had had half a dozen kids and they'd all produced five or six children so he wouldn't be in the spotlight all the time.

"Amen," Jesse said.

Logan raised his head to see his mother pick up the platter of eggs and hand them to his father.

Wyatt took a portion and passed it to Logan. "Your grandpa says that you were at the cemetery yesterday."

"I was," Logan said.

He'd heard all this so many times that there was no new way for them to approach it. Too bad they had to spoil such a good breakfast with this arguing. They should know they were not going to win. There was nothing that hadn't already been said more than a dozen times, and nothing that would change his mind about Emmy Jo.

"The church committee had a meeting yesterday afternoon," Jesse said.

Logan inhaled and let it out slowly. The conversation was going to be about church business and not his relationship. There were dozens of committees that took care of decisions like business or prayer concerns. He didn't care which one had had a meeting or what they'd discussed.

"It's boiled down to this," Jesse said. "You stop seeing Emmy Jo or you can't live in the garage apartment. You have a week to get out if you decide to stay with her."

"Dad!" Wyatt exclaimed. "It's my church now. This sort of thing can't happen."

"That committee meeting had a member from each of the church groups. I'd say it can," Jesse pointed out.

"Runnin' me out of the apartment because of Emmy Jo isn't right." Logan slammed his hand down on the table, making the eggs quiver on their plate. He wished he could make his grandfather quake the same way.

"You've got to be kiddin'," Paula shrieked. "This is our son. I might not agree with his choice of a girlfriend, but I agree that this is wrong, Jesse. I can't believe that you spearheaded such a horrible thing."

"Someone had to step up and take charge." Jesse folded his arms over his chest.

Logan pushed his plate back. "I'll start packing tonight, and from now on I'll attend that little church where Emmy Jo goes. So far they haven't thrown her out."

"Tandy goes there," Jesse growled.

"So do a lot of other citizens in Hickory, some of whom are my clients at the bank. And it seems like they might have a little more forgiving nature than y'all do." He laid his napkin on the table.

"You are making a big mistake." Jesse's face turned scarlet.

Logan hoped that Jesse's blood pressure didn't cause him to stroke out right there. "Depends on whether you are wearing my shoes or yours, Gramps. I'll see y'all around. Am I still welcome in the parsonage for Sunday dinner, Mama?"

"Of course you are. We are family, and that will never change." Paula shot a dirty look across the table toward Jesse.

"Then I'll be out of the apartment tonight, and I'll see y'all Sunday. Why did my going to the cemetery to see Emmy Jo cause all this? We've been dating for years and engaged for six months. What's the big deal about the cemetery?"

"It's just the straw that broke the camel's back," Jesse said. "I will never accept that girl into this family."

"And you are a preacher?" Logan frowned. His grandfather had always been rigid, but this went beyond even him.

"It goes way beyond my calling," Jesse answered.

"Care to explain?"

Paula's forefinger shot up, pointing straight at Jesse. "I'd like to hear that explanation, also."

Wyatt gently took her hand in his. "And so would I, Dad."

"Let sleeping dogs lie," Jesse said through clenched teeth.

"We would if it didn't involve our son," Wyatt said. "And I agree with Paula. You've gone behind our backs with this, and it's just not right. I have three months left on my contract with the church. If this is the way it's going to be, Paula and I might look for something else."

Jesse raised his voice two notches. "You don't want him to get tangled up with her, either."

"Maybe not, but this shouldn't have anything to do with the church," Wyatt answered.

"What does it have to do with, Dad?" Logan asked.

"She'll drag you down in whatever career

choice you make," Paula said, taking over the conversation. "You know what kind of women she comes from. We've tried to let it run its course, but your chances at being something more than a loan officer are limited when they start doing background checks."

"Then I'll wake up every morning and be happy with Emmy Jo. See y'all at Sunday dinner. Dad, you might want to ask someone to take over my Sunday school class. I won't be there." Logan waved as he shut the door behind him.

He'd maintained his cool, and for that he was proud of himself, but he wanted to kick holes in the side of his truck. Anything to get rid of the anger burning in his gut.

When he reached the bank, he cornered his best friend, Jack, in the kitchen area and told him what had happened. "So does the offer still stand to share your trailer with you?"

"I'll bring my truck and we'll get you moved out right after work. I've got an extra bedroom that's sitting empty. I told you that living that close to your folks would never work," Jack said, puffing his blond hair out of his face with his words.

As tall as Logan, but fifty pounds heavier, Jack had been Logan's best friend since they were kids, and he was engaged to Emmy Jo's best friend, Diana.

"Thank you. I'll be glad to split the lot rent and utilities with you," Logan said.

"And I'll be happy to let you." Jack clamped a hand on his shoulder.

Logan hadn't had a single doubt that he could move in with his friend, but hearing him say it was okay took a heavy load from his shoulders. He'd been spending more time with his grandpa, and it had seemed like things were getting better. It must've just been the calm before the storm.

"You going to tell Emmy Jo why you are moving?" Jack asked.

"We don't keep secrets from each other. See you at closing time, then? And thanks again."

"You are very welcome, Logan. I'll have to run home and change into jeans. Don't want to ruin my good slacks. You can go on to the apartment and start packing. I don't envy you the job of telling Emmy Jo." Jack lowered his voice to a whisper as they left the kitchen and went to their workstations.

"I just hope I get to her before the rumors do." He waited until his ten o'clock break to text her and then only gave her the basics: *Not going so well at home. Moving in with Jack tonight. Can't wait to see you at lunch tomorrow. Will call after work.*

The message that he got back simply said: *I love you.*

CHAPTER FIVE

Seth had just finished the first page of the *Dallas Morning News* when the phone rang and Oma Lynn brought it to the deck, stretched the cord to a wall jack, and handed him the receiver.

"Good mornin', brother," Nora yelled into his ear.

He held the phone out six inches. "You don't have to shout. It's a telephone, not a tin can."

"Just a minute," she said. "Is that better?"

"Yes, what did you do?"

"I fixed it. Don't matter how I did it. If I explained, you wouldn't understand; you're too stubborn to get into the techie age. So how's Emmy Jo working out for you?"

"She's still here." He tried to think of a reason that he should get off the phone, but nothing plausible came to mind. It was eight thirty, which meant that Nora didn't have anything going at the retirement home for at least an hour and a half. He'd be crazy by then.

"I knew she was spunky from talking to her on the phone. Admit it, brother. You like having someone to help you," Nora said.

"Like I would love a boil on my butt." Maybe

if he made her mad she would just hang up on him.

Nora laughed so loud that he smiled. When she got really tickled, he could hear his mother's laughter. "Seth Thomas, you are an old geezer, but you've still got a soft heart hidden in your chest."

"Don't you bet on it, Nora. I'd hate for you to bitch at me because you lost a bunch of money. What I like best about this arrangement is Tuesdays and Thursdays—her days off," Seth said.

"I was lyin' there last night almost asleep when I finally figured out that she is kin to Tandy Massey. I didn't make the connection when I hired her, but she'd be . . . what? A granddaughter? No, Tandy had that baby out of wedlock not too many months after we graduated. This would be Tandy's great-granddaughter, right? She and I aren't far from the same age, and I have great-grandchildren about Emmy Jo's age. Tell Emmy Jo to give my best to Tandy. She was one of the few girls who was nice to me," Nora said.

"You tell her. I'm not saying anything to her about Tandy. The girl's main job is to take me to the cemetery on Sunday. Now I have to go. I've got things to do even if you don't," he said. He wasn't about to bring up Tandy's name to Emmy Jo. She could ask more questions than a sane man could answer without encouraging her.

It didn't do a bit of good. Instead of saying good-bye, she asked, "How did Sunday go at the cemetery?"

"Fine." Maybe if he answered with only one word, she'd finally get the hint.

"That's all. Just fine?" Nora asked.

"She sat in the truck with her boyfriend for an hour and left me alone. Is that enough information for you?"

Nora giggled. "Did you go to the home place? What did she do there?"

"We talked." *God almighty! Did she want a play-by-play?*

"About?"

"Should I write a damn book about what all we said?" *Surely that would make her throw the phone at the wall.*

"You don't have to get huffy. Retirement hasn't been good for you, brother. You were a lot easier to talk to when you worked sixteen hours a day at the real estate office. I thought maybe you'd get out more and get to know people once you retired. You need something to get you out of that rut you live in." Nora's tone went cold.

"I like my rut. It's comfortable, except when you meddle in my life." Seth glanced over at the empty chair beside him.

"A rut is a horrible place to be, especially when you are old. Spice up your life or dry up and die an unhappy old man," Nora argued.

"You might be old, but I'm not," he said.

"You will always be thirteen months older than me." She laughed. "Good-bye, brother. I'll call again in a few days, and if you don't answer, I'll hire a limo to drive me to Hickory."

"Don't you dare!" he sputtered.

"Oh, I will and you know it. I'm rich as Midas and can do whatever I damn well please. If Oma Lynn tells me you can't come to the phone, I'll be there in four hours."

"Okay, I'll talk to you," Seth said. *Damn woman! She would try the patience of Job. No, she'd make Lucifer turn tail and hide out in a cave.*

"Good. Don't get too lonely now. Emmy Jo will be home at five."

"This is not her home," Seth said quickly.

"It is until the end of May. 'Bye, Seth."

The line went dead before he could say another thing. He put the receiver back on the base, picked up his newspaper, scanned the first three pages, and laid it aside. This would never, ever be Emmy Jo's home.

The breakfast crowd at Libby's had thinned out by the time Emmy Jo got there on Tuesday morning. She slid into the booth in the back corner, ordered a cup of coffee, and opened her laptop to read through the story she'd started. The library opened in thirty minutes and she planned to spend her morning there, but until then she would take notes with her trusty pen in a red composition book. Somehow she knew that what Seth had told her was the tip of the iceberg to the big fight between the three old people. Just how those two people riding through town in a wagon connected the whole thing was a mystery, but maybe Emmy Jo could get it to unfold with some research into their backgrounds. Wasn't that how all those detective shows on television worked? They started with a crime, which was the big secret in her case. In order to understand what was going on, they went back to see what had happened in the past.

She nodded at her own thoughts. She'd figure it all out down to the tiniest detail.

"Hey." Diana slid into the other side of the booth and set a plate full of pancakes down on the table. "Why haven't you called me?"

"You've got my number on speed dial, and you were the one who wouldn't let me stay with you. Why didn't you call me?"

"I have nothing to apologize for. My heart said that you were makin' a mistake and I wasn't goin' to aid in that," Diana said defensively.

"What does your heart say now?"

"That I miss talkin' to you. We haven't gone this long since we were in the third grade and had that fight over Theresa Jones." Diana laid a hand on Emmy Jo's. "Can we forgive and forget?"

Emmy Jo slid out of the booth and hugged Diana. "Of course we can. Lord, I missed you and I would've called, but things have been crazy. I wish you could see the room I've got up there, Diana. The house is absolutely beautiful, but it's so lonely. It's like it's callin' out to me to make it happy."

Diana hugged her tightly. "And Seth?"

"Oh, he's eccentric, but I kind of like the old guy." Emmy Jo went back to her seat on the other side of the booth. "He's got a soft heart hidin' in that tough old skin. And you've never seen anyone work as hard as he is at getting mobile again."

"So?" Diana waved a hand over all the work on the table. "You settin' up shop in here? Mama might charge you rent if you are."

"Only for half an hour. You helping out your mama on your day off?"

"Yep," Diana said as she poured maple syrup on the tall stack of pancakes.

"So how's things at the office?"

"'Bout the same. Everyone still thinks you are bat-shit crazy for taking the job, but I'm dyin' to hear everything, so start talkin'. You said the house is lonely. How can a building have feelings?"

"I'm not sure, but it's this big old monster of a place that needs people in it." She picked up a fork and stole a bite of Diana's pancakes.

"I guess you heard that the church pitched a fit and made Logan move out of the apartment," Diana said.

"I'm furious over that. What kind of people are they? And, girl"—Emmy Jo closed her laptop and leaned forward—"they might take your Sunday school class away from you if they see you talking to me."

"I already told Brother Wyatt that he'd have to find someone else. I felt so bad about not letting you stay with me on Friday night that I couldn't sleep, and on Sunday morning I felt like a hypocrite in my class. Of all the things that we were studying, it was the story of the Good Samaritan. Felt like someone was putting a knife in my heart and twisting," Diana said.

"You are forgiven, and it's forgotten. I felt bad that I put you in that position, but my gut was right. The job isn't bad at all." Emmy Jo chuckled. "I'd sure like to know what it is about all this that put my granny on edge, though."

"Maybe it goes back to when Seth, Jesse, and Tandy were all in school together," Diana said between bites. "And if you want to stay with me the week between when you finish this job and when you and Logan get married, you are welcome."

"Thank you." Emmy Jo smiled as she made a note to check old newspapers for anything from when those three were in school together. "Where is Libby?"

"In the kitchen helping Daddy with the prep work for the lunch run. I'll have to get back there soon, but I wanted to talk to you. Thanks for understanding." Diana laid a hand on Emmy Jo's and squeezed. "Oh, and your favorite client, Miz Edna, sends her greetings. Everyone at the office took on a couple of your clients until you come back, so I got her. She's a darlin' old gal. I love it when I get to visit with her."

"Give her a hug for me and tell her I miss her." Emmy Jo pointed at the clock. "Library is open now. That's where I'm spending my morning. I'm off on Tuesdays. Maybe next week we can have breakfast together."

Another squeeze and Diana removed her hand. "Sounds good to me, and if you ever just want a place to hang out on your days off, the spare key is taped to the bottom of the mailbox."

"I just might take you up on that." She envisioned a quiet place to work all day on her story if she could get Seth to open up again and tell her more. "Tell Libby hello for me," she said as she gathered up her things and headed out of the café.

During her high school years, she and Diana had both worked any spare hours they had at the diner. The job not only put clothes on Emmy Jo's back, but it helped out a lot of times when Tandy would have had to make a choice between paying the electric bill or going to bingo.

The librarian, Edith, opened the doors when Emmy Jo parked. "Hey, girl. What are you doing here during your workday? I heard you were Seth Thomas's new assistant."

"Just doing some research on my day off," Emmy Jo answered. "You got any of the old yearbooks?"

"At one time we did, but water damage in that part of the library a few years back ruined some of the oldest ones." Edith flipped on the lights. "What's it like working in that house for Seth?"

"It's a job." Emmy Jo hurried off to the little room off to one side so she could use the machine to bring up copies of all the old Young County newspapers. If Edith got started, she'd talk for hours, and Emmy Jo had work to do. Still, she felt a little guilty about brushing the old girl off.

The names of the newspapers and the dates they were published were taped to the front of the desk. The one she was interested in that day was the *Graham Leader*, which had been in business from 1870 to 1970.

She took out her notebook and started to scroll through the first one, looking at headlines for anything that mentioned a wagon wreck in Hickory between 1917 and 1919. She hit pay dirt in a July 1918 newspaper. The article didn't make the front page but appeared on the second page near the top. It said that an unidentified couple traveling with a small child had been killed when their wagon overturned on the outskirts of Hickory. For no apparent reason, the two horses had gone berserk. The woman hit her head on a rock and died instantly. The man's neck was broken.

"Hmm." Emmy Jo paused. Seth had told her that a piece of wood pierced his grandmother's leg and she'd bled out in seconds. She read through the article again and decided that Seth probably had information from documents he'd found in his research that the newspaper reporter didn't have back then. She decided to believe Seth's story and read on, learning that a local pastor and his wife took the little girl child into their home until relatives could be found. The couple had worn wedding bands, so it was assumed they were married and the baby belonged to them.

Seth hadn't told her the part about the preacher and his wife taking Mary into their home. She would have been an upstanding member of the church and of Hickory. Emmy Jo scrolled through the rest of that paper and several more and finally found that Preacher Roberts and his wife had officially adopted the child of the wreck. No one had come forward in two years to claim her, so the judge declared it okay for them to proceed with the adoption. Emmy Jo looked through several more papers but couldn't find anything on Mary Roberts until she found a marriage license listing in August 1934 for Mary Roberts and Samuel Thomas. She flipped back six months and went slowly. There was no mention of an engagement and nothing in the paper about a reception in the church following the courthouse news.

Emmy Jo did the math in her head. Seth was born seven months after the marriage. "Oh, no!" She clapped her hands over her cheeks. Maybe that's why they'd shunned her. Eighty years ago that would have been a big black taboo, for the preacher's daughter to get pregnant before marriage.

She glanced at the clock and realized it was almost noon. Time to gather up her things and go meet Logan at the Dairy Queen for lunch.

Edith poked her head around the door. "I'm so sorry I didn't have time to come help you, but I had to get a whole raft of books shelved. Folks read more in the summertime. And now it's lunchtime. Well, you best get on and meet your feller. Helen O'Malley is bringing some of her chili, and she and I are going to have a little visit. Maybe we can visit longer next time you come in."

"Yes, ma'am, and I'm sorry for my short answer. I was in a hurry," Emmy Jo said.

Edith waved her away. "Looks like we both had things to do this mornin'."

Emmy Jo didn't realize how hungry she was until she walked in the Dairy Queen and got a whiff of a mixture of burgers, onions, and tacos.

Logan stood up and wrapped her up in a bear hug. "Well, hello, beautiful!" he said, brushing a kiss across her lips.

She hugged him tightly. "You are so sweet, but I look like warmed-over sin today."

"Then warmed-over sin is beautiful." He took her hand in his and kissed the palm, sending shivers down her backbone. Then he motioned for her to scoot across the booth seat so he could sit beside her.

"I absolutely love you, Logan." She rested her hand on his thigh and asked, "Did you get all moved in last night?"

Logan chuckled. "Yes, we did get moved in. I was going to call you, but it was way past midnight when we were done. I slept like a rock. Should have moved in with Jack right out of college, but I was trying to get the folks to come around to accepting you and me."

"Never going to happen. Not with them or Tandy," she said.

The waitress set their food on the table. "Anything else?"

"You ordered!" Emmy Jo planted a kiss on Logan's cheek. "I'm so hungry and I thought we'd have to wait. I love you even more than I did an hour ago."

"Bacon cheeseburgers, fries, and sweet tea," he said. "Anything else?"

She shook her head. "This looks so good."

"Then I guess that's all," he told the waitress. Logan was so thoughtful that sometimes she wondered how the devil she'd gotten so lucky.

"Tell me the whole story about the moving-out business," she said as she popped a hot fry into her mouth and removed the paper from her burger.

"I already did," he said.

"But I couldn't see your expression. I'm so sorry about the way they're acting, and it's all because of me. Logan, what are we going to do? I was sure they'd come around eventually, but now I'm worried that later you will resent me for it." Her eyes filled with tears. Family, crazy and mixed-up as it was, was important. To have them shun Logan because of her hurt Emmy Jo deep down in her soul.

"This will not come between us, I promise. I can't figure out why us meeting in the cemetery set the church committees on their ear so bad. I can kiss you right here and no one says a word about it. We've probably even been seen coming out of a motel together. So what's the big deal about the cemetery?"

"It's Seth," she said. "Did you know that his

mama and daddy were only married about seven months when he was born? Back in those days that would have been pretty bad. That might have been the start of why everyone looked down on his mama."

"But that wouldn't keep Tandy and Gramps from liking him. They were born about the same time. It would have been their parents that had a problem with Mary, not them." He picked up her hand and kissed each knuckle. "Where did you go after the cemetery?"

Her heart kicked in an extra beat at the touch of his lips. "We went down to the house where he grew up. I didn't even know that place existed and I've lived here my whole life. It's this tiny little house with probably only two rooms in it. There's a rocking chair on the porch where he likes to sit and think. He's a lonely old soul, but he's a softy. He loved his family and especially his mama."

"Maybe folks like Gramps and Tandy hate him because he's gotten rich. He might have been poor back then, but I hear he's got enough money to buy the state of Texas these days," Logan said. "No . . . that's not right, either. What if Jesse and Seth both loved Tandy and she jilted both of them?"

"Yeah, right. God, this is good. Do you think something happened when they were kids in school?" Emmy Jo's brows drew down into a deep frown. "I'll just have to keep going. Today I found out about the fact that Mary was pregnant when she and Samuel got married. I'll go deeper and find out more."

"My love, the sleuth." He chuckled.

"It's something that's been laid on my heart, Logan. I've been writing it down in story form in the evenings after supper. I feel this crazy connection and a gnawing desire to find out what's going on. I can't put my finger on any of it, but it's drawing me," she said.

"Are you sure that's healthy?" he asked.

"I don't know what it is, but I can't stop."

"Then good luck. Now let's talk about us. I've offered to work every Saturday morning while you are up at Seth's place. That way I can take Thursday afternoons off and we can spend them together. And I put in for a week's vacation starting the day of our wedding, so we can have a honeymoon." He flashed a brilliant smile.

"Honeymoon!" she squealed.

He'd mentioned it before, but she'd thought he was kidding. With the expense of renting a place and getting started, she hadn't thought they could afford even a weekend away from Hickory and their jobs.

"Yes, darlin', a honeymoon, and there will be no sleuthing on the honeymoon unless you lose your bra and we have to track it down."

She giggled. "Shh, someone will hear you."

"Okay, then, let's talk about the trailer coming open for rent the first of June in the Hickory trailer park. We might think about renting it until we can save up enough for a down payment on a house," he said.

"You've been busy." She grinned. "How far is it from my granny's place?"

"All the way to the back side of the park. We can even drive in and out the rear gate if you're afraid she'll bring out that shotgun again." He brushed her hair back behind her ear and whispered, "And no one can hear us when—"

She put a finger over his lips. "But they can now."

"You are blushin'," he teased.

"Of course I am. You know I get all heated up when we touch. You'd better finish your lunch. You've got to be at the bank in fifteen minutes."

"Party pooper. I was enjoying the visions in my head about our honeymoon, and now I've got loan applications on my mind."

She squeezed his thigh under the table. "Not me. I'm still thinkin' about our honeymoon—and not jobs, people, or nothing can interfere with us being together then."

"You keep playin' with my leg and I'll call in sick this afternoon," he whispered.

She slid her hand up another six inches. "Is that a promise?"

"You're killin' me, woman," he drawled.

She leaned over and whispered, "But what a way to die."

He kissed her on the cheek and slid out of the booth. "If I don't leave right now, I'll get fired. As it is, all I'll get done this afternoon is think of you."

"I love it when you say things like that." She watched him through the window until she couldn't even see his truck, and then she went back to the library and spent the afternoon looking through the newspapers from the early 1940s until 1953. Nothing was mentioned about Seth Thomas except that he and Tandy Massey were both pictured with the graduating seniors of 1953.

Granny was beautiful. Emmy Jo leaned in closer to the screen to see the tiny picture better. "And look at Seth with that dark hair and those brooding eyes."

Then she went forward a couple of pictures and there was Jesse, light haired, a smirk on his round face. Logan looked nothing like him, thank goodness—she'd never seen that cocky look on his face. Jesse must have thought he was something special in those days.

What made him so popular? Was it because his folks had more money than the other people in town? It sure wasn't his looks. Seth was ten times more handsome than Jesse.

But he'd been the quarterback of the football

team that almost went to state their senior year. The editor said that if he'd been able to play the team would have been a shoo-in for the title, but a few days before the playoff game, a gang had attacked him and come near to killing the boy.

She fished her phone from her purse and called Logan.

"Your timing is great. I'm on break," he said.

She read the newspaper article to him, word for word. "Has Jesse ever mentioned this? I don't have a clue about it. Granny never says anything but cusswords when she talks about him or Seth."

"Yes, he has, many times. I've heard all about how they had the state title cinched up tight, but then he got beat up by a bunch of rival kids and the team lost the whole thing. It was the only year in history that Hickory came close to winning the big trophy," Logan answered.

"Is that what he talked about when he was trying to get you to play football?" she asked.

"Oh, yes. All about the wonderful world of sports that he and my dad both lived in during their high school glory days. Dad was a crackerjack basketball player, and Gramps went in for football," Logan said. "I don't see how any of this would have a thing to do with Seth or Tandy, though. Seth didn't play, and there weren't girls' sports to speak of, so that leaves Tandy out."

"Everyone in town would have known if they

were involved with the sports scene somehow, I guess," she said. "Call you later. Love you."

"Love you, too," he said.

She went back to the screen and studied the write-up about each senior class member. Jesse wasn't only the star of the football team; he was the class president all four of their high school years and had been voted most likely to succeed.

She moved forward a few spots to Tandy Massey. She was in Future Homemakers of America. That was it, nothing more. That meant she did not run in the same circles with Jesse Grady.

Moving forward again, she stopped on Nora Thomas. The black-and-white picture did not show what color her hair was, but it was curly and not dark, maybe red or strawberry blonde. Her eyes looked to be the same shade as Seth's. Under her picture, it said that she was salutatorian of her graduating class.

"I bet that caused a ripple in the rumor mill," Emmy Jo said. "She wasn't voted into anything, but she was smart."

Then she moved over to Seth again. Same eyes as his sister, Nora, and there was nothing at all under his picture. She read the article that included who was voted what among the seniors, and his name was not listed. He went to school, he graduated, and that was all.

She moved ahead to the next few papers. In July, Jesse joined the navy and there was a splash complete with picture about that. The next week, Seth joined the army along with three other guys, and his article was buried on an inside page.

Speeding ahead four years to 1957, she found a front-page article with Jesse's picture, telling about him getting out of the navy. The last two years he'd spent his time as a chaplain, and the smirk was gone from his face. Maybe he had learned something while he was floating around in the ocean on a big ship.

There was nothing about Seth coming home to Hickory from the service, but there was a small article on page five in an August edition saying that Clifford O'Dell had hired an assistant. Seth Thomas would be working in the land, loan, and real estate business on Main Street.

"Why would he be nice to Seth when the rest of the town ignored him?" she muttered.

She made a note to talk to Logan about that. If Logan asked Jesse, would he tell him why one man hired him when it appeared that no one else in town gave a flip about a poor kid named Seth Thomas?

At four thirty she closed her notebook, now with as many questions as her pages and pages of information. She waved at Edith and got back to Seth's at fifteen minutes until five. She set her tote bag and purse on the steps and rushed through the living room and into the dining room, where Seth was already seated at the supper table.

"Did you miss me?" she asked cheerfully.

"Were you gone?" he shot back.

"Ah, so you did." She gave him a quick pat on the shoulder on her way past him.

"Like I'd miss a case of the plague," he grumbled.

"I love you, too, Seth Thomas," she said. "But right now I love Oma Lynn more than you, because the menu says we're having fried chicken with all the fixin's. Don't pout. You get to spend the whole day with me tomorrow."

"Well, ain't I just the luckiest old guy in Hickory?"

She went through the door into the kitchen, where she picked up a bowl of mashed potatoes and carried them to the table. "Don't stick your finger in those while I'm bringing out the corn on the cob. Old sourpuss like you would spoil them."

"I will do whatever I please," he declared.

She moved the bowl to the other end of the table so he couldn't reach it.

"You are worse than my sister," he said.

"I'll take that as a compliment." She and Oma Lynn made two more trips before she scooted the food close enough that he could get to it.

"So what did you do today?" Oma Lynn sat

down and passed the chicken to Seth, who took a leg and a thigh and sent it on to Emmy Jo.

"I had coffee with Diana this morning at Libby's, went to the library, had lunch with Logan, and went back to the library this afternoon." She put a breast on her plate and gave the platter back to Oma Lynn.

"You spent the whole day in the library?" Seth asked. "Doing what?"

"Research," she answered. "What did you do other than count the hours until I came home?"

Oma Lynn chuckled under her breath.

Seth shrugged. "Are you sure you aren't Nora's granddaughter? Maybe she had a child none of us knew about."

"Nope, my great-granny is Tandy Massey, my granny was Rose, my mama was Crystal, and now there's me, the fourth generation of wild Massey women giving Hickory plenty of fodder for the rumor mill," Emmy Jo answered.

Oma Lynn almost choked. "Don't say things like that when I've got a mouthful of sweet tea. You got to admit, Seth, she brings some life into this old house."

"I liked it fine the way it was," he said.

Emmy Jo flashed a bright smile toward Oma Lynn. "Thank you. At least someone appreciates my efforts."

Oma Lynn nodded. "Did you talk to Tandy today?"

"Well, crap!" Emmy Jo slapped her forehead. "I meant to call her. I'll do it on Thursday. Maybe she'll meet me in town for ice cream."

"She won the five-hundred-dollar pot at bingo last Friday night," Oma Lynn said.

"Well, then she might not want to see me, since she'll think that getting rid of me made her lucky." Emmy Jo giggled.

"I'd think I was lucky if I could get rid of you," Seth grumbled.

"You'd have to drop dead to get rid of me." She accentuated every word with a poke of her fork. "And I'd cry if you died, so you have to live until the end of May. Look at it this way—there's a light at the end of your tunnel. Granny is going to be kin to me the rest of her life, no matter if she likes it or not. At least you don't have to claim me."

"Praise the Lord," he said.

Emmy Jo was pretty sure he was biting the inside of his lip to keep from grinning.

CHAPTER SIX

Before she died, Seth's mother's favorite time of the year had been spring. This would have been the time to plant the garden, to sit on the porch in the evening after a day's work was done and to open the windows to air out the house. A time to wait for his dad, Sam, to come home from work and hope that he was in a good mood.

Sitting there on the patio that morning, Seth could almost hear Mary humming as she went about the daily chores. That made him think of that first time he heard Emmy Jo humming the Eddy Arnold tune. A bright smile covered his face, but it soon faded. Spring had turned from the best time of the year into the worst. Sam had started drinking again not long after the first of the year. Six weeks later, when the potatoes had been planted at the first of spring, he and Lottie McDonald, a barmaid who worked at one of the bars south of Hickory, ran away together. In mid-May, just as summer was pushing spring into the history books, his mother had died. The potatoes weren't even ready to be dug yet.

Oma Lynn poked her head around the door in the middle of the morning. "Snacks on the patio or in your office?"

It couldn't be midmorning already. Seth glanced at his watch and then at the stack of papers that he hadn't touched. "Patio today. It's too pretty a day to waste by stayin' inside."

"Reminds me of the cool mornings when Mama would make us go pick the green beans," Oma Lynn said. "I loved fresh green beans cooked with bacon and new potatoes, though I did not like to pick beans or to snap them, either. Emmy Jo, can you come on inside and help me carry out the popcorn and hot chocolate?"

Seth could almost taste the smoky flavor of a pot of green beans with a big hunk of his mother's warm corn bread to sop up the pot liquor. He would have to remember to put that on the menu for the next month.

Emmy Jo laid aside the paper. "I cannot believe how people air their dirty laundry in a public newspaper. I've been looking at the old papers, and they had advice columns in them but they weren't like this."

"There were more restrictions on what a person could put in a paper back then. Besides, most of us were more concerned with having enough to eat." Oma Lynn was still rattling on about the Depression as Seth went back to his paper, but still not one headline caught his attention. He laid it aside and watched a robin gather dead leaves and small sticks to build a nest.

"Enjoy your baby birds," Seth muttered. "Some of us never get the privilege of having a family of our own."

"What was that?" Emmy Jo said at his elbow as she sat a big crock of hot buttered popcorn on the table. "Were you talking to me?" She filled an oversize mug with hot chocolate and handed it to him.

"No, I was talking to myself," he said.

Emmy Jo picked up the hot chocolate and held it in her hands. "That's a sign that you are getting old or crazy."

"I'm already old, and the crazy part is debatable if you ask folks in town," he said.

"You are only as old as you let yourself be, and that means you'll always be young." Emmy Jo sipped the hot chocolate. "This is really good. Homemade, right? It tastes like what Granny makes. Diana and I hated that instant crap after we'd had the good stuff. When we were in high school, we'd talk Libby into making us a cup like this after evening cleanup at the café."

"Jeff." He nodded.

"What? Who is Jeff? Is that a fancy chocolate or something?"

"I used to come in there to get a carryout meal when Libby had fish night. The tall waitress with the brown hair was Jeff. You were Mutt," he said.

"Oh, now I get it—that old cartoon thing." Emmy Jo smiled. "I don't remember you."

"I was only in there five minutes. Got my order and got out," Seth said.

"Well, you should've stuck around and had some hot chocolate. It tasted like this," Emmy Jo said.

"We had popcorn and hot chocolate for supper on Sunday nights," Seth said wistfully. The aroma of warm butter always brought on a vision of his mother shaking her biggest pot over the old gas stove so the popcorn wouldn't stick. "Mama said that's what they had when she was growing up, because her adopted dad had to preach and he didn't want anything heavy on his stomach before services."

"Which church?" Emmy Jo asked.

Lord, have mercy! This girl could ask more questions than anyone he'd ever known. "We didn't attend church. Mama gathered us all around in the living room and told us Bible stories."

"Even when you were a teenager?" she asked.

"Yes, even when I was a teenager. When Mama died I was barely eighteen, and Nora was seventeen. She and Walter got married the day after we buried Mama, and he took her and my younger brother, Matthew, to Amarillo, where Walter owned an oil company along with his father. Matthew was only ten that year."

"How old was Walter?"

"Twenty, but his granddad had seen a future in oil back in the boom days and made a fortune.

When Walter graduated high school, the grandfather retired and gave the company to him and his father jointly."

Emmy Jo whistled through her teeth. "I can't imagine having that kind of luck fall into my lap."

"Neither could Nora, but she married him for love. He was a good man and they finished raising Matthew, plus they had three of their own."

"It must have been wonderful to have siblings." Emmy Jo sighed. "I always envied the kids that had a brother or a sister."

He wished he could pull a sister from thin air and give it to her. Too bad Nora was past eighty, or he'd offer to share her with Emmy Jo.

"And while they were fightin' and fussin', they probably were jealous of you because you didn't have to share anything," he said.

"I never thought of that. Bless Nora's heart, though. Being so young and taking on the raisin' of her younger brother," Emmy Jo said.

"Nora was always older than her years." A vision flashed into his mind of the day that he'd gotten on the bus to leave for basic training and waved good-bye to the family. Matthew had been so excited to be going to a new place. The bus and the 1952 Ford pulled away from Hickory at the same time, leaving their mother's fresh grave behind.

"Where is Matthew now? Amarillo?" Emmy Jo

asked. She hadn't run across his name in any of the research she'd done.

"Matthew was planning to make a career of the army, but he died in a training session when he was only twenty. Nora insisted on burying him in Amarillo, and in those days—well, it seemed like the right thing to do."

Emmy Jo's eyes filled with tears. "I'm so sorry. She takes care of him and you take care of Mary. That is so sweet."

"Thank you." He swallowed hard to get the lump in his throat to go away as he remembered the military funeral. Those were sad days, but nothing compared to the day he'd had to stand beside his mother's plot as they buried her.

When they'd finished their chocolate, Emmy Jo filled the two empty mugs with coffee and sipped at hers. Anyone who could drink coffee as strong as he liked it and not even wince was a good kid—even if she was nosy.

"I wonder why Mary fell in love with your dad," she said after several minutes of silence.

"She didn't." He wished he could take the words back the moment they left his mouth, because they'd bring on more questions.

Emmy Jo sat up straighter and set her mug on the table. She was four feet away, facing him when he looked her way. "Are you going to explain?"

"Might as well, or you'll hound me until I

drop dead," he said. "Remember the story of the wagon overturning?"

It was that instant flash of a smile as well as the sarcasm that reminded him so much of Nora when she was that age. Telling Emmy Jo things was like talking to Nora when they were teenagers and shared everything.

"Samuel Thomas, my dad, was about five years old that day. His parents had gone down to Beaumont to see about some kind of job in the oil well boom and left him with his grandparents," he said. "Mama never knew this, at least not while she was alive."

"How did you find out?"

"When Daddy left us, I was sixteen. He put a letter under my pillow explaining the way things happened and the way he felt. I could never bring myself to tell her, and looking back I imagine it was the most difficult thing he ever felt compelled to write." Sadness filled Seth's heart, and he felt a twinge of the same nausea that he'd had the day he took the letter to the woods to read it.

"Do you still have the letter?"

"Yes, and it's locked away in a safe with everything else that I've uncovered about my family. Do you want to hear this or not?" he snapped.

She clamped her mouth shut and bobbed her head a couple of times.

He picked up his coffee and drank several sips, getting his thoughts all together before he started again. He took a deep breath and let it out slowly as the words on the letter came back to his mind.

He'd found it early on a Saturday morning and recognized his father's tight handwriting when he opened the five pages. The first words said that the letter was only for his eyes, because Samuel felt that he owed him an explanation. Tucked into his shirt, close to his side, it had practically burned a hole in his skin at the breakfast table.

"Where's Daddy?" Nora had asked.

"He didn't come home last night," Mary had answered. "I expect he worked all night unloading feed down at the store. They get a shipment in on Friday evenings some time. He'll be here in a little while, and we'll have to be quiet so he can rest."

Seth shut his eyes some sixty-six years later and could smell the warm biscuits that Mary took from the oven that horrible morning. She'd set them in the middle of the table along with a bowl of sausage gravy and asked his brother, Matthew, to say grace. The letter felt like hot coals against his skin one minute and a snowball the next as he forced food down.

More than sixty years later, his stomach still knotted up thinking about that time in his life. He didn't look at Emmy Jo when he talked.

"That day my mother's folks were killed, my dad's grandparents told him that his parents weren't coming back and he had to live with them forever. He said that his grandma was weeping so hard that his grandpa had to tell him that his father and mother had been killed in a bank robbery that had gone bad. They'd simply been in the wrong place at the wrong time."

"Oh, no! Poor little guy." Emmy Jo's big blue eyes misted over.

"He was so angry that he ran out of the house and down the hill to the dirt road going into town. He said in the letter that the woman in the wagon was singing when he threw a big rock at the horses. He thought that no one should be happy and singing when his parents were dead and he'd never hug them again. Then it all happened so fast and yet it took forever. The horse that he hit in the leg stumbled and the other one went wild. The wagon fell off to one side and the two people went flying out into the air."

"Oh. My. God!" Emmy Jo covered her eyes. "Your father caused the deaths as a little boy. What happened to him?"

"He never told anyone about it, kept it bottled up inside him. He became an unruly child and never finished school. His grandfather died when he was fourteen. His grandmother really lost control of him. She died when he was twenty and he inherited the family farm. He lost it in a poker game one night to Jesse Grady's daddy and won our house the same night from an old guy that only lived in Hickory a few months."

Emmy Jo's voice was barely a whisper. "He told you all that in the letter?"

Seth nodded. Nothing was ever the same after that. He knew why his father left and yet he couldn't tell his mother without coming clean about what Samuel had written about her. And he could not bear the pain in her eyes every time she looked at him if he knew the shame that she'd suffered. And the bad thing was that none of the sequence of events up to that day or the ones to follow were a damn bit her fault.

"What did you say to him when you saw him again?" Emmy Jo asked.

"I never did see my dad after that. He and Lottie McDonald got into her old car and they never came back to Hickory. We didn't know where he went, but many, many years later, long after Mama was gone, I discovered they'd gone to California and were buried somewhere around Orange Grove."

Emmy Jo frowned. "Who was Lottie McDonald?"

"A barmaid that he'd been having a fling with for several years."

"No!" Her voice came out in a screech. "He left

your mother to face that kind of embarrassment. Why would he do that?"

"He said in the letter that he'd always been in love with Lottie and that he'd only married my mother because he was trying to atone for his sins," Seth answered.

"How on earth did your mother survive with three kids to take care of and no husband?" Emmy Jo asked.

"That's a story for another day. It's almost lunchtime. Let's go inside," he answered. Telling that much had lifted some of the burden from his heart, but he could not answer that question—not today and maybe not ever. Other than his mother's death, the days that followed his father's disappearance had been the hardest that he'd ever faced.

"Does Jesse know about the poker game?"

"Oh, I'm sure Jesse knows, and if I was to ever see that old bastard again, he'd goad me about it," he answered.

"No doubt about that. He'd glory in it," Emmy Jo said.

"Oh, yes, he would." Seth swung his legs out to the side and put a hand on each side of his walker. Getting up after sitting so long was tough, but it was getting easier.

The story that Seth told played through Emmy Jo's mind as she helped Oma Lynn bring lunch to the table that day. For dessert, she'd made a chocolate sheet cake that looked exactly like the ones that Tandy stirred up. Looking at it made Emmy Jo so homesick that she had to brush away a tear. She missed her granny, and even if she was cussin' mad, at least Emmy Jo could hear her voice.

Oma Lynn brought out three glasses of sweet tea. "I heard that Wyatt and Paula have been offered the church over in Graham."

"That didn't take long. Logan only moved out Monday night." Emmy Jo dipped into the soup. "Good Lord, Oma Lynn. You should run a restaurant."

"No, thank you. I was waitress at one over in Graham for more than twenty years. I like this job much better," she said.

"So you think they'll really move from Hickory?" Seth asked.

"If they do it'll be the first time in my lifetime that a Grady hasn't been a preacher at that church," Oma Lynn said.

"So Jesse's daddy was a preacher?" Emmy Jo's eyes widened.

"As well as a farmer. He owned a big spread out west of town," Seth said. "Got religion about the time that Jesse was born and started preachin' on the side."

Emmy Jo wondered just what sins Jesse was trying to atone for by becoming a preacher.

• • •

Thursday morning found a nervous Emmy Jo waiting in Libby's Diner for her grandmother to show up. Tandy had been cool on the phone the night before, but she had agreed to meet Emmy Jo for breakfast—if Emmy Jo was paying.

Emmy Jo heaved a long sigh of relief when she saw Tandy park her old Ford outside the café. But then she held her breath when Tandy just sat there as if she was trying to make up her mind whether to leave or get out of the car. Finally, the door opened and Tandy swung her legs out, then stood up and took another full minute to close the door. Emmy Jo held her hands tightly to keep from clapping when Tandy took two steps toward the café. She ignored Emmy Jo's wave when she was inside and stopped to talk to Henry, who was having doughnuts and coffee. Until she slid into the seat on the other side of the booth, Emmy Jo still wasn't sure if she'd actually join her.

Libby brought two cups of coffee to the table. "So what's goin' on in your world besides winning big at bingo?"

"Not much. I bought a new set of tires for my car and paid the electric bill with the money," Tandy answered. "I got enough left to play again Friday night. Probably ruinin' my luck by havin' breakfast with this renegade."

"Or maybe you're doubling your luck." Libby laughed. "What can I get you girls this morning?"

"I'll have the breakfast special," Tandy said. "With a short stack of pancakes and fruit on the side."

"Same here," Emmy Jo said.

Libby smiled. "Be right out. Won't take long. The morning rush is done over. Any time you want to go back to work, we'd sure hire you, Miz Tandy. We ain't had a waitress as dependable as you were since you left us."

"Thanks, Libby, but these old legs have stood on concrete long enough in their lifetime. I feel lucky I ain't had to have my knees or hips replaced," Tandy said.

"Well, the offer is always there if you want to work a few hours a week," Libby told her as she headed toward the kitchen.

Tandy tucked her chin-length gray hair behind her ears and leaned forward. "I heard that Logan moved in with Jack in my trailer court and that Wyatt and Paula are thinking about taking a preachin' job in Graham. And that Jesse Grady is about to have a fit over it all. Good! That old son of a bitch."

"Granny!" Emmy Jo exclaimed and whispered, "What else did you hear?"

"Well, for the first time in history, instead of being the outcast, I was the queen. Everyone wants to know about that house and Seth, and since you work there . . ." Tandy let the sentence dangle.

"You want me to gossip?"

"No, gossip is just facts that might be true. I want the real deal," Tandy replied.

"Tell you what: You tell me something about Seth and Jesse when they were in high school and I'll tell you something about the house. Like I want to know why that rival team only whipped Jesse and not any other members of the Hickory football team. Why didn't anyone ever identify those guys who did the beating?" she asked.

"That was a long time ago and I don't remember the details." Tandy looked over Emmy Jo's shoulder, a sign that she was lying. "Now tell me about the house. I don't give a damn about Seth, but I would like to know what the inside of that big place looks like."

"Don't seem like a fair trade to me. I didn't get anything, so why should I give anything?" Emmy Jo said.

"Don't you take that tone with me. I don't care if you are grown and about to get married. This is not a trade-off and I'm not talkin' about things that happened more than sixty years ago," Tandy said.

"Then I'm not talkin' about Seth or his house. And since you are so old that you don't remember, let's talk about my wedding," Emmy Jo said.

Tandy narrowed her eyes and set her mouth in a firm line. "I have the memory of an elephant but some things is best left alone. And I don't want to talk about your wedding."

"Can I use your mama's wedding ring as my something old? I still want to wear your pearls. I want to tie the wedding ring into my bouquet or maybe sew it into the hem of my dress. I think it would bring good luck to my marriage."

"You'll need more than Mama's ring for that. Them Grady men is like wolves in sheep's clothing. They talk a pretty picture, but they don't deliver nothing but bullshit," Tandy told her. She picked up her coffee cup. "But we're here now, so we might as well visit about something. Are you really not going to tell me a thing about that house? Is it all fancy as hell inside?"

"Not really." Emmy Jo slid out of the booth and bent to hug her granny just like she'd done with Diana earlier in the week. She had no illusions about things going that smoothly with Tandy, but maybe it would soften the old girl up a little bit. "It's nice, but it looks like it was furnished in the sixties and hasn't ever had an update. My room is really big and I have my own bathroom," she said as she moved back to her spot.

"Well, la-di-da!" Tandy waved a hand in the air. "I guess he got it all ready for that citified woman and when she got smart and called off the wedding, he didn't have the heart to change anything. He always was too softhearted for his own good."

"Why did the woman call off the wedding?" Emmy Jo asked.

Tandy shrugged. "She came here and saw Hickory. It ain't Amarillo."

"Did you ever see her?" Emmy Jo asked.

Libby brought their food and set it in front of them. "I'll have those pancakes out real soon. Don't want them to get cold while you are enjoying the omelets."

"Thank you." Tandy picked up her fork and set about eating.

"Well?" Emmy Jo asked.

Tandy held up a finger. "Girl, you have gotten to where you ask more questions than you did when you were a three-year-old. I swear to God, you've gotten so nosy that it's goin' to get you into a mess of trouble. But yes, I saw her once. Me and Rose were at the drugstore. She came in with Seth for a cold drink while we were there filling a prescription."

"What'd she look like?" Emmy Jo picked at her hash browns.

"Did you bring me here to pump me for information or to have breakfast with me?" Tandy asked, cocking her head to one side at her great-granddaughter.

"Maybe both." Emmy Jo smiled. "Didn't you come for gossip?"

Tandy sighed. "It was a long time ago, but best I can remember she was tall and skinny, had blonde hair and big blue eyes, and was dressed fit to kill. I never thought I'd be having this conversation more than fifty years later, so I didn't get my picture made with her." Evidently, Tandy thought that was funny, because she giggled like a little girl. "Why are you askin' about Seth's woman, anyway?"

"You brought it up and just got me curious. Reckon we could make this a weekly deal. Or maybe you could make some of your famous brownies, and we could sit around the kitchen table at home and have a visit."

Tandy motioned for Libby to put the pancakes on the griddle. "If you bring the milk and brownies, we'll meet at the park and share them. I'm still mad at you for choosing Seth over me."

"I did not choose him over you. He's my employer. You are my granny," Emmy Jo argued.

"Who are you livin' with?" Tandy shot back.

"I'm not having this conversation. Tell me about my father," Emmy Jo said abruptly, hoping to throw her off her determination not to talk about the past.

"He was just a kid like Crystal. When she died, he was pretty broken up. He got religion about then and changed from a wild boy into a missionary. He went to one of those third-world countries and never came back." Tandy spoke in a practiced monologue.

"You told me that years ago. Didn't he ever call or ask about me?"

"The first year he kept in touch, and then he got married and died a few years after that. I've told you all that," she said.

"But what did he look like? There's tons of pictures of Rose and of my mother in the house, but none of him. Did he graduate from Hickory with Mama?"

"Two years before her," Tandy said. "He was rotten to the core in those days, and I tried every way in the world to get her to break it off with Bubba Dale. But she wasn't having no part of it. She had the same stubborn streak that you've got with Logan Grady."

"Logan's handsome enough to keep anyone's attention. What did Bubba look like? I used to picture him as tall with dark hair and . . ."

"Gregory Dale was his real name. And, honey, he was like a little cocky rooster. Maybe five feet six inches tall, red hair, and a scruffy, hippie-lookin' beard like somebody dragged him through a bunch of red fuzz. But your mama was took with him, and couldn't nobody talk her out of it."

"Like me and Logan, right?"

Tandy laid a hand on Emmy Jo's. "You got that right. What's got you all tied up and askin' questions about your parents now? I thought we got all that settled when you was a little girl.

You wanted to know why I was so much older than everyone else's mamas in your classroom at school."

Emmy Jo loved the touch of her great-grandmother's old, wrinkled hand on hers. "Granny, until this minute I never realized how much you gave up for me. You were retirement age and should have been having the time of your life, yet you were raising another child. Thank you. I love you."

Tandy's nod was a bit jerky. "And I love you, but I'm not going to forgive you for leavin' me and goin' up there with him."

"It's enough today that you love me," Emmy Jo said.

"I guess if you brought the milk and brownies you might come visit me. But you call first. I might be entertainin' a guest."

"Granny, do you have a boyfriend?" Emmy Jo asked.

"No, and I wish to hell *you* didn't. And I wish it was anybody in the world besides Jesse Grady's kinfolk," Tandy said in soberness and set about eating her food.

Emmy Jo followed her lead, thankful for the few tidbits that she'd gotten that morning. They didn't play into the story, but then maybe there was a lot in what wasn't said.

When Tandy had polished off the last of her pancakes, she pushed the empty plate back and stood up. Her hair might be gray, and there were wrinkles in her face, but she was still a beautiful woman.

"Okay, kiddo, I've got to go home and get some laundry done," Tandy said. Emmy Jo wanted to jump up and dance a jig right there in the café. Her grandmother called her by that endearment when she was happy with her.

"Reckon we might do this again next Thursday, Granny? And maybe I'll stop by the trailer on Tuesday with brownies in my hand?"

Emmy Jo was pushing her luck, because Tandy had said she might meet her at the park on Tuesday, since she was still too mad for her to come to the trailer.

"Oh, okay! But you bring the brownies. And if I win at bingo on Friday I'll buy breakfast on Thursday. If I don't, I might not even show up," Tandy said.

"But I can still come home on Tuesday, right?"

"You could sweet-talk a dead man into buying a coffin." Tandy laughed. "See you Tuesday."

Emmy Jo stood up at the same time Tandy did and hugged her tightly.

She walked out into the bright morning with Tandy and waved until she'd driven out of sight and then went straight to the library. Edith was busy with story hour for a whole group of preschool children when Emmy Jo found the section with old yearbooks and carried several to the little room she'd used before. She found her father's senior picture a couple of years prior to her mother's. Emmy Jo squinted at the small photo and wondered why in the world she'd never thought to look for her parents in the old yearbooks before. She did look a lot like him, except that his eyes were dark, or at least appeared so in the picture. No wonder her granny hadn't liked him; he had the same smirk that Jesse Grady had in his senior picture.

"The more I dig, the more I want to know," she muttered.

"Were you talkin' to me?" Edith asked.

The elderly woman's sudden presence startled Emmy Jo so badly that she almost fell out of the chair.

"No, ma'am, I was talkin' to myself again," Emmy Jo answered.

"Well, I'm going to have lunch in the office and just wanted to tell you. What is it that keeps you coming back to these old papers?"

"My past. I just looked up a picture of my father in that old high school annual." Emmy Jo nodded at the open book.

"Oh, honey, I remember him very well." Edith pulled up a chair. "He was a"—she lowered her voice—"very bad boy. Your mama was such a sweet little thing. Quite a reader. She came in here every week to check out books. But your father, never saw him one time here."

137

"So I read about Jesse Grady gettin' beat up. Do you remember that?"

"Jesse wouldn't have anything to do with your past, honey. But I do remember that time very well. He was a senior and I was only in the seventh grade. Folks in town were already talkin' to a sign maker to get us a big thing to go at the edge of Hickory that would say 'State Champions,' with a list of all the players. It all fell through when them hateful boys from the other team came nigh to beatin' Jesse to death," Edith answered. "I must get to my lunch, darlin', but if you have any questions that I can answer, I'd be glad to help you out. You makin' a family tree?"

"Something like that. I should be going, too."

Edith smiled. "Got a date with that feller of yours?"

Emmy Jo nodded. "Yes, ma'am, and I don't want to be late." She gathered up her things and headed out to the parking lot. The message on her phone said that Logan was already at the trailer with takeout from the Asian place in town. She took a deep breath and focused on getting to be with Logan for the afternoon as she drove to the trailer and parked.

When he stepped out onto the tiny porch, the whole story of Seth's past and her library research disappeared.

All that mattered was Logan.

Wearing jeans and a T-shirt, no shoes and a big smile, this was the Logan she liked best. The carefree boy she'd fallen in love with when they were in high school. She was proud of Logan the college graduate, and Logan the bank employee, but she was in love with the guy who stood in front of her.

Their gazes locked across the tiny yard as she hurried toward him. He opened his arms and scooped her up like a bride, carried her into the trailer, and kicked the door shut behind him.

Four hours later she rushed back to Seth's house, wondering the whole way how time had passed so quickly. When she parked in the garage, she checked her reflection in the rearview mirror. Her hair was a mess, her face was still flushed, and she'd dressed so fast that she'd forgotten to put on her bra. A glance at the dashboard clock told her that she had twenty minutes, which was plenty of time to dash upstairs, get one on, brush her hair, and still get to the kitchen in time to help Oma Lynn put supper on the table.

She took the steps two at a time. Her phone pinged four times while she was putting herself together, and the messages from Logan put a crimson flush in her cheeks. She wished she had a lemon to suck on as she splashed cold water on her still-smiling face. She reached presentability when she breezed past Seth at the dining room table and headed into the kitchen.

"Beans and ham, fried potatoes, fried okra, and sliced tomatoes. You can carry the corn bread and the ketchup to the table," Oma Lynn said. "What have you been doing all day?"

"I saw Tandy this morning for breakfast," Emmy Jo answered, still aware of the smile twitching at the corners of her mouth.

"That's good, but seeing your granny didn't put that look on your face," Oma Lynn said.

Emmy Jo spontaneously hugged Oma Lynn. "No, this comfort food did. I'm starving."

Oma Lynn clucked like an old hen gathering her chicks before a storm, though her eyes glittered. "Don't know where you kids get that kind of sayin'. This is plain old country cooking."

"It brings comfort to our bodies and makes us happy when we eat it. Macaroni and cheese is a comfort food, too," Emmy Jo said.

Oma Lynn carried the last dish to the table.

"I hate macaroni and cheese. If you want it, you'll have to order it at Libby's on your days off," Seth said.

"Why?" she asked as she pulled out a chair and sat down.

"I swear, Seth, she's like a two-year-old," Oma Lynn said. "Every other word is *why*."

Emmy Jo giggled. "That's the same thing

Granny told me today. The pair of you shouldn't gang up on me. I'm tough enough to fight you both. And for the record, I get even meaner when I'm hungry."

"Just like Nora," Seth muttered. "Meaner than a junkyard dog."

"A hungry junkyard dog." Emmy Jo picked up a bowl and ladled out beans, making sure to get several large chunks of ham.

"A smart-ass mutt," Seth said.

"Smart—whatever!" She ladled beans into Oma Lynn's bowl and then filled her own. And that's when she remembered the takeout containers sitting on the countertop at the trailer. Unopened and still full.

CHAPTER SEVEN

Logan, Jack, and Diana quickly found a seat on the back pew at Tandy's church and each picked up a hymnal from the pew pocket in front of them.

"Smaller," Jack whispered.

"I know most of these people, though," Diana said.

Folks came in from Sunday school and milled around a few minutes before getting settled into their seats. Logan noticed Tandy two pews up when a couple of older ladies patted her on the back, one stopping long enough to congratulate her on the money she'd won at bingo on Friday night. He made a mental note to tell Emmy Jo when he saw her that afternoon in the cemetery. She'd mentioned that if her granny didn't win, she'd swear it was bad luck brought on by seeing her. But now that she had, Emmy Jo would be Tandy's good-luck charm.

Edna Weatherly, one of Emmy Jo's patients at Hickory Health whom Diana had inherited, pushed her walker through the back door and stopped in the middle of the aisle beside the back pew. "Is that really you, Diana? Well, darlin', I'm sitting by you." She maneuvered around to sit in their pew. "Is Emmy Jo going to join you? I love that you are coming by to take care of me, but I sure do miss her. She's been my girl for two whole years."

"No, she has to work on Sundays with her new position, and she's getting married on June tenth, so it'll be the end of June before she's back on the schedule," Diana whispered.

"She has such a lovely voice. Did you know that she sings in the choir?" Edna sighed.

"Yes, ma'am, I did," Diana answered.

"You and these good-lookin' fellers should be up there in our choir. I'll talk to the preacher about that this week. We need the young folks to take on responsibility," Edna said and then straightened up when a tall woman tapped on the microphone at the pulpit.

"Good morning, everyone, on this blessed Sunday. I'd like to welcome our newcomers Logan Grady, Jack Ramsey, and Diana Watson. We are glad to have you kids. Now if you'll open your song books to page thirty, we'll all sing together."

Many of the old folks sang off-key and out of tune, but their enthusiasm, as they clapped to the music coming from an old upright piano, was infectious. After another congregational song, the preacher took the stand. Logan tried to listen, but his mind kept wandering to Emmy Jo and what she would look like in a pretty white dress walking down the aisle, whether it was in this church or somewhere in an outdoor setting.

After the benediction, Logan fetched Edna's walker, brought it to the center aisle, and offered her an arm to help her. Folks angled past, stopping to shake hands with Diana and Jack and asking them to come back the next Sunday.

"Well, hello, Tandy," Edna said.

Logan looked over her shoulder; Tandy's eyes bored right into his.

"How're you doin', Edna?" she asked.

"Doin' great. Any Sunday I can get out of bed and make it to church is a good day. Ain't it wonderful to see these kids in our church this mornin'?" Edna asked.

Tandy winked.

Logan blinked.

"Of course, it is," Tandy said. "Why don't you go with me to that Asian place for lunch today, Edna? I hate to eat alone, especially on Sunday. We'll go in my car and I'll take you home afterward so you don't have to call the senior citizen van."

"Love to," Edna said.

Tandy took over Logan's job of helping, and the two old gals moved toward the doors to shake the preacher's hand. Logan stood there in awe for a long moment. Was the wink telling him that she was going to finally accept his relationship with Emmy Jo, or was it saying that he'd better watch his back?

• • •

The silk lilacs on Mary's grave weren't faded that Sunday afternoon, but Seth replaced them with a fresh bouquet as he always did. Emmy Jo made sure he was settled in his lawn chair with the tattered old quilt in his lap before she hurried away to the black truck waiting down the road.

"It's been a week with that girl, and there's something happening, Mama. I'm feeling different. Not physically—oh, I'm stronger every day and Emmy Jo has even said that I'm progressing really well—but there's something I can't put my finger on inside my heart." Seth's lips barely moved. No one other than a shy little cottontail bunny peeking out from around the tombstone could hear him. "It's beginning to look like I'm going to have to endure the sassy redhead for the entire time, and that's okay with me now."

He shut his eyes and raised his chin, catching the sun's rays on his thin, wrinkled face. "I told her things that I've never shared with anyone in my life. Not even Nora. Every time I reveal a little more of the past to her, it's like I'm letting go of the burden I've been carrying all these years."

He lowered his head and hugged the old quilt to his chest. "I wish you could meet her . . . she reminds me of Nora. Most days I wish she wasn't in my house. But when she has days off, I end up watching the clock until it's time for her to come back. Don't make a bit of sense, does it?"

The bunny hopped around the tombstone, and two little guys followed her. Seth sat very still and watched the two babies bravely get out a few feet and then hop back to their mother when something spooked them. "I hated those two years after Daddy left, Mama, but you were like that bunny. You took care of us and you were strong. I don't think I've ever thanked you for the food we had on the table or the shoes on our feet."

He was still baring his soul when he heard the truck door slam and the engine start up. It was too soon for Emmy Jo to return. Maybe she'd broken up with that kid. Nothing good ever came from Jesse Grady's bloodline. He checked his watch and was surprised to find that an hour had passed and it was time to go.

"Where to? Dairy Queen for ice cream?" she asked cheerfully.

"That's the routine." He waited for her to bring the walker before he stood up. He'd tried getting around in his bedroom that morning without the cursed thing and had done fine. But the uneven ground might send him tumbling, and he didn't want to endure an assistant for more than eight weeks.

She drove to town and pulled up to the drive-through window, ordering a small cup of vanilla and a medium cup of the same. She handed off one to Seth and set hers in the cup holder below the console.

"So you decided on a cup instead of a cone?" He grinned.

"Yep." She nodded. "When I saw how much they put in your cup last week, I figured out that you get more for your money that way."

He chuckled. "Well, then, maybe you are smarter than you look."

"Hey, now!" She shook her finger at him.

"I'm just speakin' the truth. Take it however you want."

"Then I will take it as a compliment. Now to the cabin?" she asked.

He shoved a spoonful of ice cream into his mouth and nodded again.

She hummed the whole way across town to the two-room house and was still at it when she retrieved his walker. He remembered the days when he'd hummed all the way home from the creek banks. In those days, he'd been in love, too.

When they were settled on the porch, she turned up the cup and drank what ice cream had melted before she dug in with the plastic spoon.

"Look, Seth!" She pointed past him toward the end of the porch. "The first rose of spring. Was pink your mama's favorite color?"

"No, purple was. She loved lilacs best of all,

but she had green thumbs. She started those roses from slips. She put a stem in the ground and covered it with a glass jar until it rooted." He waved a hand toward the end of the house. "She's got red ones at the back porch, pink ones on this end, and yellow ones under the kitchen window."

"Holy smoke! Some of the roots on those things are more than seventy years old?" Emmy Jo exclaimed.

"Or older. There were roses here when my folks got married, too," he answered.

"My granny is good with roses, but she's real partial to red. Her flower bed is the best-kept one in the whole trailer park. Her mother started some of the roses that she's got. Makes me wonder if some of hers might have come from the red ones in your backyard. Maybe her mama and yours swapped slips way back when."

Emmy Jo was like a hound dog on that subject, but he didn't want to hear about Tandy Massey. Not her flower beds or her roses. He didn't want to picture her back when she was a feisty teenager.

Emmy Jo had continued talking through his silence, perhaps accepting his avoidance of that topic. "I've been thinkin' about your mother and how life must've been with her growing up in the church. It had to be hard on her not to go back there."

Seth had been there the day that the ladies in

the church had shunned her, and he'd seen her walk out of the church, her head held high and her back ramrod straight. He'd been so angry that he'd wanted to set fire to the place.

"It wasn't as hard to leave the church where Jesse preached as it was the church where your grandmother goes now," he said.

"She went to both?"

"Yes, she did," he answered.

Emmy Jo waited, afraid to press him for more. Yet there was something inside her that wanted answers, that wanted to know about Mary, about Seth, that superseded natural curiosity.

"Mama finished school a year early, so she was only sixteen when she graduated. She was engaged to a man named Luke Simmons. They were planning a Christmas wedding that year. He already had a little church over near Loving and he was going to start as their preacher right after Thanksgiving."

He paused and stared at the lonesome little rose for a long time. Emmy Jo bit her tongue against the dozens and dozens of questions begging for answers.

"It was July 4." His voice cracked and he swallowed hard.

Emmy Jo wanted to hug him, but she thought he might push her away, so she stayed in her place.

"There was a picnic at her best friend Lillian's house. Her father, Alfred Conroy, was a deacon in the church."

Another long pause. Emmy Jo didn't know if that was all she'd get that day or not. Then he went on. "Alfred offered to take her home at the end of the evening."

His gray eyebrows knit into a solid line, and he sighed. "I didn't think deacons were supposed to drink. Maybe he didn't except on holidays, but from what Dad said he was very drunk. Instead of taking my mother back to the parsonage, he drove down to Hickory Creek and—"

"Oh! No!" Emmy Jo didn't want to hear the rest of the story.

"He raped my mother, and then he drove away and she had to walk all the way to the church in humiliation with her clothes all mussed. Sam Thomas was sitting on the curb in front of a bar south of town when she walked past. He didn't say a word to her, but he knew something bad had happened. He figured her father would kill whoever hurt her, and he staggered back here to sleep off his drunk."

Emmy Jo fought back tears. How would she ever write this chapter in her story?

"She told her father and mother, and they not only refused to believe her, they packed her bags and kicked her out. You can imagine how the rumors went. I expect that the preacher and his wife took the easy way out—it could have ended his career. That don't make it right."

"Where did she go?" Emmy Jo whispered.

"She went to Luke's house. But he'd heard something. I imagine the good reverend took the time to talk ugly about my mother so her words wouldn't mean anything. Luke met her right on the porch and turned her away. He said that he couldn't marry a woman like her."

Emmy Jo's chest tightened. Her heart ached. Her stomach turned. She couldn't begin to imagine the pain Seth had gone through at sixteen when he found this out about his mother. It was so painful to her, all these years later, that she thought she wanted to throw herself on the ground and weep for hours. "No!" She slapped the porch post.

"Yes." Seth's voice was packed with emotion even in one word. "She had a few dollars in her purse, so she went to the hotel."

Emmy Jo frowned. "Hotel?"

Seth shrugged. "It used to stand where the grocery store is now. My dad sobered up and went back to the bar that evening. You can imagine what all the men were talking about. Instead of drinking, Sam went straight to the hotel and proposed to my mother. He promised her that he would never drink again if she would marry him."

"My heart hurts for her." Emmy Jo swiped an angry tear from her cheek.

"Mine broke when I read that letter," Seth said. "Dad felt responsible for her miserable state. If he hadn't spooked those horses, she wouldn't have been adopted and she would have been raised by her real parents. He felt like everything that had happened to her was his fault. Marrying her would fix it, I guess he thought."

Seth's chin quivered, but he went on. "At first she refused, said she wasn't worthy anymore to be any man's bride. He was finally able to convince her that it was her only social option—the town had turned its back on her. They went to Graham the next morning and got married at the courthouse."

"Oh, Seth, that's horrible. I can't begin to imagine how you must have felt when you read that," she said.

"The first time made me violently ill. I carried a lot of anger with me for a very long time," he admitted. "It's still not all gone."

"Well, that's understandable," she said.

They sat in silence for the rest of the hour, Emmy Jo trying to digest what he'd told her. Trying to feel the emotions that Mary did that evening and the next few days as her whole world crumbled around her—going from a parsonage to this small house, from being a preacher's daughter to the town's slut.

So that's why everyone in town still gossiped about Mary Thomas. They didn't have any idea what had really happened, and if they did, they still wouldn't believe a deacon would be capable of such a horrible thing. *Oh, my!* She slapped a hand over her mouth. *Was Seth the product of that rape?* She couldn't ask, and yet she couldn't get it out of her mind.

He went on, his voice sounding as if it were coming from far away. "The next Sunday she got dressed and walked to church, held her head up high and went right to the front pew. Her mother went over and sat down beside her, whispered a few words in her ear, and she got up and left. Dad said she came home with tears flowing down her face," Seth said.

"And that's when she started going to the other church?" Emmy Jo asked.

"No, she didn't go to church again until seven months later, when I was born. I was so tiny that the doctor said I wouldn't make it through the night. I was probably three months premature and only weighed about three pounds. In those days, babies who were born that early didn't live. Dad said that she promised God she'd go to church somewhere if he'd let me live. She started going to the little church where Tandy goes now, and she never missed a Sunday until after my dad left us."

"Seven months! I bet the rumormongers had a

field day with that," Emmy Jo said, glad that he didn't belong to that horrible man.

"Right after I was born, Luke married Lillian, and Alfred escorted his daughter down the aisle. Preacher Roberts performed the ceremony. The morning that my mother was kicked out of the preacher's house and went to Luke's place, she told him what had happened, but he didn't believe her. Or maybe he did, but he knew that marrying a woman who—well, you understand—would kill his career as a preacher. I don't know what was in his mind, but my dad said that he played the poor, put-upon fiancé who'd been jilted for the town drunk. Then when I was born early, it solidified his standing."

"She should have yelled it from the rooftops and told the police," Emmy Jo said.

"I guess after her parents and Luke all turned their backs on her, she didn't figure anyone would ever take her word over Alfred's. He was a pretty big name in Hickory in those days."

"And her best friend turned on her, too. That's too much for any woman to have to bear," Emmy Jo said. "I wish you could tell me that your dad buried them in the woods." She made a mental note to ask Edith about Alfred next time she went to the library.

Seth smiled. "So did I at one time. That's enough for this day. It's time to go home and heat up leftover chicken and dumplings for our supper."

After that story, Emmy Jo could agree that it was enough for that day, but on another day, she wanted more. She had to know everything.

Warm wind whipped the sheer curtains back away from the open balcony doors that evening when Emmy Jo opened her computer. She quickly wrote down Alfred, Luke, and Lillian's names so that she could look them up in the newspapers on her next day off. Edith would surely remember something, too. That lady loved to talk.

Then she began to write. Emotions flooded through her as she imagined the day at Lillian's house, how they'd likely giggled and talked about Mary's upcoming marriage to Luke and maybe even discussed whom her friend was interested in. After a picnic meal shared on a quilt with Luke and his friends, there would have been fireworks and then . . . why didn't Luke take her home? Was he called away on a visit for someone who was sick?

She inserted a line of question marks to fill in later and with a heavy heart went on to the next part of the chapter. Did Alfred tell her that he knew she'd been putting out to Luke? What kind of language would they have used in 1934? They might have said she'd been sleeping with Luke rather than having sex, since that word was still mentioned in whispers in Tandy's circles. She made a note to look up the wording when she could hook up to Wi-Fi.

When she finally crawled between the sheets that night, the emotion of the day sent tears to her eyes again. Her phone pinged, so she picked it up from the nightstand and found a text from Logan: *Call me. I'm worried.*

She checked her messages and found that he'd sent six more texts since they'd parted in the cemetery. She quickly hit "Speed Dial," and he answered on the first ring.

"Is everything okay?" Logan asked. "I was about to call you."

"It's fine. What's going on there?" she answered.

"You sound like you've been crying. Are you sure everything is okay?"

She knew every nuance in his voice, and his tone spoke volumes. "Just a little tired, but Seth and I had a good day. He's opening up to me and talking to me more, so I feel like I'm accomplishing a little of my goal to make him like me." She wiped away a tear. "Now tell me about your day."

"Diana came over and made supper for us, so I washed up the dishes to give them some alone time," he said. "I just wanted to hear your voice tonight. Go to bed and dream of me, darlin'. In only a few weeks we'll be together forever."

"That day can't arrive soon enough," she whispered.

"Amen," he said.

She laid the phone to one side and shut her eyes, but then they popped wide open. "But today didn't have anything to do with Seth and Jesse and my grandmother. That's still a mystery."

Chapter Eight

Tuesday morning Emmy Jo arrived at Libby's to find her grandmother already in a booth awaiting her with a smile. Breakfast had been ordered, but Emmy Jo didn't think that had anything to do with her mood.

"Did you win at bingo?"

"If you weren't up there in that godforsaken mansion, you'd know the news and the gossip. But yes, I did win. Did you bring the brownies?"

"I did. I was surprised when you called and said that we could have breakfast before we went to the trailer for brownies and milk," she said.

"I've decided that you might bring me luck," Tandy said. "And I'll take a couple of brownies with me. I've got to go to the church; I volunteered to do some cleaning today."

"Well, at least we get to have breakfast together. Maybe next week I'll come to the trailer."

"Sure," she said. "Now tell me about what's happened since I saw you last."

"Pretty much just settling into routine. I really like Sundays, when we go to the cemetery and then to the cabin."

"Cabin?" Tandy asked.

"The place where he grew up." Emmy Jo dug into her food.

"You mean that shanty?"

Emmy Jo bristled. "He calls it a cabin. It's peaceful there, even if it does need a little paint."

"Don't you take that tone with me," Tandy shot back.

"Then don't call it a shanty. It sounds . . ." She paused.

"You can make a purse out of a hog's ear, but it don't make it a fancy one," Tandy said. "*Cabin* makes that place sound all la-di-da, like his big old mansion up there on the hill, but it is what it is."

"What it is, is peaceful and I like being there. I can almost feel his mama's spirit in the place."

Tandy sipped her coffee. "Well, who in the hell would want to feel the spirit of Mary Thomas's ghost? For God's sake, Emmy Jo, you know about that woman. What kind of spell has Seth got you under to be wanting to commune with his dead mother?"

"I'm not under any spell," Emmy Jo said. "And I do feel peaceful at the cabin, as if angels are watching over me."

"And you don't feel peaceful in our trailer?"

Emmy Jo counted to ten before she answered. "Of course I do, Granny. Let's eat; our eggs are getting cold. I remember a sassy old girl who told me once that cold eggs ain't even fit for the dogs."

Tandy grinned. "She's a pretty smart old girl."

"Oh, yes, she is."

Customers trickled out of the little café as they finished, so Diana's mother had time to pull up a chair and visit. The three of them chatted about Diana's Christmas wedding, which would now happen in Tandy's church. Emmy Jo noticed that Tandy couldn't hide her smile at the thought that Jesse Grady's family was missing out. No way would Tandy ever set foot in the church where Wyatt Grady preached.

It was after ten when Emmy Jo finally reached the library. Edith was busy straightening books and Emmy Jo tried to sneak into the newspaper room, but the woman had the hearing of a bat.

"Well, good morning. I wondered if I might see you," Edith said. "What are you researching today?"

Emmy Jo glanced over at the magazine table surrounded by four comfortable chairs. "Would you have time to tell me what you know about some of the older residents? I can look it all up, but if you already know . . ."

"Oh, honey." Edith beamed. "Come right on over here and sit down where we can be comfortable. Who are you interested in? My family has been in Hickory since the sixth day of creation, so I know all about everyone."

"It's Alfred Conroy."

"Oh, he was a pillar in town. Deacon of the

church. Had his finger in lots of goin's-on around here. Was on the town council, I think, and even served as chamber president for a few years. Almost got appointed to be the mayor, but then the bad thing happened," Edith said.

"What bad thing?" Emmy Jo held her breath.

"His only child died. You see it was like this." Edith went on to tell about how Lillian and Mary Roberts had always been friends and how the friendship ended when Mary took up with Sam Thomas.

"Lillian comforted Mary's fiancé, as you might guess. They got married and it was the biggest, prettiest wedding Hickory has ever seen. Seven bridesmaids. My mama was one of them, and she talked about it until the day that she died. Then the flu epidemic hit, and Lillian was taken with it. Her death devastated Alfred. He never was quite right after that."

"Did Lillian ever make up with Mary?" Emmy Jo asked.

"Oh, no, honey! Mary cooked her own goose when she up and threw away Luke to marry Sam"—Edith lowered her voice to a whisper—"and then when Mary had Seth before they was even married eight months, well, you see, there was no way Lillian could be a party to that kind of thing. Poor old Luke. Mama talked about it right up until she died. It was quite the rumor in those days when a girl did something like that.

Nowadays, it happens all the time, but eighty years ago . . . oh, my goodness."

"Lillian and Luke never had children?"

Edith shook her head slowly. "Poor Alfred only had that one child and not even a grandbaby. Then his wife died the next year. Mama said it was from a broken heart when she remembered those days. I remember that she was real glad I was too young to get involved with Seth and too old for his younger brother. She used to feel sorry for the women in town who had girls their age."

"What happened to Alfred?"

"He became a recluse. Didn't get out much. He died"—she tapped her check with a fore-finger—"I can't remember when exactly, but it was after I was grown and married. On the other hand, I was in junior high school when Mary died. Seth left town, for the army, I think, or maybe it was that he went with his sister and their younger brother. Anyway, the sister did well with her life, but I don't know about the brother. Never did hear what happened to him. Seth came back about the time I was ready to graduate. Mama sure gave me a lecture about him." Edith laughed. "But I didn't need to be told. I was already in love with my late husband by then."

"Well, thank you so much. I was just wonderin' about them. So did you ever meet Mary?"

"Oh, yes. She was a tall lady with beautiful eyes

and very polite. You'd never guess by lookin' at her that she . . . well, you know."

Emmy Jo nodded, thoughts of Seth's revelation on her mind.

The library door opened, and half a dozen kids filed in ahead of two ladies.

"Well, it looks like it's about time for my story hour, so I'll leave you to your research. We'll talk again." Edith hurried off to greet the children.

Wednesday went by in a blur. The routine was the same as always. Seth was ready to argue with everything she said, and she was more than ready to give him tit for tat. She spent Thursday morning in the library again but kept stopping her research to stare off into space. Edith was busy all morning with patrons, so she didn't come back to talk to her and the clock seemed like it stood still.

A few minutes before noon, she got a text from Logan saying that he was on his way to the trailer with a pan of pasta and a pepperoni pizza from the local pizza shop.

I'm not interested in food so much, she texted back as she waited at a stoplight. She'd parked right beside his truck when her phone pinged again. The message said: *Be cool.*

He wasn't waiting on the porch, so she rang the doorbell and waited. He threw open the door and rolled his eyes toward the ceiling as he stood far to one side and invited her inside. Had something catastrophic happened? He always hugged her and gave her a kiss even in the Dairy Queen or at Libby's—right out in public. So what was the deal today?

The aroma of pizza, pasta, and warm chocolate greeted her when she entered the trailer. Leaving the bright sunlight, her eyes took a while to adjust to the light, but when they did, she could hardly believe what she was seeing. "Granny, what are you doing here?"

Surely, she was seeing things. She blinked half a dozen times, but her grandmother did not disappear like a vapor into the thin air.

"I came to visit. When someone new moves in, I bring brownies. I admit I've been slow in getting them down here, since Jack has lived here all this time, but now that Logan has moved in, well, I thought it would be a good time to kill two birds with one pan of brownies." Tandy grinned.

Kill two birds. The memory of Tandy standing on the porch with a shotgun flashed through Emmy Jo's mind; a quick glance over at Logan told her that he was thinking the same thing.

"So are you going to invite me to have pizza with y'all or not?" Tandy asked.

"Of course, Mrs. Massey," Logan said. "I hope you like pepperoni, but in case you don't, I do have a pan of pasta."

"Love anything Italian. You can say the grace, Logan, and then I expect we can help ourselves. After we eat, we'll have brownies, and I've got a Monopoly game out in my car. We can play that all afternoon," Tandy said.

Emmy Jo's heart fell to her toenails, but Logan was smiling like he'd just won the lottery. He must think that Tandy was finally accepting him, when the real issue was that she had control now that Logan lived in "her" trailer park. There would be no more Thursday afternoons in the bedroom. If Emmy Jo's car and Logan's truck both showed up at Jack's place, Tandy would be there, brownies in one hand and a board game in the other.

Of all the games, Emmy Jo hated Monopoly the most. She'd far rather be sitting in the library going over old articles and taking notes. She studied her grandmother from the corner of her eye. From her lucky bingo pants to her T-shirt blinged out with rhinestones around a four-leaf clover, the old girl didn't look like the devil Emmy Jo knew she was trying to be. She'd even applied makeup and . . . was that hairspray in her hair?

"So this is the end of your second week at the Thomas house," Tandy said immediately after Logan said grace. "How are you settling in?"

"Just fine," Emmy Jo said.

But I'm going to be cranky all week, since I

have to share my precious Logan afternoon time with you.

Tandy helped herself to a slice of pizza and some pasta and started toward the small table for four. Logan went over to pull out her chair and see to it that she had a glass of sweet tea before he turned back to getting his own food.

How could her granny not love a man that thoughtful?

"I heard you're on a winning streak at bingo," he said.

"Humph." She almost snorted. "Woman can't burp in this town without the whole dang town knowin' that she ate hot dogs for dinner. I had a little luck at bingo and I'm hoping it stays with me."

Tandy and her superstitions. Maybe she was being nice because she'd gotten it in her head that she'd win at bingo the next night. *Lord,* Emmy Jo almost whined out loud, *why couldn't she be nice to someone else today?*

Logan seated Emmy Jo and gently squeezed her shoulder as if to say that everything was good. "We enjoyed being in your church last Sunday," he said with a glance toward Tandy.

"It ain't my church. It belongs to God," she said in a sharp tone and then softened her voice. "The bunch of you should come around on Wednesday night for choir practice."

"We might just do that. We've all been part of

the choir at my dad's church since we were in junior high school," Logan said.

"I hear your mama and daddy are lookin' at a church over in Graham," Tandy said. "Is that right?"

"They are praying about it," Logan answered. "It would still be close to Gramps so they could help with him. He doesn't drive anymore since his cataract surgery."

"That's nice." Tandy smiled.

You aren't happy that they'll be near, but because Jesse can't drive. Emmy Jo bit her tongue to keep from saying the words out loud.

"Think Jesse will step in and preach until they find someone?" Tandy asked.

Now Tandy was just being nosy, trying to get the scoop first in order to spill it at bingo tomorrow night.

Tandy poked her on the shoulder. "You sure are being quiet today."

"Just thinking about the past," Emmy Jo said.

Tandy went slightly pale. "What about it?"

"I went down to the library and looked up a picture of my father in the old yearbooks. I was surprised to see that they ran senior pictures all the way back to when you were a graduate, Granny. You reminded me of the pictures of Rose. Did you know some of the yearbooks were destroyed when there was a leak in the library?"

Tandy lost a little more color. "Yes, I did know

167

that, and Rose was prettier than I ever was."

"Why'd you name her that?" Emmy Jo asked.

Pink flushed Tandy's face. "It's a pretty name."

"Did you know someone named Rose?" Logan asked.

"No, but a boy I knew back then brought me roses that he picked from his mama's bushes. I thought the name fit her right well with her little rosebud mouth."

"What was her middle name?" Emmy Jo wondered if that boy could have been Seth.

"Her full name was Ann Rose."

"Hmm." Emmy Jo finished her pizza and went to the bar to get the pan of brownies. "Why Ann?"

"I liked the name," Tandy answered. "And she named her daughter Crystal Ann."

"Where'd she get the name Crystal?"

From the aggravated expression on Tandy's face, Emmy Jo knew she was tired of all the questions, but she hoped to make her mad enough to leave.

"Hell if I know. I hated the name. It sounds like something you drink out of, not something you name a little baby girl, but it was Rose's baby, so I didn't say a word," Tandy said.

Logan lifted the first brownie from the pan and made appreciative noises when he tasted it. "This is great, Mrs. Massey. Does Emmy Jo have this recipe?"

"Yes, she does. It's in my mama's cookbook, but we've made them so often that we don't even have to look at the recipe anymore. Y'all hurry up so we can play Monopoly. You can get the game from my car, Logan."

"Yes, ma'am, but first I'm having a second brownie. My sweet tooth is never filled," he said.

"Just like your—" Tandy stopped and took a long drink of tea.

"Your what?" Emmy Jo pressed.

If you can ruin my afternoon, you can finish the sentence.

"Just like your grandpa, Logan. He always had candy in his pocket when we were in school. Mostly hard candy, like peppermints, because it wouldn't melt like chocolate. But I do remember him loving chocolate cake when it was served in the cafeteria for lunch. In those days they didn't have all these laws and such about what is good for a kid and what ain't. They put food on the tray and we ate it. Jesse would trade anything on his plate for chocolate cake. Sometimes he'd eat five pieces." She glared at Emmy Jo.

I bet that hurt to talk about him.

"Seth has a sweet tooth, too," Emmy Jo said.

"Wouldn't know about that. Let's clear off this table so we can play. I do love a good game of Monopoly," Tandy said.

Logan popped the last bite into his mouth and headed out to the car. "Be right back."

Tandy wrapped her long, bony fingers around Emmy Jo's upper arm. "Don't you think for one minute you are going to spend every Thursday afternoon shacked up with him in this trailer. I intend to be here every single time you park out there, and believe me, I will know. I've got eyes everywhere in this town."

So she'd been right. "It's okay if I go down to Hickory Creek and roll around in the sand with him, but I can't spend time in this trailer?" Emmy Jo asked without an ounce of warmth in her tone.

"Hell, no!"

"He's a good man."

"He's got a good mama; I'll give him that much. But I'm going to fight you to my death over marrying that boy. I refuse to be shirttail kin with Jesse Grady."

"Why?"

"Because he can deck himself out in the robes of righteousness, but underneath it all he'll always be a jackass," she hissed. "You want to play Monopoly all afternoon or make an excuse to leave this trailer?"

"What do you want to do?" Emmy Jo shot back.

"I want to get out of here," Tandy said. "I've had enough Logan Grady to last me a lifetime."

"And here it is! I should warn you ladies, I'm really good at this game," Logan said cheerfully as he carried the game into the living room.

"Yay!" Emmy Jo clapped her hands. "Let's set it up on the coffee table. Granny, you can sit on the sofa and me and Logan will take the floor."

Tandy groaned under her breath and carried her half-empty glass to the living room, where she eased down on the sofa, all the while shooting the meanest side-eye imaginable at Emmy Jo.

Emmy Jo kicked off her sandals and plopped down on the floor. *You sowed the seeds for today. Now you can reap the harvest.*

Two and a half hours later Emmy Jo was bankrupt and Logan had two dollars in the bank. Tandy had wiped them both out when she put hotels on both Boardwalk and Park Place.

"It's been fun, but I've got to go to work now." Emmy Jo reached for her shoes. "Walk me out, Logan?"

"Sure thing. You want to play another game with just the two of us, Mrs. Massey?"

"I've got to get home. One of my favorite shows comes on in fifteen minutes," she said with another look at Emmy Jo. "I'll walk out with you. Maybe I'll see you again next Thursday."

"And we'll play canasta," Logan said. "I hear you love that game."

"I sure do." Tandy smiled. "Thanks for the pizza. You keep the rest of the brownies. Jack might like some when he comes home."

"Thank you." Logan gathered up the game and carried it in one arm. The other one was draped around Emmy Jo's shoulders. When they reached her car, he kissed her chastely on the forehead and whispered, "Call me as soon as you can."

Her head bobbed gently. "Will do. 'Bye, Granny. See you next Tuesday morning for breakfast? You want me to drive you down to your place?"

"No, I need the exercise," Tandy called back.

"I really have to go or I'll be late." Emmy Jo wrapped her arms around Logan's neck and pulled his face down for a long kiss. "We'll talk after supper."

"I can't wait." He grinned.

To Seth, Thursday lasted a week. From the time breakfast was over until snack at midmorning, Seth kept a watch on the clock. *Dammit!* She'd be gone at the end of May, and he'd be there all alone again. That's why he didn't have a dog or a cat or even a blasted pet fish. They all went away at some point and left him, so why even start?

When he heard the car engine in the garage, he smiled, but when she breezed through the dining room, he hid it behind his book. She went straight to the kitchen to help Oma Lynn bring in the supper and then sat down in her chair. He could tell by her expression that she was ready to chew nails and spit out staples, so he didn't ask about her day.

"So I hear that you spent the day at Jack and Logan's trailer playing Monopoly with Tandy," Oma Lynn said.

"Damn telephone!" Seth muttered under his breath.

"That's right." Emmy Jo dipped into the green beans and passed them on to Seth.

"I hate Monopoly," Seth said. "But then, I hate all board games except Scrabble."

"So do I," Emmy Jo said after she'd swallowed. "And so does Granny."

"Then why'd she bring the game to Logan's?" Oma Lynn asked.

"She didn't want everyone to think we were shackin' up in the bedroom," Emmy Jo answered.

Oma Lynn sputtered and came close to spewing sweet tea across the table. "The way you young people talk these days!"

Seth grinned at her directness.

"So I asked her if we should go to Hickory Creek and roll around in the sand," Emmy Jo said.

Seth chuckled. Oma Lynn slapped a hand over her mouth.

"And then she asked me if I wanted to make an excuse and leave or stay and play Monopoly all afternoon," Emmy Jo said.

"And?" Oma Lynn asked.

"I asked her what she wanted to do, and she said that she wanted to get the hell away from

Logan as fast as she could. So I decided to play Monopoly."

Seth laughed so hard that he spewed tea all over the table. He and Tandy did agree on a couple of things. One being that Emmy Jo had no business marrying Logan Grady, and the other was that Seth would want to get the hell away from any offspring of Jesse's as fast as he could, too.

Oma Lynn fussed the whole time she cleaned the tea up with a dish towel. "What's so damned funny about that?"

Emmy Jo got so tickled at the way Seth was guffawing that she snorted and then got the hiccups, just like Nora still did when she laughed. The crazy break-glass giggles were infectious. He couldn't remember the last time he had to wipe his eyes because he'd gotten so tickled. It had to have been when he was slapstick drunk once in the army. The hangover the next morning made him swear off liquor other than the occasional shot of Jack Daniel's when he had a sore throat.

He would never admit it to his sister, but he did like the girl's sense of humor.

As soon as supper was over and Seth had gone to the balcony to listen to his radio, Emmy Jo raced up the stairs and called Logan.

"So what was that today?" he asked.

"What was what?"

"The tension reminded me of that last morning

at Mama's. And just so you know, I also hate board games except for Scrabble. I only like that one because of all the fun we have when we play with Jack and Diana."

She told him exactly what had been said between her and Tandy, leaving out none of the details. "I can't understand this big thing that's between my granny, your grandpa, and maybe even Seth. Whatever it is has enough anger in it to survive more than sixty years. But on a more positive note, I made Seth laugh. One goal accomplished, and it took less than two weeks."

"He's a tough old goat to hold out that long," Logan said.

"Yep." She padded across the floor to the balcony, unable to hide a laugh of her own. "But I did it."

"How do you women say nice things to one another when what you really want to do is have a hissy fit? That tension in the room today was the worst."

"We are from Venus, darlin'."

"What are you talking about?" Logan asked.

"It's from a book that I read for one of my psychology classes. You guys, on the other hand, sprang from Mars, where they teach cage fighting and how to spit," she told him.

His laughter shot through the phone and out toward the stars. "You are funny, but probably right. Thank goodness for y'all ladies to soften us. Next Thursday we are going to Graham. I won't let her catch us again."

"I'll make the reservations." She grinned.

"I'll bring dinner, and if anyone, including Tandy or my grandpa, shows up at the door, we aren't going to answer it."

"If that's in a contract, just show me where to sign. If they are sitting in the parking lot when I get there, leave the bathroom window open and prop a ladder beside it on the outside."

"Sounds like a solid plan to me," he said. "Good night, darlin'. See you Sunday."

"'Night. I love you to the moon and back," Emmy Jo said.

Just as she hung up, a star burning its way across the heavens caught her attention. She watched it shoot from the place it had occupied for maybe a million years in a long white trail until it left the horizon. Tightly shutting her eyes, she made a wish. *I want to know this whole story. Something is asking me to figure it out.*

CHAPTER NINE

Seth had been in a good mood on Friday and Saturday. He didn't laugh again, but he did smile at least once a day, and on Sunday when they were sitting again on the porch of the old home place, he complimented Emmy Jo on her dumplings.

"They're almost as good as what Mama made for us every Sunday," he said as he ate the last few bites of his ice cream.

"Really!" She was shocked that he'd say that but glad that he'd opened the door for her to ask questions. "So you have some good memories of this place?"

"The best." He nodded. "Growing up in the Depression, we weren't the only poor people in Hickory. Lots of folks left to go to California, where there were jobs. Those of us left behind lived hand-to-mouth most of the time. Daddy had part-time work at the mill and did odd jobs for folks who had the money to hire him. Mama made do with what he brought home, but we always had chicken and dumplings for dinner on Sunday after church."

"And homemade bread?"

Seth shook his head. "Not until Nora got to be about ten years old and found out she had a knack for bread making. Mama could make biscuits that would melt in your mouth and the best strawberry jam in the world, but she never was much of a hand at yeast rolls. But now, Nora—that girl could do a fine job with them."

The chair squeaked as it rocked back and forth on the old wooden porch. Seth looked happy, so maybe now was the time to ask the question that had been on her mind for the last two days.

"So after your dad left, how did your mama make it?"

Big black clouds obliterated the sun and Seth's expression changed in a moment to match the sky. His blue eyes drew down into slits, and he inhaled so deeply that his chest puffed out. His body went ramrod stiff in the chair and didn't change as he let the air out slowly.

"I thought everyone in town knew about my mother," he said.

"I've heard the rumors," Emmy Jo said.

"When Daddy left, Mama went everywhere in town looking for a job to make enough money to keep us kids fed. Every day for a whole week, she swallowed her pride and asked all those people who'd been ugly to her for a job. She would have cleaned their outhouses or cooked for them or ironed their clothing—anything to make money. But most of them slammed doors in her face. Then she heard that Jesse Grady's mama was looking for a housekeeper, and she walked three miles out to their farm to ask if she could have the job." He paused and ran a hand over his forehead.

"If someone had a job to be done, why wouldn't they hire her?" Emmy Jo asked.

"Jesse's mama told her that no one was ever going to hire her because she'd left poor Luke practically at the altar for a shiftless fellow like Sam Thomas."

"But that was what? Like years and years before?" Emmy Jo couldn't wrap her mind around such pure meanness. The years should have softened the townsfolk somewhat in the years between the time she was seventeen and in her thirties. If not for her, then for the children she was trying to support.

"The first time was seventeen years before. The second time happened when I was sixteen. Nora was just shy of fifteen. The next day we decided that if Mama couldn't find a job, we'd work. I went to the lumberyard, and the manager said he was barely making it. As I was leaving, Jesse and his daddy came into the place."

He stopped talking, and the sadness in his face said he was remembering that day all too well. She waited, afraid to ask another question and yet aching to know the rest of that story.

"Jesse's daddy had a lot of pull in the community by the time my dad left. He was a churchgoing man who even preached sometimes in those days. You have to remember that he wasn't a religious man until after he'd won my grandparents' farm in the poker game. When that happened, he doubled the size of his property. Maybe he decided that it was time to clean up his act. Who knows?"

"Did he say something to the manager?" Emmy Jo asked.

"They went over in a corner and talked real low. Jesse stood there with a cocky smirk the whole time that his daddy and the manager talked. It was only a couple of minutes, but finally I realized that I wasn't going to be hired. So I left."

"Did Nora have any luck?" Emmy Jo asked.

Seth shook his head. "Not a bit. She was in tears when she came home that evening. Several ladies said they'd give her a job, but times were tough and nearly everyone was struggling."

"And your mama? She must have been frantic, havin' three kids. The food was probably getting down to the bare bones," Emmy Jo said.

"Mama sat on the porch all night with her Bible in her lap. I slept poorly, wondering what we would do. The property belonged to Daddy, not to Mama, so she couldn't sell it. We had no money to leave Hickory, and you are right, there was little food in the house by then."

"Surely the people in Hickory wouldn't stand by and watch y'all starve. Didn't they bring in pots of beans or something to keep y'all fed? We have that food pantry nowadays."

Even with Tandy's horrible reputation, her friends would have supported her in a situation like that. And she'd worked at Libby's as a waitress until she retired back about the time that Emmy Jo was born. So there was proof that Hickory cared about its people, even if they did stray from the narrow pathway.

"I think they might have liked to watch us starve to death," Seth said. "The word was that Mama had finally gotten her just due. Everyone still felt sorry for Luke because he'd lost his wife, since he'd never married again. And the fact that Daddy had run off with a barmaid, well, it made them feel righteous to punish Mama."

Kind of like the way Jesse Grady feels about me. All powerful and self-righteous, because I'm not legitimate. And yet, Granny is carrying that feeling over to Logan. Lord, what a mess.

"Then of course all the old garbage surfaced. Maybe Mama's parents weren't even married. What if they were serial killers . . . By the time we were down to the last flour in the bin, she was nothing but a blight on the town and they were determined to run her out or die trying," he said.

"But they didn't get what they wanted, did they?" Emmy Jo asked, not really wanting to hear the rest of the story. Mary had suffered enough in her lifetime. To be totally shunned in her time of need was beyond horrible. It was downright evil.

"No, but I wished they had. She sent me to town that Saturday morning for red paint. Used the last of her money to buy it, and she went out to the shed and painted an old lantern."

Emmy Jo held her breath so long that light-headedness set in and she had to force air into her lungs. "I was hoping that you weren't going to say that. I'd heard things about her, but . . ."

Seth held up a palm and went on. "She carried it to the front porch and hung it beside the door while it was still wet. I still hate the smell of paint today, and I hate the color red. Hanging that light on the porch meant that she was opening her doors to make money sleeping with the men in town. Overnight she became the town prostitute."

"Lord, you were only sixteen. You must have felt helpless."

He nodded. "She gathered us around her and said, 'The people in Hickory don't want us here, but we don't run from our problems. My kids will not go hungry.' That night the sheriff came and told her to take down the light. It was against the law. I don't know what she told him, but the light stayed up and he never came back."

"Blackmail?" Emmy Jo asked.

"Maybe. She must've known something on him, because he steered clear of our place from then on," he said. "But those women who wouldn't give her a job . . ." He cleared his throat and hesitated again. "Every time one of their husbands left the house, they wondered where he was, right? And then the husbands had to let her stay in town because she could have told the wives. What a tangled-up mess."

"And you and Nora were old enough to know who came and went," Emmy Jo finished for him.

"Yes, we did." His smile was barely more than a grimace. "And Alfred Conroy was the first one to arrive at the house. He begged her with tears to take money from him and take down the light. She told him that it was too late to do what he should have done in the beginning, and she shut the door in his face. I never knew why she wouldn't let him in the house until I read Daddy's letter."

"I see why you hate red," she whispered.

Seth's eyes softened. "Before the next Sunday, the preacher's wife came calling and told Mama that it would be best if she didn't come to church anymore. That made it the second church that she'd been thrown out of in town."

Tears spilled down Emmy Jo's cheeks and dripped onto her bright-yellow shirt, leaving wet circles. How could this be the town she grew up in? Even Tandy had had help.

"Don't cry," Seth said softly. "Mama didn't. She held her head high and told the woman that

God was not confined to a building, so she could worship him right there in her house with the red light on the porch."

Emmy Jo wiped the tears away with the back of her hand and then dried it on her jeans. "I want to grow up and have Mary Thomas's strength. She must've been made of steel."

The chair began to rock again. "To everyone but her children. There she was a softhearted mama. And now it's time to go home for supper. How about a game of Scrabble after we finish? I bet you five bucks I can beat you."

"You're on." Emmy Jo popped up from the porch.

She'd been dating Logan since she was sixteen, and his parents had always disapproved of her because of Tandy's reputation. But good grief! It was nothing like what Seth had endured. No wonder he was a recluse.

It had been years since Seth had taken the old game from the cabinet. Those first few months after he sold his real estate business and leased out the building, he'd played a lot—against himself. Emmy Jo had been so upset when she heard about the red light that he wanted to take her mind off it. Hearing rumors was one thing; hearing facts was a whole different ball game, especially when she had already heard about the other things Mary Thomas had endured. Bless

184

Emmy Jo's sweet heart for taking on the burden of even listening. He was grateful to her, because each bit that he talked about softened up another hard spot in his heart.

But now it was time to play a game, to get back into their bantering mode to take their minds off the sadness.

"I should tell you," she said as she set the board up on the kitchen table, "that Tandy hates Scrabble, so I played it most of the time by myself."

"Just to be fair." He turned the tiles upside down and shuffled them. "I did the same thing."

"Well, I haven't seen a board in maybe five years, so we're starting on fairly even ground." She slid over her share of tiles. "Did you go to college after you got out of the service?"

"I took some classes in business while I was in the service. When I got out, I took what I needed to get my real estate license, but I do not have a degree. Did you get any college at all?" He set his tiles up on the wooden holder.

"Kind of." She rearranged the tiles. "I went to vo-tech and got my CNA—certified nursing assistant degree—and then went to work for Hickory Health Care right out of high school. I enrolled in night classes and got my LPN last year. You can go first." She grabbed a tissue in time to catch a sneeze.

He played a word and drew four tiles from the

pile in the middle of the table. "Allergies?" he asked.

"Could be. I'm never sick. I was the only kid in school who didn't miss a single day in all twelve years," she answered and then sneezed again.

"My doctor is coming to check my incision pretty soon. He can give you a goin'-over to be sure that it's just allergies. I don't want you gettin' me sick," he said.

"Jeez, Seth! I don't need a doctor over a couple of sneezes. Don't be so paranoid," she said.

"You will be checked." He tipped his chin high enough that he was looking down his nose at her.

"We'll see," she said. "Play your next word. I feel lucky, so you better be careful."

He played the word *math*. "My favorite subject."

"Mine, too," she said. "That and English. Not so much with science or history, though."

"Did you like school?" he asked.

"Loved it, but I was not class president or a cheerleader. I didn't have time for that. I worked at Libby's after school and studied in between customers. In today's world they call me a nerd. What was the word for the unpopular crowd in your day?"

"I heard the word *nerd* when I was in school, but mostly the boys who weren't popular were called hubcaps. I don't know about the girls," he answered.

She played a word and frowned. "So were you a hubcap?"

"I wasn't even a lug nut," he answered. "The Thomas kids weren't even worthy of jokes. We were invisible for the most part, and we liked it that way."

She played the *Q* on a triple word slot and jumped ahead of him in points. "I'm going to wind up with your five dollars."

"Don't count your chickens before they are hatched," he said.

"Don't get too used to having that five in your pocket," she shot back, grateful that they were back on familiar ground with each other.

It was well after ten when they wound down the second game. At the end of the first one, Emmy Jo was richer by five dollars. When the next one was finished, she'd given the same bill back to Seth.

"A profitable evening." Seth yawned.

Emmy Jo sneezed again and reached for a tissue. "Good night. See you in the morning."

"Good night." He stood without the help of his walker.

"Good job." She grinned.

His heart doubled in size at the compliment from her. "So you think the doctor will be pleased with the progress?"

"Oh, yes, he will. Some of my patients don't do this well even with therapy."

Seth would have danced a jig if he'd been able.

On Tuesday morning, Tandy had something going at the church and Emmy Jo was secretly happy, because she needed another couple of days away from her grandmother after the previous Thursday afternoon. When she reached the café, the breakfast run was over and Libby and Diana were sitting at a table with a platter of pancakes and bacon between them and a pot of coffee off to the side.

Libby waved her over. "Grab a cup from behind the counter and a plate and we'll share."

Emmy Jo wasn't hungry, but a cup of hot coffee did sound good. She got a mug, poured it full, and sat down with the two women. "Libby, did you know the story about Seth's mama and the red light?"

Libby's dark-brown ponytail was twisted into a messy bun with a pencil stuck in the middle to secure it. She swallowed and nodded at the same time. "My mother mentioned it when Seth came in to pick up his takeout orders. She always said that she knew that boy would come back to Hickory and set it on its ear for the way it treated his mama."

Emmy Jo sipped her coffee. "What else did your mother say?"

"My grandmother knew Mary Thomas and said

there wasn't a finer woman in the world. She never did believe that story about Mary cheating on her fiancé. Said she wasn't that kind of girl. Something happened that night that the preacher and his wife kicked her out into the street. Rumors had it that she'd spent the night with Sam Thomas and was drunk. My grandmother didn't believe it, but . . ." Libby shrugged.

Emmy Jo nodded. "Anyone else ever think that?"

Libby shook her head slowly. "I wouldn't have any idea. Once a rumor is started and folks believe it, you might as well write it up in stone and prop it up by the church house doors, because ain't nobody goin' to believe anything else."

"So, there were a few women who didn't think Mary was treated right?"

"Mama told me that if my grandmother had had the money to hire Mary or Nora or even Seth, she would have done it, but in those days this little café was barely paying the bills. People could hardly afford to buy groceries, much less go out to eat. So yes, it was just a handful of people, those who had a little money, who banded together and tried to run Mary out of town. Self-righteous bastards!"

Emmy Jo finished off her coffee. "Can I pour all of us another cup?"

"Yes, and thank you," Libby said.

"So the café goes way back in your family?"

Emmy Jo filled all three mugs and set the pot on a hot pad in the middle of the table.

Libby smiled. "My great-grandmother and grandfather put in the original café and named it Libby's. That was her name, and she was an amazing cook. The place burned and was blasted by a tornado a time or two. After the last one, they bought this building and it's been here ever since."

"Then your mama ran it when Seth and my granny and Jesse were in high school?"

Libby pushed her plate back and propped her feet on an empty chair. "Not really. My grandmother was still the owner then, and my mama was in school with those three."

"Did she ever talk about them?"

Libby blushed.

Emmy Jo laid a hand on Libby's shoulder. "Hey, I know the history. It's okay."

"Your granny was a wild one. Seth was a nobody and Jesse was a cocky son of a bitch. That's what she told me when I asked questions."

"Pretty much what I get from everyone," Emmy Jo said.

"Now, you two get on out of here and spend the day together. Diana has a vacation day and you've got the whole day off. Y'all go talk weddings or drive up to Wichita Falls and window-shop for just the right cake. Just get out of Hickory for the day."

Emmy Jo would rather have spent the day in the café or in the library. She might get some more answers to all these questions.

"But Mama, you need help. I took the day off to spend it with you," Diana argued.

"I'll call one of my standby waitresses to help out. It's been a while since you girls have had a day to play," she said. "Now shoo! Get out of here. I'll expect to hear about wedding stuff next time I see you, not all this old gossip that's been around for sixty years or more. That's depressing."

Diana left her apron hanging on the back of the chair and followed Emmy Jo out to their cars, parked side by side. "Let's go to my place and eat junk food, watch old movies, drink a beer or two, and giggle instead of spending all day riding to Wichita Falls and back in a car."

"That sounds amazing. It's been a long time since we had a day like this. Let's do *My Big Fat Greek Wedding* and . . ." Emmy Jo paused.

"And *The Longest Ride*," Diana said as she got into her car. "See you there."

The traffic light stopped Emmy Jo, so Diana was already in the house when she arrived. She'd found a movie, had it in the DVD player, and pointed toward the kitchen when Emmy Jo walked through the door. "Get whatever you want to nibble on and kick off your shoes. You can have the recliner and I'll take the sofa."

"I've got lunch with . . . ," she said as she removed her sandals.

Her phone rang, the tone letting her know that it was Logan. She answered as she headed toward the kitchen.

"Bad news, sweetheart. I've got a meeting of the employees over my lunch hour concerning safety issues. Can't make it today, but I'm lookin' forward to Thursday," Logan said.

"Me, too, but nothing can keep us apart on Thursday, not family, friends, or foes," she said. "I'm at Diana's. We're going to watch movies and visit."

"Have fun," Logan said. "Love you."

"Me, too," she said and hit the "End" button. "Hey, Diana, can I get you anything? I'm only going to have a glass of apple juice."

"Bring me one, too. After that big breakfast, I don't need a thing," Diana yelled. "Movie is ready to start when you get here."

She set the two glasses of juice on the end table between the sofa and recliner. Once she was settled and had a fluffy throw tossed over her body, Diana hit the "Play" button and *My Big Fat Greek Wedding* started.

"I wish I'd been born into a big family like this," Diana said.

"Me, too, but with my luck, all those old women would act just like Tandy." Emmy Jo giggled. "I'm already thinkin' about her wedding dress. I don't want anything that big, but I do want the big affair."

"I'm not so sure anymore. I'm about ready to burn my wedding book and make a run to the courthouse one afternoon," Diana said.

"Bite your tongue!" Emmy Jo shook her finger at Diana. "We've got years and years of work on our wedding books. We can't ditch them this late in the game. Besides, you are the only chance I'll ever have at being a maid of honor."

"Okay, okay!" Diana said. "I'll have the wedding, but I want it to be a small one without much fanfare. You can have the huge thing."

"That's better," Emmy Jo said.

At four thirty the last of four movies ended, and Emmy Jo popped the recliner's footrest down. "I've got to go, but this has been such a good day."

"Yes." Diana yawned. "I slept through part of the last one."

"Shame on you. The ending was the best part." Emmy Jo gave her a hug. "I'm so glad that we aren't—"

"Me, too," Diana interrupted. "Now get out of here before you are late and get fired. I want to be the bridesmaid at the biggest wedding Hickory has ever seen."

"Thanks for the day. Tell everyone hello at the office for me." Emmy Jo put her sandals on and waved at the door.

When she got home, Emmy Jo left her research bag in the car and took the steps two at a time. As usual Seth was sitting at the head of the table and Oma Lynn was bringing out the food.

"So how are you feelin'?" Seth asked.

"I'm fine. Diana and I spent the whole day together at her house watching movies and I didn't sneeze one time," she answered.

"Well, my doctor is going to look at you tomorrow anyway," Seth said.

"Over a sneeze or two? That's crazy," Emmy Jo protested. "I work in home health. I know about sickness, and if I was feelin' bad I would be smart enough not to work around elderly folks."

"Elderly, am I?" One of Seth's snowy-white eyebrows shot up.

"Well, darlin', you ain't a spring chicken."

"Oma Lynn, she has insulted me. Call Nora and tell her that I'm firing her. Get your bags packed, young lady," Seth said.

"Don't tease me. I've had a wonderful day, and I'm not wasting money on a doctor over nothing more than a bit of pollen up my nose."

"Either you'll let the doctor check you or I really will call Nora," Seth said seriously.

Emmy Jo threw up her palms. "Okay, okay, but since it's your idea, you will pay for it. I'm not throwing my hard-earned money down the drain."

"Deal," Seth said.

"Once he gets set on something, wild horses couldn't change his mind," Oma Lynn said. "You can come help me bring in the biscuits and gravy."

Emmy Jo headed toward the kitchen. "What doctor in this area makes home visits?"

"Not one in this area. He'll fly over from Fort Worth," Seth answered.

"Fly?" Emmy Jo asked.

"The roof has a helicopter pad," Oma Lynn answered. "They took Seth to the hospital for his hip replacement and brought him back that way. Dr. Everson agreed to come to the house to check on him."

"Dr. Everson, as in the best bone doctor in Texas?" Emmy Jo was totally amazed.

"You think he'd let just anyone cut into him?"

"You're going to have Dr. Everson check me for nothing. Lord, he'll charge a fortune," Emmy Jo declared.

"Stop worrying. He's one of them high-powered surgeons, but surely he's got enough sense to know if you are starting to get sick," Seth yelled from the dining room.

"And if you are a little bit sick," Oma Lyn whispered, "you ain't goin' to be fired. He hates to listen to Nora bitch and moan, and she would be an old bear if he fired you."

Emmy Jo picked at her food. She'd nibbled all day, so she wasn't hungry and the fact that she'd wasted a whole day started to weigh on her. She would spend the evening working on her story and notes to make up for the time when she should have been in the library. When Oma Lynn brought in the lemon pie for dessert, she was thinking about why Samuel Thomas had run out on his family. She tried to put herself in his shoes as she finished supper. Had he really loved the barmaid he ran away with, or was he going through a midlife crisis? Try as she might, she could find no sympathy for him. Leaving his family, especially his three children at the ages they were, was inexcusable.

"What are you thinkin' about?" Seth said. "I've asked you twice what movies you watched. The old theater here in Hickory has been closed for years, so where did you go?"

"We didn't," she said. "She owns several movies and we watched them on television at her house."

"Humph." Seth snorted. "Television is the ruination of the world today. Folks don't read the newspaper or talk to one another anymore."

"Oh, come on," Emmy Jo said. "Nothing can be the total blame for the world's problems."

Seth gave her a sideways look meant to chill her to the bone, but she giggled. "Don't you look at me like that. I've lived with Tandy Massey my whole life, and you aren't nearly as mean as she is."

A smile twitched at the corners of his mouth and finally turned into a wide grin. "You are right about that. Now finish your supper so we can play a game of Scrabble before bedtime."

Rats! I wanted to go over my notes and get some writing done, she thought.

Too bad. You wanted to be his assistant, so this is your job. You are not part of his family but the hired help. The argumentative voice in her head sounded a heck of a lot like Tandy's.

CHAPTER TEN

Oma Lynn brought a hot toddy to the room before she left that evening.

"What is this for and why are you here so late?" Emmy Jo asked.

"Seth asked me to stay until bedtime so I could make you drink this," she said.

"I don't need it, Oma Lynn. I'm really not sick."

"I know that and you know it, but Seth is paranoid about catching anything right now and having to go back to the hospital, so drink it."

"Yes, ma'am." Emmy Jo nodded. "See you in the morning, then?"

"Bright and early," Oma Lynn said as she closed the door behind her.

The thought of a hot toddy reminded Emmy Jo of Samuel again. Maybe he had resorted to alcohol as escapism when he realized that his life was never going to be any better. A wife he'd married out of guilt and three kids who had to be fed and needed shoes at least once a year. With all that responsibility, she might fall into a bottle, too, especially if it tasted this good.

The phone rang.

"I'm bored and you are my assistant. You need

to come down here to the patio and sit with me," Seth said.

"What if I get you sick?" she asked.

"I'll sit on one side of the patio and you can sit on the other."

"I was teasin' you. We had supper together and our heads weren't three feet apart while we played Scrabble. I'll be down in five minutes. Shall I bring the hot toddy with me or down it up here before I come down?" she asked.

"It does more good if you sip it," he said. "So bring it with you."

When she arrived, Seth held up his drink. "I'm having a toddy, too. No self-respecting germ would ever live in this stuff. It's prevention medicine."

"To a good doctor's report tomorrow." She touched her glass with his.

"You didn't see Logan today?" Seth asked.

"Not today. He had a meeting at the bank. I'm hoping to spend Thursday afternoon with him." She sat down and held the glass up and looked at the moon and stars through the crystal. "Have you ever drunk enough of these to get tipsy?"

"No, but I discovered when I was in the army that I had a taste for good whiskey and I did get drunk. After the first few times, I decided that I had to leave it alone or I'd end up like my father."

She tipped it up and finished off what was in the glass. "I've never been drunk. Granny let me have hot toddies when I was sick and I've had a beer with pizza many times, but losing my senses and throwing up the next morning isn't my thing."

He turned on the radio and they listened to several classic country music tunes before she finally got the courage to ask the question on her mind. "What really happened between you and Jesse to make y'all carry a grudge for more than sixty years?"

Seth finished listening to the song that was playing, then turned off the radio. He leaned back on the lounge and took another sip of his drink. "By the end of summer after Mama put out the red light, I thought everyone had moved on to other gossip and we Thomas kids would be ignored like we'd always been. My brother, Matthew, was in elementary school, and some kid made a rude remark about our mother on the first day. He'd probably overheard it at home and was repeating the word, but callin' Mama a whore didn't set well with Matthew."

"How mean!" Emmy Jo frowned.

"He was a firecracker, and he came right back by saying that the kid's daddy gave Mama the money for his new shoes." Seth grinned. "The fight was on and the other kid wound up with blood all over his shirt and a black eye. Matthew had a bruise on his arm and his new pants had tears on both knees."

"Did he get in trouble?" Emmy Jo asked.

"Oh, yeah, both at school and at home. Mama did not abide fighting or cussin', and Matthew had done his fair share of both that day. The principal gave Matthew and the other kid each three licks at school and Matthew had to wash the supper dishes for a whole month."

Emmy Jo cocked her head to one side and frowned.

"Washing dishes was girls' work," Seth explained. "She told him that it would knock some of that cockiness out of him."

"Did it work?"

Seth's head slowly went from side to side. "Not one bit. The next morning another kid caught him going home after school and kicked Matthew in the seat of the britches, sending him flying across gravel and making a mess of his hands. Plus, it tore the knees again out of the britches Mama had just gotten for him."

Emmy Jo's fists knotted. "Did he fight back?"

Seth chuckled. "The kid was Jesse Grady's cousin. He and Matthew locked up horns. It took the principal and two more teachers to break up the fight. The principal got out the board and Matthew got three licks again, and the other kid got suspended for starting the whole thing."

Emmy Jo waited and was almost ready to go inside to her room. But then Seth went on.

"Matthew told Mama the whole story. She said he'd be doing supper dishes until Christmas."

"And?" Emmy Jo urged him on.

"He said that it was worth it and that the water would heal his busted knuckles." Seth grinned. "We thought it was over, but a few weeks into our junior year, it fired up again."

The smile faded, and his eyes went so sad that she wanted to hug him in the worst kind of way. With her hands clasped tightly in her lap, she held her breath.

"We were in history class, and the teacher was talking about why so many black folks had surnames like Thomason or Jackson. She asked if anyone in the class knew why?" Seth's eyes misted over and he swallowed hard. "Nora raised her hand and said that it was because when they weren't slaves anymore they took their master's first name and attached *son* to it, becoming the son of Thomas or the son of Jack."

He threw back the rest of his toddy and set the glass down with a thud, reminding her of the old Western movies that Tandy liked to watch on late-night television. "The teacher said that was right. But then Jesse raised his hand. I knew he was about to make a smart-ass remark. I could feel the tension in the air."

From the anger in Seth's eyes, Emmy Jo could feel part of what he had that day in the school-room. "Please tell me that you were wrong."

"Oh, no, I was dead-on right," Seth said. "And I can still see the smirk on his face and feel the burn on mine when he said, 'Then, teacher, if a feller's mama is a tramp, he could be called Trampson, right?' And his gaze never left my eyes the whole time he talked."

Emmy Jo felt Seth's pain. Even in telling it, he was reliving that horrible nightmare when those words echoed over the whole schoolroom.

"The whole class roared with laughter, and the teacher sent Jesse to the office. He was back in no time with nothing more than a warning to watch his mouth. They weren't going to do anything to him, because Hickory High School was in the football playoffs the next night. Jesse was the quarterback," Seth said.

"Was that the night that a gang beat him up? I read about it in the papers when I was looking up stuff about my granny and my mama," she said.

"That was the afternoon that I followed him home. There was no gang, Emmy Jo," Seth said. "He could have gotten away with putting me down, but he'd called my mama a tramp, and it was his mother and her cronies who'd forced her to do what she did by not giving her work."

"You beat him up, didn't you?" Emmy Jo whispered.

"I tried to kill him and would have, but Nora found me and dragged me off him. She took me straight to the creek and cleaned me up as best she could, then we went home. I told Mama that I couldn't talk about what had happened, but that Matthew would have some help with the dishes every night for the rest of the school year," Seth said in a monotone. "I thought Jesse was dead when we left him. I wish he had been. If he had, it would have changed the course of my life."

Emmy Jo started to argue. If Jesse had died, there would be no Logan. But she managed to hold her tongue. "So didn't he tell on you?"

"While he was still conscious, I reminded him that if he told anyone that 'Trampson' had whipped his sorry ass, he'd be the laughingstock of the whole school. And then I raised his bloody face up and told him if he ever said another mean word about my mother again, I would kill him. After that I pounded him until Nora grabbed my hair and pulled me away from his unconscious body. We left him lyin' out behind his daddy's barn," Seth said.

"He made up that story about a gang, didn't he?"

Seth nodded very slowly. "Everyone in school felt sorry for him. We lost the first round of playoffs that Friday night. Basketball season started without Jesse being the hot dog on the team and we didn't have a good year there, either. When he came back to school after Christmas, he treated me like an invisible person, and that was fine with me."

There was the story all tied up with a bow—except there was nothing about Tandy in the story. Not one single word. Why did she hate both Jesse and Seth so much?

One day at a time, sweet Jesus. The old church hymn floated through her mind. One day at a time until Seth was ready to tell her more of his story.

Or maybe Granny will tell me before she dies. She shivered at the visual of a funeral with Tandy Massey laid out in a casket in the front of the church. One thing for dead sure—no pun intended—heaven had better get ready for some drastic changes when Tandy showed up.

"And you've been enemies ever since, right? Did he ever apologize?" Emmy Jo searched the sky for a falling star so she could wish one more time for legitimate kids no one would ever make fun of. But the stars weren't streaking through the sky that night.

She started to get up.

"You too tired to stick around for a little longer?" he asked.

She sat back down and pulled a blanket up over her legs. "Not a bit."

"You love Logan, don't you? What if you found out something really bad about him?"

"Do you know something really bad?" Emmy Jo asked.

"No, but if you did?"

"I'd cross that bridge when I got to it. Were you ever in love?"

Seth toyed with his mustache. "One time."

"The woman who left you just before the wedding?"

He raked his fingers through his thick gray hair. "I thought I loved her at the time. But there's really only one deep love—the first one. Others don't have the fire that the first one does. Is Logan your first love?"

"First and only, unless you count Hunter Price when I was in the third grade. Broke my heart when he moved away." She laughed.

"I fell in love with a girl when I was a senior in high school. She was quite a beauty in her day. We met down at the creek up under an old weeping willow tree on Sunday afternoons. She was as wild as a Texas tornado, and I was as green as spring grass."

Tandy! Emmy Jo's eyes widened. *That sounds just like her.*

"I loved that girl with every ounce of my heart, but we had to keep our love secret. Mama would have pitched a fit if she'd known what I was doing, and her mama would have thrown an even bigger one if she found out that the girl was seeing Mary Thomas's kid."

"What happened?" Emmy Jo pushed the cover back and turned to face him.

"She got pregnant and told me about it the

night we graduated from high school. When I asked her to marry me, she laughed in my face. She said that she would never marry the son of a whore and then told me that the baby belonged to Jesse Grady. She'd been sleeping with him on Saturday nights under the same willow tree."

She thought of things she'd heard about Tandy's reputation again. Was he talking about her grandmother? That could be the connection between the three of them.

"What did you do?" she asked.

"I doubled up my fists, but I could never hit a woman, especially one I loved so much. I told her that the only difference between her and my mother was that she gave it away for free. She slapped me so hard that it rocked my jaw." He ran a hand down his cheek as he remembered that night.

"Then I said that I hoped Jesse left her high and dry. And he did. He joined the navy not long after that," Seth said.

"What happened to her and the baby?"

"That's a story for another day," he said. "You'd best get on up to your room and get some sleep. The doctor will be here right after breakfast, and you are going to let him check you."

"Yes, sir!" She saluted sharply. Next week she was going to ask Edith who'd had a baby about the same time that Tandy had Rose. Good Lord, what if Seth really was talking about Tandy and

Jesse was her great-grandfather? Was that why he'd asked that question about Logan?

She wished that she'd taken the elevator by the time her weak knees carried her to the top of the stairs. If Tandy had been sleeping with Jesse Grady, then that made Logan her cousin—far enough removed that it wasn't illegal for them to marry, but still shirttail kin. And if Jesse knew, then why hadn't he told Logan in the beginning?

Throwing herself on the bed, staring at the dark ceiling and listening to her heart pound rapidly in her chest, she thought for a few minutes that she might really be sick. Only it wasn't a cold or a flu but pure old nausea. How on earth did she find out for sure if Tandy was the woman Seth was talking about and if Jesse was her great-grandfather?

She sat up and slung her legs over the bed. The nausea subsided, and she began to pace from one side of the room to the other. She couldn't tell Logan—not yet—but she had to hear his voice. She dragged out her phone and scrolled until she saw his name. She took a deep breath and threw the phone on the bed. She made three more laps around the room and picked it up again and hit his name before she lost courage. It went to voice mail after four rings, and she was about to leave a message when he answered with a sneeze.

"Sorry about that. It's that time of year for allergies," he said. "I was about to call you.

I have to work Thursday after all. We've got a couple of folks who are taking an early vacation, and I can't say no since I've asked off for the week of our wedding."

"Being away from you so much is tough." The words were true, but she heaved a sigh of relief. She needed a few days to sort this thing out and find out the facts before she told Logan what she suspected.

"Hopefully by the next Thursday we'll be back in our routine. God, I miss you."

"I feel another sneezing fit coming on. I love you."

"Love you, too," she answered.

Diana called before she could lay the phone down. "Let's talk weddings. I'm all fired up after watching all those romance movies."

Of all the things in the world that Emmy Jo wanted to talk about, weddings were the last on the list. She wasn't sure just what she could say or what kind of trouble she could get into with the privacy issues and what Seth had told her. And again, she didn't want to say anything until she confirmed things.

Since there was no way out of the conversation, she inhaled deeply and said, "Putting you on speakerphone."

"I've decided on the cake. Have you?" Diana asked.

"I'm thinking about a small cake for Logan

and me to cut, and then fancy cupcakes on one of those tiered stands. Or maybe cupcakes on each end of the bridal table. One with different kinds of chocolate for the groom's end and one with lemon, wedding cake, and Hawaiian wedding cake on the bride's end." She'd never had to fight against tears so hard in her life. Her dreams were about to be shattered if Jesse had fathered Rose.

"You always come up with the best ideas," Diana said. "So are you still thinking about a morning wedding?"

"I think so," she said. "That way I won't be pacing the floor all day. Get up, get dressed, and get married. Have a reception and be off on our honeymoon by early afternoon. I've penciled in a ten o'clock ceremony with a waffle brunch immediately afterward. It's just me and you to get ready, and we're used to getting up early. Besides, it won't be as hot in the morning," she said.

"Outside then for sure?" Diana asked.

"Yes, ma'am. Granny's church won't be big enough to hold everyone."

"You'll have to have a backup if it rains," Diana said. "Turn to page four of the wedding cake pictures. Remember when we put this one in as a possibility? If you aren't going with the satellite cakes, I might. Each one could be a different flavor, like you are doing with cupcakes, and the main three tiers could be wedding cake."

"That's a great idea," Emmy Jo said.

"I've got a text from Jack. We'll talk more later," Diana said, and then she was gone.

Her phone rang an instant after she'd ended the call. Expecting it to be Diana, she didn't even check the caller ID. "That was quick, but let's talk about something other than weddings."

"I told you that was an evil place and you'd be sorry you went up there." Her grandmother's voice was high and squeaky. "And now you've come down with the plague."

"Good Lord, Granny! What are you talkin' about?"

"Mono. I heard you've got that horrible stuff. Don't you come to the trailer until you are well," Tandy said.

"Granny, I sneezed a couple of times. I'm not even sick," Emmy Jo argued. "Who told you I had mono?"

"If you aren't sick, then you need to come home where you belong. Whatever you are allergic to is up there around that house of Seth's and you got a double dose of it."

Emmy Jo rolled her eyes toward the ceiling. "Seth's doctor is flying in and he'll check me. Does this mean that you'll come up here and take care of me if I get the plague?"

"Hell, no!" Tandy sighed. "If you got something other than allergies, you keep your butt up there and give it to Seth. Maybe that old bastard will die. I should come up there and drag you home. That's what I should do for sure."

"Granny, you couldn't drag me two feet, much less all the way out to the street. I've got to go. We'll talk tomorrow night. Unless you want to tell me who Rose's father was?"

"Tomorrow night. Before nine so you don't interrupt my television show," Tandy said, and the phone went dark.

Emmy Jo tossed the phone off to the side. She changed into a pair of pajama pants and a tank top and crawled into bed. She slept poorly and dreamed of her wedding. Hundreds of people were there and Seth walked her down the aisle. But when she got to the front of the church, Jesse was standing there with a sneer on his face. There was no groom or groomsmen.

"Hello, Trampson," he said.

She awoke with a start, her heart racing. "I have to find out the truth and soon," she muttered as she headed to the bathroom for a shower.

CHAPTER ELEVEN

In those few minutes after opening his eyes to see the first rays of sunlight coming through his bedroom window, Seth decided what he was going to do when the doctor arrived. He slung his legs over the side of the bed and pulled the old phone book from the drawer in the nightstand. Running his finger halfway down the page, and hoping that Tandy had not changed her phone number, he finally found it. He picked up the receiver and poked in the buttons.

A starting point.

"Hello." Her voice had changed with age, but then the last time they'd spoken had been sixty-four years ago.

"Tandy Massey?" he asked, to be sure he was talking to the right woman.

"Who in the devil calls a woman at six o'clock in the morning? Are you crazy?"

"This is Seth Thomas," he said.

The silence was so long that he thought she'd hung up, but then he heard her breathing. *Fire, probably, and if it could come through this receiver, it would scorch the hair right out of my ears.*

"Is my granddaughter alive?" Icicles dripped from Tandy's tone.

"Why would you ask a fool question like that?"

"Because it's the only reason I can think of that you'd call me or that I would talk to you," she said bluntly.

"She was when she went up to bed last night. She usually doesn't come down until about seven thirty," Seth said.

"Then what the hell are you doing calling me?"

"You told me that you were pregnant with Jesse's child. Did you tell him?"

"That ain't one bit of your business," Tandy said, as if to cut him off.

"I think it is, because I was sleeping with you, too," Seth said.

"Rose belonged to Jesse. I kept track of the days when I could get pregnant and the only one I slept with on those days was Jesse. I was determined to marry him so I could get out of Hickory. Anything else you want to know?"

"Then why in the hell are you letting her marry Logan? They are cousins." He raised his voice a few notches.

"Don't you yell at me, Seth Thomas. And if they are kin, it's only third or fourth cousins, and that ain't illegal. You got no right to judge me or come around askin' questions now," Tandy said.

"They are still cousins," he said tersely.

"She's not yours, if that's what you are thinking. God almighty, man. Look at that red hair. If that's not a throwback to Jesse, then—"

"Thank you, Tandy," Seth said and laid the receiver back in the cradle.

He got dressed, went to the kitchen, and put on a pot of coffee, muttering the whole time. "My uncle had the same color hair and eyes as Emmy Jo, so it might *not* be a throwback to Jesse. But I do know how to figure this out once and for all. Hell, Tandy! If she's Jesse's great-granddaughter, then they are cousins. That just ain't right, and I'm getting to the bottom of this."

Seth had seen Rose a few times through the years, and he hadn't felt a thing toward the child. Surely if she'd been his daughter, there would have been something. And he'd watched Crystal grow up in the small town of Hickory. She'd had light hair and blue eyes, but then so did Wyatt Grady, Jesse's son. But there was something about Emmy Jo that was so much like Nora that it made chill bumps on his neck. It was past time for him to find out the truth.

Oma Lynn arrived at seven and went right to work in the kitchen. Emmy Jo appeared in the dining room thirty minutes later. Her hair was pulled up in a curly ponytail and she was dressed in jeans, sandals, and a T-shirt, ready to face the day.

"You ready for breakfast?" Oma Lynn asked. "Rumor has it that you've got mono."

Emmy Jo sighed. "Mono presents with chills

215

and aches, loss of appetite, and fatigue. I only sneezed a couple of times."

"The doctor will be here at eight thirty, and he's going to check you out. I'm not going back to the hospital because of a summer cold or the flu."

Oma Lynn brought out the breakfast and put it on the table. "You will drink two glasses of this orange juice. Vitamin C is good for whatever you've got."

Emmy Jo shrugged, poured a glass of juice, and downed it. "Why two?"

"Because if one is good for you, then two is twice as good," Oma Lynn said.

"Okay, you win," Emmy Jo said. "And I'll let the doctor check me, but it's a waste of his time and your dollars."

"Thank you," Seth said. "It would be a shame if you couldn't take me to the cemetery."

"I'm taking you to the cemetery," she said. As if an infection of any kind would stop her from that basic duty!

The noise of the helicopter coming in for a landing on top of the roof made Seth put down his coffee cup and straighten up out of his chair. He reached for his walker and made his way to the office, with Emmy Jo right behind him.

"You can stay out here until I call you," he said when they reached the door.

"I'm a home health nurse. I've seen the stitches and the staples from hip surgery. This is literally my job," she argued.

"Okay, then, but only because I'm afraid you'll back out of letting him check you."

"You old coot!" she mumbled under her breath.

"What did you say?"

"I said you are an old coot," she repeated.

"Well, thank you. I'm living up to my reputation," Seth said. "Come on in here, if you are coming. I swear, you young'uns sure are bossy these days."

"Well, thank you," she threw back. "I'm living up to my reputation."

Not long after the whirring noise stopped, the elevator doors opened and a man with jet-black hair and green eyes stepped out. He seemed young to be an orthopedic surgeon, but then anyone under sixty was young to Seth.

"Good morning."

"Mornin' to you. Meet my assistant, Emmy Jo." Seth made introductions. "And this is Dr. Everson. She is a nurse's aide, so if you need any help, just tell her what to do."

The doctor nodded. "Why don't you lie on the sofa here and let me take a look at the staples."

Emmy Jo stood back until the doctor had carefully pulled down Seth's loose-fitting pajama pants. The wound looked clean to her, no redness around the staples or swelling.

217

"What do you think, Emmy Jo?" the doctor asked.

"Looks fantastic. Give me a gauze and I'll hold the staples while you remove them," she said.

"I agree. Has he been getting exercise?"

"He's been walkin' around the house, and he's doin' a lot better about getting up and down without depending on his walker as much," Emmy Jo answered.

"All good news. Got clean hands?"

"Yes, sir, but I'll go wash them again if you'll let me take those staples out," she said.

The doctor smiled. "Thanks for the offer, but I'll do it."

"Thank God!" Seth said.

"You can assist me," Dr. Everson said, quashing Seth's enthusiasm.

Emmy Jo was as nervous as the first time she got to remove stitches on her own. Diana would never believe that she'd even been able to assist the great Dr. Everson.

Seth didn't even wince when the first few staples came out.

"You could at least cuss or moan with one of those staples so I'll know you are human," she muttered.

"It don't hurt, so why should I carry on like a girl? Doc, what does it say on my records about my blood type?"

"AB negative. Rarest type there is. Why are you asking?"

"That proves I'm human, Emmy Jo. Even if it's rare, it's human blood." He shot a look over at her.

"Oh, he's human, all right." The doctor removed the last two. "No one who isn't throws fits like he does when he doesn't get his way."

"I didn't want to go to that damned rehab place with all those people," Seth said. "Now Doc, I need you to check Emmy Jo. She's not feelin' up to par, and if she's really sick with some dread disease, I don't want to catch it."

She rolled her eyes. "It's nothing but allergies. I only sneezed twice. He's paranoid."

"I am only protectin' myself from havin' to go back to the hospital," Seth said.

"Well, let's take a look anyway, just to make him happy." The doctor checked her ears, nose, and throat, listened to her lungs, and nodded. "She knows what she's talking about. I can't find a thing wrong with her. Probably just snorted some pollen up her nose." He winked at Emmy Jo. "Anything else?"

"Nope, that'll do it until next time," Seth said. "And thanks."

"See you in two weeks. You keep a check on the wound, Emmy Jo. If it starts to look red or there's swelling, call me. Pretty nice to have a live-in nurse and assistant." The doctor pulled Seth's pajama pants back into place.

"Not too bad, but she does have a lot of sass," Seth said.

"Good for her. She'll need it to take care of you."

"Newspapers on the patio," Seth said the minute the doctor was in the elevator and the whirring noise of the helicopter started. "We'll have to read fast to get them done by snack time."

"Why?" Emmy Jo frowned.

"Why what?"

"Why don't we read slower and not worry about the clock?" she asked.

He shrugged. "I need schedule in my life."

"Schedule is one thing. OCD is another." She followed him out of the office, opening doors for him all the way to the patio. "Looks like rain today."

No sooner had she said the words than the first few drops made big splotches on the stones and the walls. She hurriedly grabbed up the newspapers and carried them into the house. "Now what?"

"We read them in the office." He turned his walker around. "And Emmy Jo, I am not obsessive. I just like a schedule. It makes my days go by better since I retired. Leave the doors open. We'll get the smell of fresh spring rain."

Seth settled himself on the sofa and propped

his legs up on an oversize hassock. She laid the papers beside him and melted into a rocking chair. He picked up the top newspaper, and she took the one from the bottom of the stack. She flipped it open to the lifestyle section and shook her head as she read more about people's dirty laundry.

"What are you reading?" he asked.

"These crazy advice columns again. They're like a car wreck. It's hard to not look at them even when you know you should move on down the road and leave it alone. Why do they write this stuff?" She yawned.

"Because when folks read it, then their problems don't seem so bad."

She popped the paper up in front of her face and continued reading the rest of that column. The next question came from a woman who had not seen her father in more than twenty years and now he wanted to get back in touch with her. They'd been estranged when he'd divorced her mother, married, and had children with a new woman who wanted nothing to do with her. He was divorced again and wanting to reconnect. She laid the paper aside and pulled out another one, read through the comics, and picked up a pencil to work on the crossword puzzle. So what if it was for children under twelve?

"Did you know my father?" she asked.

Seth frowned, his white eyebrows knitting

together. "No. I knew his name and saw him around town a few times."

"Granny says he had red hair and blue eyes like mine and that after my mother died, he got religion and went off to another country to do missionary work," she said.

"That's what I heard, too," he said.

Emmy Jo wanted so badly to ask outright if Tandy was the woman he'd loved, but she didn't have the courage.

CHAPTER TWELVE

Rain. Rain. And then more rain.

Every day until Sunday afternoon and then the gray skies parted, letting the precious sunshine through for a few hours. Logan was not sitting in his truck waiting for her in the cemetery this time, because his parents had asked him to go with them to look over a church in Wichita Falls. So she spent the hour that Seth talked to his mother in the car trying to get the courage to ask Seth what had become the big question that was on her mind constantly. Tandy wasn't going to tell her anything, and there was no way she'd ever approach Jesse with such a thing. So Seth was the only one she could turn to, and the problem was that she was terrified of the answer.

When Seth stood up and turned around, she scrambled to get his walker out of the back, but he'd taken three steps without it by the time she got to him.

"Not so smart on uneven ground," she scolded as she set it in front of him.

"Don't tell me what to do," he grumbled.

"Don't scare me like that. I was afraid you would fall."

"I'm ready for ice cream," he said. "And I'm

not going to use that damned contraption a minute longer than I have to."

"Are we going to the home place today, or will the chair on the porch be too wet?" she asked.

"I'll sit on the quilt if it is."

"Then ice cream and the cabin it is." When they reached the place, Seth carefully unfolded the quilt, revealing a fluffy throw inside. He handed it to her before he arranged the quilt the way he wanted it in his rocking chair.

"Thought you might need that to sit on, since the porch is wet," he explained.

"Thank you." She managed a smile, but it didn't lift her spirits.

"I haven't heard you sneeze today," he told her.

"I told you from the beginning that I was fine."

"Nora has always had a bout with sneezing in the spring and in the fall," he said.

Emmy Jo wondered why he'd think of Nora, but it did open up a way to get him talking. "Tell me about her. Were y'all good friends? Did you share things, or were you fighting siblings? I never had a brother or a sister."

"Nora is an angel with a set of horns," he answered. "She has always had a temper and a smart-ass attitude, but her heart is made of pure gold. She took Matthew with her to Amarillo, and she and her new husband made sure he was taken care of. She's short like you, has red hair and blue eyes, and she'd fight a forest fire with nothing but spit for her family."

"Why didn't you go there when you got out of the army?" Emmy Jo asked.

"Mama said that we didn't run from our problems. Besides, I had my reasons."

"Which were?" she pressed on, hoping that he'd shed some light on her heritage.

"You remember I told you about being in love with a girl who got pregnant and then insulted my mother because she was going to marry Jesse Grady. She wanted to get out of Hickory so bad that she tricked him into marriage by getting pregnant. Well, I was on the creek banks with her the night we all graduated."

"I remember." Emmy Jo's chest tightened.

"Nora and Walter, the man she married the next week, had taken Mama home, because Nora thought that's where I went. Then they took Matthew to Libby's for ice cream. When I came in, my mother was lying in a pool of blood on the floor. She was able to tell me she had tripped and fallen." Seth's voice cracked. "And then she died in my arms.

"If I'd been there I might have gotten help and saved her, but I was on the creek bank with a girl who didn't want anything to do with me," Seth said. "And I don't expect you to understand, but I . . ." He stopped and looked out over the yard.

"I think I do understand. Hickory was home

and you felt guilty. You hoped that by coming home you could show that woman you loved that you weren't that boy with nothing to offer anymore. That you were becoming a respectable citizen. And you wanted to be close to your mama's spirit," she said.

"Pretty smart for a kid." Seth grinned.

"So what happened when Jesse came home?" she asked.

"Jesse never did acknowledge the baby he'd produced. He married his wife, Nancy, after he got his education to be a preacher and moved into the pastor's position at the church. That other girl was pretty wild, so maybe he thought she was lying when she told him. Or maybe he thought he'd never be accepted as a preacher if folks knew. Hell, Emmy Jo, I don't even know for sure that she did tell him. Maybe she was just saying that to me so that I'd quit begging her to marry me," Seth said.

"Does she still live here in Hickory?"

Every single, solitary clue led straight to Tandy. Even her heart said it was Tandy, and that made sense. That would explain everything—the whole enchilada about why the three of them had been at cross purposes since they were in high school.

"I'm tired now. Let's go home and eat some dumplings and then have a game of Scrabble. I think I could beat you tonight." He avoided her question.

She pointed at him. "Dream on, Seth. It's my turn to win." She had a thousand more questions, but there was still time, and it seemed as if he could only stand to tell her bits and pieces at a time.

Seth didn't like things undone. Everything had a place, should be in its place, and that included this new thing with not knowing whether he or Jesse was the father of Tandy's daughter. He sincerely hoped that it wasn't him, because the guilt for not taking care of his only child would be a burden to carry. Then, in a moment of pure insanity, he would wish that Emmy Jo was his great-granddaughter, so that he wouldn't come to the end of his days with nothing but a bank account that would choke a king to show for his entire life.

That would sure make Tandy madder than a wet hen after an F-5 tornado. He smiled. *It would be her comeuppance after the way she talked about my mother. But she's had her just due. She lost her daughter and then her granddaughter, and now she's on the outs with her great-granddaughter. I will never forgive her for what she said that night, but I can't help but feel sorry for her.*

"Who's winning?" Emmy Jo asked as she settled him into the passenger seat.

"We aren't even playing yet, so how do I know?" he grouched.

"You were fighting with the voices in your head. I could see you were winning and then you were losing and then you were sad." She parked the car in the garage and then hustled around back to get his walker.

And if that's not Nora Thomas talking to you. She said the same thing to you more times than I can count. I swear. His mother's voice came through loud and clear in his head. *Why don't you just accept the fact that she's yours? You already know it in your heart.*

Because—he sighed—*I don't want to be disappointed again, Mama.*

He couldn't keep his mind on the board game and she won three out of three, netting her five dollars. It was well past dark when they parted company and he went to the patio to listen to the radio for an hour before turning in. Instead of turning the radio to his favorite old country station, he put it on one that played the newer stuff. Every song that played that evening brought back memories and visions, most of them having to do with his family before his mother died and/or Jesse and Tandy.

"How Do You Like Me Now" by Toby Keith especially spoke to him. The lyrics didn't exactly match his and Tandy's situation, but the idea behind it was the same. Then an artist he'd never heard of named Jon Pardi sang "Head Over Boots." He'd been in that place with Tandy all those years ago, and he'd never gotten over her. Too bad she hadn't given him a chance. He'd have made her a queen just like the singer said. After that Randy Travis sang something called "Three Wooden Crosses" that said something about a hooker and a preacher that caught his attention more than the rest. The lyrics warned that what was left behind when you left the world wasn't as important as what you left behind you when you died.

"I've got to know," he muttered as he left his walker beside the chair and went to the three-foot wall, where he paced from one end to the other and back again. After five trips, his hip began to hurt, and he went back to his walker. He rolled it into the kitchen, where he cut a slice of pecan pie, poured a glass of milk, and was in the process of eating at the cabinet by the moonlight pouring into the window when the lights came on.

"Holy hell!" he grumbled. "You almost blinded me."

"Sorry about that. I couldn't sleep and I remembered those leftover chocolate cupcakes."

"Well, make a little noise from now on," he said.

Emmy Jo didn't argue, which surprised Seth. She always had a sassy comeback to whatever he said.

She uncovered a container with three cupcakes inside. "I'll share."

"I'll take one, since I had pie, and you can have the other two," he said.

"Fair enough." She backed up against the cabinet and removed the paper wrapper from the first one. "I love chocolate—cupcakes even more than candy bars."

"Tomorrow we need to drive over to Graham and have the car serviced. I made a ten o'clock appointment. There's a fancy little doughnut shop not far from the place where I get mechanic work done. I thought we'd get our midmorning snack there. They make amazing iced doughnuts, and they even sprinkle them with tiny little chocolate chips," he said.

She carried her second cupcake and the gallon of milk on the counter to the table, along with a glass. "And you are just telling me this now?"

"Forgot about it," he said. "You are my assistant."

"Yes, I am and I'm more than ready to go somewhere." She smiled. "Why do you go to Graham? There's places to get a car serviced here in Hickory."

He stole long glances at her. Nothing about Tandy there except the fire in her temper and her humor. Lots of Nora, and those eyes were Thomas blue. He remembered another song he'd heard that evening. Tanya Tucker sang "What's Your Mama's Name," a song about a man who was hunting a woman he'd loved many years before. He was interested in a little green-eyed girl because her eyes were Wilson green. It made Seth want to find out for absolute sure what Rose's daddy's name was, since her eyes were definitely Thomas blue.

"What are you thinking about?" Emmy Jo asked.

"I was listening to some different stations on the radio. Some of them really spoke to me. And to answer your question, I changed when my favorite mechanic took a job in Graham. No underlying secret reason other than that and I like the pastry shop over there and I really like the air-conditioned waiting room at the garage," he said.

"Which songs?" she asked.

"Just some that I hadn't heard in a while and a couple I'd never heard. Nora fusses at me for not stepping into the modern world, so I did a little bit tonight."

"You didn't come home for four years after you left? Not even once or twice to see Nora and your family?" she asked.

He removed the paper from his cupcake and took a bite. "I believe you young kids say that it was a time when I found myself."

She fidgeted, wanting him to go on and tell her more, but he took his own good time in eating the whole cupcake and then refilling his glass with milk.

"I was away from Hickory for the first time. The people around me had no idea about my mother or me. I was just another recruit with no hair and a scared look in my eye."

"I can't imagine you without hair," she said.

"In those days, I wore it really short anyway, so it wasn't as big a deal as it would be now. I got acquainted with a few guys in Kentucky, though I left them all behind when my training was done. From there I went to a place called Wildflecken, Germany, and saw real snow for the first time in my life. Got there in February and thought I'd freeze plumb to death by the time spring came."

"We have snow," she argued.

"We get snow and then in a few days at most, it melts. We had snow from February until May, knee-deep in most places," he said. "I got so homesick that after the first year I declared I'd never leave the state of Texas or complain about the heat. Where all have you been, Emmy Jo?"

"I've been to Oklahoma and Arkansas, but that's the limit of my travels. Did you get homesick for Nora and your brother?"

Seth's head bobbed once, and his eyes misted over. "Nora wrote to me twice a week and Matthew wrote pretty often, but he was a ten-year-old kid and he was in a new place, so I didn't expect much from him. I hid every time I read the letters because I cried, and men, especially in those days, did not show emotion. Then one day while I was in my hiding place, which was the corner of the mess hall after hours, I met Markita. She was a German girl who had been hired to translate for the base."

Emmy Jo's ears perked right up when he mentioned a possible romance. "What did she look like?"

"Dark hair, big blue eyes, and almost as tall as me. She sat down beside me and didn't even smile when I wiped my tears away with my fist. She asked me if the letter was from my mother or my girlfriend."

"And?" Emmy Jo asked after the pause lasted three minutes past eternity.

"And I told her neither. What I said was that my mother had been dead for more than six months and the letter was from my sister, who was raising my younger brother. That started an amazing friendship that helped me get through the next years. It went to a relationship within six months, and when my time was up we were in love."

From the sadness in his eyes, Emmy Jo wasn't sure she even wanted him to go on, and yet she had to hear the story.

"I didn't have a thing to offer her in Texas. The home place was there, but I couldn't bring her to a tiny cabin that didn't even have an indoor bathroom. I had to come home and get a job, at least rent a decent house and do a million things before I could ask her to marry me."

"You didn't even give her the choice?" Emmy Jo fussed at him.

"She cried the last night we were together, and I promised that as soon as I had a job, I'd send for her. She promised that she would be ready. But . . ."

Emmy Jo shook her head emphatically. "No *but*s. Don't say that word. You deserved some happiness after all you'd been through. Tell me that she came to Texas and y'all had some good years together."

"No, I came home, got a job, and we wrote letters. At first it was every day and then every couple of days, and then after a while we did good to write once every two weeks. Then six months later I got a long letter from her saying that she'd found someone else, a sweet German fellow who worked at the base, and they were in love. She was breaking it off with me so they could get married. By the time I got the letter, the wedding was already over, and I never heard from her again," Seth said.

"Did that break your heart all over again?" Emmy Jo wanted to hear about a happy time in Seth's life. He was a good man, and he deserved something good instead of so much sadness.

"No, the whole thing had just kind of died in its sleep. It was a disappointment, but the more I thought about it, the more I realized that she'd never like Hickory, Texas, and I'd never have the money to send her home for visits."

"But you did have that kind of money," Emmy Jo argued.

"Not at first. That didn't come until later. We'll talk about that part of the story another time. We'd best turn in since we've got a trip planned tomorrow," he said.

Emmy Jo made sure the milk was put away and the lights were all turned off before she went up to her room. Really, it was an excuse to wait until Seth was in his bedroom and hadn't gotten too brave about getting around without his walker. When she reached her room, she opened her laptop and began to type in what he'd told her as fast as she could so she wouldn't forget any of the details.

Suddenly, she stopped typing and sighed. *What if Seth is really Rose's father? Surely if he thought that he would have said or done something, right?* Would Logan have to go for genetic testing before they had kids? They both wanted a big family, since they'd been raised as only children. What would it do to his family if he confronted them with this news?

She began to pace the floor. Her hands grew sweaty, and her head started to throb. She found two Tylenol in her purse and swallowed them with a glass of water from the bathroom.

Staring at her reflection in the mirror above

the vanity, she turned every which way, trying to see some of Jesse in her face or maybe some of Seth. All she recognized was the same face shape and red hair that her father had had in the senior picture she found in the newspaper.

"I need to know," she whispered.

Her phone pinged and she hurried across the floor to the nightstand, grabbed it up, and quickly hit the button to talk. "Logan, I'm so glad you called."

"You sound better. Are we going to make that Thursday date?" he asked.

"I'm hoping that we will. We are going to Graham to get the car serviced at some auto place over there and we're going to get doughnuts at this little place and . . ." She paused to suck in more air.

He chuckled and lowered his voice to a seductive whisper. "I know I keep saying it, but I can't wait until June, when we will be together forever."

Her throat tightened and formed a lump the size of an orange. "Me, too."

"What's wrong?" His tone went from sexy to worried.

"I really, really don't like being apart from you like this," she answered. It was the truth, even if there was an underlying possibility that her life would parallel Seth's, in that she'd found her only true love and nothing else would ever work out.

"Me neither, but it's only three more days and then we get to spend a whole afternoon together."

She sighed. "I hope so."

"Emmy Jo," he said, "what's wrong? Something is eating on you and I know it. Talk to me."

"I've got a lot on my mind, but I don't want to talk about it on the phone." She couldn't make herself tell him about her suspicions.

"You'd tell me if there was something else, right?"

She smiled and nodded, then remembered to speak. "I'll be fine when I get a kiss from you. I didn't even get to see you today. Texting isn't the same as hearing your heart beat as we lie together."

"I love you," he said simply. "And darlin', it's only forty-eight more days until our wedding. Have you decided where it's going to be held?"

"Not yet. Good grief, Logan, it's midnight and you've got to work tomorrow. Good night. I love you."

"Me, too," he said.

Three seconds after she ended the call, she got a text that covered her screen with little red hearts. She smiled as she went to sleep and dreamed of her wedding again. This time Logan swept her up into his arms and carried her to Seth's fancy convertible and they drove off together with her veil flowing in the wind.

CHAPTER THIRTEEN

The room had air-conditioning, all right, but it smelled like motor oil and cigarettes. Half a dozen well-worn magazines were scattered about, with names like *Hot Rod*, *Motor Trend*, and *Car and Driver*. There wasn't a single one that had to do with brides or getting married. A coffeepot sat on a table in the corner, and four folding metal chairs had been lined up against a wall. A few disposable coffee cups in the trash can said that Seth and Emmy Jo weren't the first customers of the day.

The door opened, letting in more fumes that let Emmy Jo know she was not in a beauty parlor. Seth and Willard, an old bald guy in coveralls, greeted each other warmly with hearty handshakes and smiles. Willard asked about Seth's hip, and Seth asked him about his family. Then they got down to the business of discussing the car and what Seth wanted done that day. After a lot of chin rubbing and decisions, Willard headed back into the land of oil changes and tire rotations.

Seth left his walker by the door and poured two cups of coffee, handing one to Emmy Jo before he sat down beside her. "Willard makes good strong coffee. You'll like it."

She smelled the steam coming from the top. "Are you sure this is coffee, or does he just run the used oil from the cars through that pot?"

Seth chuckled. "You never know about Willard. He's all for saving a dime. Get the doughnuts out of the bag."

"Seems a shame to ruin such fine pastry with this stuff," she said.

"Trust me." He grinned. "You'll be glad for Willard's coffee to cut the sweet."

She opened the paper bag and carefully handed him a glazed doughnut before she removed the one with chocolate chips for herself. "How long does this take?"

His smile widened. "The car business or the morning snack?"

She eyed him carefully. "You are in a very good mood this morning—at least for you."

"And you aren't?" he said.

"I am, but . . ." She bit into the doughnut to give herself a few minutes to think.

A cell phone rang, and she reached for hers but then realized that the ringtone was wrong. Her brow furrowed with a question when Seth removed an old flip phone from the pocket of his cardigan and opened it.

"Hello," he said in a businesslike tone.

Thirty seconds later he thanked the person on the other end, folded the phone, and returned it to his pocket. She couldn't help staring at him.

"What?" he asked, all innocent.

"You have a cell phone?" she asked with wide eyes.

"Yes, I do, and only my doctor, my accountant, Oma Lynn, and one other person have the number. I'm not going to learn that texting crap or use it to take pictures or look up something on the infernal Internet. All that is the ruination of today's society."

"I thought that television was the ruination of the world. And who was that on the phone?" Asking was rude, but she'd said it before she even thought.

"It is of the world, but all this other is of society. There's a difference, and don't be so nosy." His tone had gone all testy. "Aren't you goin' to finally get to see your boyfriend pretty soon?"

"You're going to miss me when I have a day off," she singsonged.

"Like I'd miss another hip surgery." He wiped his sticky fingers on a paper napkin from the pastry shop and picked up a magazine.

Right then a crazy song from the kids' movie *Angry Birds* popped into her head. A while back she'd heard the song at a patient's house. The old girl loved animated movies, and when the song came on, Emmy Jo recognized Blake Shelton's voice immediately.

She finished her doughnut, stuck her purple

earbuds in, and found the video on YouTube so she could listen to the words again. "Friends," that was the name of the song, and be damned if it didn't describe her and Seth to a T—from their first meeting when she'd felt like her boots couldn't walk another mile after all the fighting with Tandy. Like the lyrics said, the cloud above her had no silver lining, and it sure didn't today.

Seth nudged her on the shoulder, and she pulled one of the earbuds from her ear.

"What?" she asked.

"What are you listenin' to?"

She popped the purple thing into his ear, leaned in closer so he could see the small screen, and started the video all over again. "This is me and you," she said. "In the past almost four weeks, we've become friends."

He tapped his foot to the music, and when it was over, he nodded. "We are friends, aren't we? But I've got to know, am I the big black bird or the white one? I like the moves that black one makes."

She giggled. "Seth, you might have gray hair now, but when you were young it was jet-black. You can be the one with the dance moves."

He handed her back the earbud. "So that's what Blake Shelton looks like. I like some of his songs that they play on the radio, especially the one about his mama and that one about being in prison and training that dog so he could escape."

"I need a friend," she said bluntly.

"Haven't heard that one," he said.

She laid a hand on his shoulder. "It's not a song. I really need a friend—someone to tell me what to do about Logan."

"And what is it that you need to do about Logan? I thought you were engaged and getting married. Are you having second thoughts?" Seth asked.

"No, but . . . is Jesse my grandfather, too? Was it my granny that you fell in love with and she was pregnant with Jesse's baby? If he is, then Logan and I . . . well, we are cousins of some kind and I'm . . . ," she stammered. "I need to know and I can't face Logan and I love him . . ."

"What is your blood type, Emmy Jo?"

"A negative," she answered.

"And did you ever take Tandy's when you were in school just to practice?"

She nodded. "O positive. Rose had A negative, and so did my mother. Granny said that she had no idea how we got to be blue bloods when she was so common."

"Did you ever test Logan's?"

Another nod. "O positive."

"Uh-huh," he said.

"Oh. My. Sweet. Jesus." She was so flustered that she slapped her palm against her forehead.

"I didn't even think to do the blood charts. What is the matter with me? I can't be related to him. Blood tells the tale."

"That's right," Seth said. "I just got a call from that other person who has my phone number. He does some digging into things for me, and he just found out the same thing you figured out. For all his blustering, Jesse Grady has the most common blood type in the world, too, as did his wife, and so do his son, his daughter-in-law, and Logan. Jesse is not the father of Rose."

Emmy Jo felt as if she were floating a foot above the chair as a weight lifted from her heart. She clasped her hands tightly in her lap to ground herself, and then more questions surfaced. "That means . . . Seth, do you know who Rose's father was? Was my granny the girl you fell in love with?"

"It's Tandy's job to tell you who Rose belonged to, not mine," he answered.

She clamped a hand over her mouth. "There is something between you and Jesse and Granny. She really doesn't like either of you. Are you and I kin? Were you Rose's father after all?"

"Like I said, that's between you and your grandmother. I just know for a fact that you and Logan are not related, so you don't have to worry about being kin to him." Seth changed the subject. "Are you excited about getting to see him tomorrow?"

"Yes, I am, and I get to have breakfast with Granny and I'll see Diana and then have an hour with Logan at lunch. After that I might go shopping in Wichita Falls," she said. "You would tell me if you knew for a fact that you were Rose's father, right?"

"I don't know anything for a set-in-stone fact. Are you shopping for a wedding dress?"

"Oh, no, Diana and I are doing that together. We picked out our cakes this past week. Want to see mine when we get home?" she asked.

She dang sure was going to corner Tandy now that she'd figured out that much. And this time she was going to have the answer, come hell or high water.

"You are talking about a picture and not a real cake, right?" he asked.

Her whole demeanor changed when he told her that she wasn't related to Logan. Her eyes glittered like they did that first day when she'd marched into his life and told him that she didn't like orange. Seth hoped that she didn't hate him when she knew the truth. If he'd known that Rose belonged to him or that Crystal was his granddaughter, he would have taken care of them as well as Tandy. He'd have to bear the burden of not digging into things, but Tandy had said that the baby was Jesse's.

"Of course it's a picture," she said. "If you

aren't crabby, I'll even let you look at my wedding book."

"Me, crabby? What's a wedding book?" he asked.

"A wedding book is a three-ring notebook with pictures and samples of everything in it that I might want for my wedding," she explained.

"Real cake samples?"

She sighed and shot him the old evil eye. "Of course not!"

"Well, I suppose after my nap we can take a look at it. Where are you going to have this big wedding?"

"Not sure yet—it needs to be outside with an inside reception. Trouble is, I can't see that happenin' in either church. Jesse would probably burn down his church before he let me have a weddin' there, even if Logan is his grandson. And Granny would do the same with her church. We could have an outside reception, but I shudder to think about flies and gnats on the cakes and drowning in the punch."

Willard poked his head in the door before Seth could answer. "It's all ready when y'all are. Got it parked out front for you."

"Thank you." Seth handed him a credit card. "We'll see you in three months."

"You bringin' your assistant with you then?"

"Probably not," Seth said. "She's only helping out until the doctor clears me for driving again."

"Well, that's too bad. It's good to see you with a friend. I'll get this rung up and bring you the receipt to sign." He disappeared back into the mechanic cave again.

Less than fifteen minutes later, Seth was staring out the side window and wondering what his life would be like today if he'd chosen a different path. He'd had no control of the events that were set into motion the day that Sam Thomas spooked those horses. Talk about the effects of a butterfly flapping its wings. One little decision could create years and years' worth of consequences.

When Emmy Jo drove through town, they passed Jesse Grady coming out of Libby's. He didn't even look up, but Seth saw him. Had the man given a second thought to the child that Tandy told him she was carrying when they all graduated? Had he ever looked at Rose and felt guilty for not supporting her? Was his aversion to Emmy Jo because he thought that she had his genes, like Logan?

He knew that's what he'd be thinking if he was in Jesse's shoes. Emmy Jo drove into the garage at eleven thirty, and they rode the elevator up to the first floor in silence.

The aroma of Italian food met them when they were in the dining room. Emmy Jo inhaled deeply and smiled. "Lasagna?"

"No, rigatoni," Seth said. "But it's Italian."

"I love anything with marinara," she said. "And Seth, thank you for reminding me about the blood types. I should have thought of that first. It was one of the things we learned in nursing training. You'll never know how much it puts my mind at ease."

"You are very welcome." He wondered if she'd thank him when she finally pinned Tandy down and demanded answers.

Chapter Fourteen

Logan awoke on Tuesday morning with an Alan Jackson song on his mind and a smile on his face. He hummed "Livin' on Love" as he shaved and got dressed for work.

Today he would see Emmy Jo—nothing could go wrong. He kept that feeling right up until he walked into his mama's kitchen. She'd invited him to breakfast so they could discuss whether or not she and his father were going to take the Wichita Falls church that had been offered to them.

"Good morning," Paula said.

"Mornin', Mama," he said as he poured a cup of coffee and carried it to the table.

Jesse shuffled in from the living room and sat down on the other side from him.

"Coffee, Gramps?" he asked.

"No, thank you. I done had two mugs while I was waitin' on you." Jesse's mouth set in a firm line, and his eyes drew down into slits.

"What's goin' on here, Mama?" Logan asked.

"A family meeting," she said.

Wyatt joined them and motioned toward a chair. "Dad, I expect you to be civil. Your whole family is here and we're going to talk about this business going on in the church without anyone throwin' a fit."

"Not the whole family. Your mother isn't here," Jesse said bluntly.

"No, she's not." Wyatt said. "And I miss her. But this is a problem for this day, so she can't help us."

Logan stacked four pancakes on his plate and checked the clock on the wall above the stove. In thirty minutes he had to get to work. "Staying in Hickory or going somewhere else is y'all's decision. I'm not sure why I'm here."

"We are not going to argue with you any more over Emmy Jo," his mother said. "That does not mean we are happy about things, but we don't want to lose you over this. Your father is going to put an ultimatum to the church committees. Either you get your apartment back or we will hand in our resignation. We've prayed about it and the rest is up to God."

"Thank you," Logan said. "But I'm going to stay with Jack. We're doin' fine in the trailer."

"I don't like this one bit," Jesse said. "The church voted and I'm not going to accept that girl."

"We're about to be a package deal, Gramps. Either you take us both or you get neither," Logan told him.

"I'll opt for neither if it comes down to it," Jesse growled.

"Y'all let me know what the decision is. I've got to go. Thanks for breakfast, Mama, and thanks for standing up for me, Dad. I'll take my pancakes with me if that's the way Gramps feels about me," Logan said.

Wyatt reached over and clamped a hand on his shoulder. "Come back any time. This is your home and you are welcome."

Logan nodded, laid his napkin on the table, and pushed his chair back. "Gramps, I hope that whatever your problem is, you get over it."

"That ain't happenin'," Jesse said.

Logan had barely turned on the lights in his office when Jack poked his head in the door. "Hey, how did the breakfast at your mama's go?"

Logan ran his fingers through his dark hair and told him what had happened. "But I told them I'm staying at the trailer with you," he finished.

"I vote that next week, we all four get together and go to the courthouse, buy a license, and get married right then," Jack said.

Logan hiked a hip on his desk. "Try getting Emmy Jo and Diana to agree with that and I'll be right there with you."

"Wishful thinking." Jack waved over his shoulder as he headed to his own desk.

The morning dragged, with the second hand on the big clock in the lobby taking at least an hour to make every round. When noon finally arrived, Logan's hands were sweating and his pulse had jacked up a few notches. He couldn't remember the last time ten days had elapsed without him seeing Emmy Jo. Even in college, they saw each other every weekend and sometimes a day during the week. The time, plus the way she'd been acting, had him thoroughly spooked when he walked into a packed Libby's that Tuesday.

She waved from a back booth and then slid out and waited with outstretched arms and a big smile. He quickly crossed the floor and hugged her tightly before tipping her chin up to brush a kiss across her lips.

"God, I wish our wedding was over." He sank his face into her hair and inhaled deeply.

"Me, too, but it won't be much longer," she said. "Sit beside me, not across from me. I want to feel you next to me this whole hour. I need to touch you more than I want the blue-plate special."

He moved across the slick booth to sit as close to her as possible, stealing another quick kiss before the waitress appeared with menus. Emmy Jo had sounded so worried when he talked to her the past few days that he really had been afraid she was about to break up with him. To see her in such a good mood and back to his bubbly Emmy Jo made him want to pull her out onto the floor and dance with her.

"How's it going? Heard you two had mono, Emmy Jo," Melody, the waitress, said.

"That was one of Hickory's rumors. I only sneezed. I probably would have had pneumonia if I'd coughed." Emmy Jo laid a hand on Logan's thigh under the table.

Yes, ma'am, everything is definitely better, he thought. *When I'm with Emmy Jo everything is fine.*

"That's great. So what can I get you to drink and are you ready to order?" Melody asked.

"I want your special and a glass of water with a lemon wedge," Emmy Jo said.

"Same here, only a glass of sweet tea." Logan said, but his eyes didn't leave Emmy Jo's lips. Thursday was only two days away, and they could spend the whole afternoon in a hotel in Graham.

"Be right back with your drinks," Melody said and hurried back to put in the order before she waited on the next folks coming into the café.

"So I'll make the reservations for Thursday. Seems like forever since we had an afternoon together," he whispered.

Emmy Jo lowered her voice. "Neither Texas wildfire nor a tornado would keep me away from that room on Thursday. What time can we check in?"

"When I call them I'll arrange it so we can have our room by one o'clock," he said.

"I'll be waiting for you in the parking lot. I'll bring—"

He put his fingers over her lips. "Bring nothing but you. Maybe even just you naked under that brown trench coat that you wear when it rains." He wiggled his eyebrows.

She squeezed his thigh again. "Oh, honey, that can be arranged. Or maybe I'll get there first and simply be waiting in a bubble bath for you."

"You are killing me." He groaned.

She leaned over and breathed into his ear. "Forty-eight hours."

Melody brought their food and set it on the table. "Oh, I'm so sorry. In this rush I forgot your drinks. Water and sweet tea, right?"

"No problem." Logan smiled. "We were talking and didn't even realize that we didn't have them."

Melody hurried off and returned in seconds with their drinks. "Thank you. Libby would hang me out to dry for that."

Emmy Jo handed him the salt before she set about cutting up her chicken-fried steak. "So I've accomplished two of my goals. I got Seth to laugh and to be my friend."

"And now the only thing left is to figure out what makes those three old coots hate one another and you'll have discovered the biggest secret in Hickory." He told her about the situation with his folks. "The tension was so thick at the parsonage this morning that you couldn't cut it with a machete. I'm glad to be living with Jack now, though I can't wait until we have our place. The trailer park manager let me look at that trailer I told you about. It's a double-wide, two bedrooms, two full baths, and it's on the other side of the park from Tandy's place. It'll be cleaned up and freshly painted, carpets cleaned and all that by mid-May."

Her blue eyes sparkled. "Then I can look at it?"

"Yes, you can, and if you like it we'll rent it until we can save up enough for a down payment on a house. Now, about the honeymoon?"

"Save the money for the house. We can spend whatever time we can take off in our new house," she said.

"Oh, no, darlin', if you are going to have your dream wedding, then we're having a dream honeymoon to go with it. I'm booking a five-day cruise for us. I wasn't going to tell you, but you'll want to pack for the tropics."

"For real?" Seeing her expression told him he'd made the right decision about the cruise.

He leaned over and kissed her on the tip of her nose. "Yes, darlin', for real. Happy?"

"Oh, Lord, yes! I can't even imagine . . ." She cupped his face in her hands and kissed him passionately. "I love you so much. I keep saying it, but I really do, Logan."

Logan floated the rest of the hour and into the afternoon. He hummed the Alan Jackson tune that had been in his head all day. He and Emmy Jo were two young people just livin' on love, and he didn't want to be anywhere else than right there in Hickory with her.

Chapter Fifteen

On Wednesday afternoon, Logan had just finished with a client when his phone rang. When he answered it, the voice on the other end said, "Seth Thomas here. Can you come to the house tomorrow while Emmy Jo is off work? I think we should have a conversation."

"Yes, sir," Logan said, and then slapped his forehead. Tomorrow afternoon he and Emmy Jo were supposed to spend the afternoon together in the hotel.

"Okay, then. One o'clock. Park in the back and come up the stairs inside the garage. I will see you then," Seth said.

He hated lying to Emmy Jo, but he vowed that he'd tell her exactly why as he scrolled down the phone and hit her name. "Hi, darlin'," she answered.

"Bad news," he said.

"No!"

"Yep, I have to work tomorrow. Have a few out with those sinus infections like we had and I can't get off," he said.

"I understand, but I'm so disappointed I could cry."

He wiped his brow, feeling as if she could see

his nervous sweat. "I'm so, so sorry. I'll make it up to you, I promise."

"Next week, then. Come hell or high water," she said.

"Or a snowstorm right here in Texas in May," he said.

"Call me when you get home?"

"I will. Got to go." He whipped his phone from his shirt pocket and found the number for the florist in Hickory.

"Bloomin' Love," the lady answered. "What can I help you with today?"

"I'd like to send half a dozen red roses to—"

"I'm sorry," she butted in, "we are all out of red roses. We have pink and we have white daisies or we have red carnations."

"Then a vase full of daisies with purple ribbons. Take them to Emmy Jo Massey at Seth Thomas's house. I don't know the address."

"I know where the house is," she said. "How do you want the card signed?"

"Missing you, Logan," he answered. "Just those words and nothing more."

"Now I need your credit card information," she said.

He rattled off the details and ended the call with her promise that the bouquet would be there within an hour. It didn't ease his conscience about lying to Emmy Jo, but it would make her happy.

He was on the way home when his phone rang. "Hello, gorgeous!" he answered.

"The daisies are so pretty, and the vase is, too. I'm going to use it on the guest book table at our wedding," she said in lieu of greeting him. "But I'm still disappointed about tomorrow."

"Me, too, darlin', and if I'd change it if I could, but it's a very important meeting." He visualized her with the daisies right there in front of her, thinking that everything was all right in the world when something had to be desperately wrong for Seth to invite him to that house.

Emmy Jo had barely ended the call with Logan when her phone rang again. She smiled when she saw her granny's picture pop up on the screen. "Hey, what are you doing today?"

Maybe, just maybe, she'd get Tandy to open up about the past if she eased a simple question or two into the conversation.

"I'm cleaning the church because it's my turn to take care of it. Right now I'm sitting on the back pew, taking a break. I heard that Logan's folks are stayin' in town. They had a showdown today with the church, and the committee said that Logan could move back into the apartment, but he's refused. Is that true?" Tandy never was one to ease into a conversation.

"That's what I heard, too. Hey, I drove Seth to the garage in Graham yesterday," Emmy Jo said.

It aggravated her that everyone in town knew their business—especially before she did.

"I knew that, too, so I figured you'd gotten over the cold or whatever to hell it was," Tandy said.

"Want to have breakfast or lunch at Libby's tomorrow? There are some things I need to talk to you about," Emmy Jo said.

"Can't do anything tomorrow. In the morning I'm baking brownies and cooking two big pans of baked spaghetti for a funeral that afternoon. The church ladies are feeding the family, although I'm not sure why. Marnelle Phillips moved away from Hickory forty years ago, and she only came back when her mama died. But her mama came to church here her whole life," Tandy said.

"Then what about Sunday afternoon? I usually spend an hour in the cemetery with Logan, but he and Jack are going to Wichita Falls right after church so Logan can get fitted for his tux."

"Maybe that would work," Tandy said. "Why don't we just talk about whatever it is on the phone?"

There it was—the opportunity to ask her the all-important question—but Emmy Jo needed to see Tandy's expression, not just hear the words.

"Because I want us to be face-to-face. It's important," Emmy Jo told her.

"What if I die between now and Sunday?" Tandy asked.

"Then you won't know and it won't matter, will it?" Emmy Jo said.

"You are just like that worthless daddy of yours," Tandy fussed.

"I'll just say good-bye, Granny, and I hope to see you Sunday. Shall I bring a dozen chocolate doughnuts and a thermos of coffee?"

"No, but you might bring cold Dr Peppers and half a dozen maple doughnuts," she said. "And if what you want to talk about is the past, then save your breath and let sleeping dogs alone. Good-bye."

Emmy Jo put her phone to the side and opened her laptop. She read through the story she'd started and put her fingers on the keys to start where she'd left off, but she couldn't force herself to type. The alarm sounded on her phone, telling her that it was two thirty. Time for Seth's nap to be over and for afternoon snacks to be served. She snapped her computer shut and carried it with her down to the patio.

"I have a confession," she said when she sat down beside Seth.

He glanced up from a Western and raised an eyebrow.

"When you first told me that story about your grandmother, it stuck in my mind and my heart. I could feel her fear and her pain there when those horses went wild, and I could relate to her being in love with a boy that her family didn't like.

So"—she sucked in a lungful of air—"I wrote it all down, adding to it as you told me more about Hickory and your life here. Only I didn't use the real names because . . . well, you know."

"May I read it?" he asked.

She opened the computer, found the file, and set it in his lap. "I brought the mouse to make it easier for you to navigate. Just roll this to scroll down the page."

"Here, you can read this." He handed her the paperback novel.

She tried to read, but nothing in the book held her attention. She bit at her thumbnail until she heard Tandy's voice in her head fussing at her. *Stop that chewin' on your nails. It makes them ugly and it shows that you are nervous. Anyone sees that, they'll take advantage of you.*

She laid the book to the side and watched a bright-red cardinal flit around the patio, finally picking up a twig and flying off with it. Red made her think again about Seth's terrible reasons for hating that color. She glanced over at him, but his face was like stone. Only his eyes moved as he read what she'd written.

It seemed like she'd aged forty years by the time half an hour passed. He cleared his throat and shut the laptop.

"So?" She held her breath.

"You have a very vivid imagination, young lady, but you are a good writer. You should finish this and let me send it to a good editor. Then I want a copy," he said.

"You'd do that for me?" she asked.

"Yes, I would," he said.

"Why?" she asked.

"Because . . . when it is all told, you'll understand why."

"Seth, tell me now. You are hiding something. I can feel it," she said.

"Have you talked to Tandy?" he asked.

"Not yet, but we've got a date to do some serious talkin' on Sunday while you are at the cemetery," she answered.

"Then we'll talk when we get to the cabin that day, I promise," he said.

"And if Tandy won't come clean?" she pushed on.

"Then we'll talk anyway," he said. "And speakin' of books, you never did bring that bride book thing for me to see. Maybe we could do that after supper?"

"Yes, and tomorrow morning you can tell me more about those first years after you came back to Hickory."

Seth picked up his book and started to read again.

She took her laptop and started to type, stealing a sideways glance toward him every few seconds. How could he get engrossed in a book with the big elephant in the room with them? But then she noticed that he hadn't turned the page in several minutes and his eyes weren't moving.

I can't wait for Tandy to read this book. Or maybe she won't want to ever see it, with the part that she's got in the story line.

Emmy Jo frowned and started to type, writing the chapter of Seth and Markita's love that didn't survive the long distance between them. Poor Seth—he just could not catch a break. Maybe he needed a little shove toward a better life and she was just the one to put her hands on his back and do that. He might be an old guy, but that didn't mean he couldn't have a little fun. The idea of a seniors' cruise or a trip to Nashville to actually visit the Grand Ole Opry came to mind.

Seth had not expected something so thick or heavy when Emmy Jo laid the wedding book on the table that evening. "All this for one wedding? Just how big is this event going to be?"

"We are posting an open invitation in both churches for all our friends and families. Basically the whole town of Hickory is invited."

Seth whistled through his teeth. "Good Lord! Why?"

"Because I want everyone to witness the fact that I am breaking the Massey curse. I'm getting married, and it will be at least nine months—but hopefully two years or more—before I have a baby," she answered.

"And you think you need to have a big affair for that?"

"You don't?" She crossed her arms over her chest and raised her brows.

He opened the book to the first page, which had pictures of various cakes she had cut from magazines or taken photos of. "The way this town gossips, you could get married on the creek bank with no one there but you, Logan, and a preacher and it would be all over the county in twenty minutes." He turned a page. "Which one have you picked out?"

She reached over and flipped through to the middle of the section marked with a tab that said CAKES. "That one." She pointed. "And then there will be all kinds of fancy cupcakes. Only a few folks will have the actual cake. Do you like those little stick things with a lilac bouquet picture on them?" She pointed to a picture of a dozen cupcakes with different things on the tops.

"Lilacs?" His voice cracked.

"Always been a favorite of mine. My colors will be shades of purple, and I'm going to carry a white daisy and lilac bouquet."

He had to swallow four times to get the lump in his throat to go away. "Purple, huh?"

"Loved it since I was a little girl. Got into lots of trouble one year when I was a little girl for picking every pansy in Granny's flower bed and the neighbor's, too."

Seth pointed at the cake. "I don't see any purple on this."

"There will be. We're not putting a bride and groom on the top like that shows. A tiny bouquet made just like mine will lie on the top, with the streamers coming down the front side."

"Then you need the lilac pictures on the cupcakes," he said.

She picked up a pen and circled the cupcake with the lilacs. "Another decision made. Thank you. Now let's go look at dresses."

"First you need a place so you know what kind of dress to get, right?" he asked.

"Why?" she asked.

He flipped to the tab with DRESSES on it and pointed to the first one. "See that big train out behind that thing? Now think about having this wedding in a park or outside. Dragging that thing behind you would guarantee that by the time you got down the aisle you'd have more cockleburs and goat head stickers than you'd have them shiny things on it."

She ignored him and stuck a finger under the VENUE tab, and suddenly he was looking at pictures of outdoor weddings. In most, white folding chairs were set up on two sides with an aisle down the middle for the bride. Some had archways at the front with flowers. Others had a gazebo-looking thing with sheer fabric flowing in the breezes.

His mind shot into high gear as he imagined the wedding out on his driveway. Concrete paving, so she wouldn't have to think about her dress. He could hire valets to park the cars out in the pasture beside his house, and the garage could be the reception hall. It was air-conditioned, so her cakes and food would be safe from the heat and flies.

Do you realize what you are thinking? Are you crazy? Nora's voice was in his head. *You hate big crowds, and you'd never let that many people have the run of your house.*

"So nix the long train." She made a note in another, smaller book. "Or else find a place that has a sidewalk for me to walk down. I'm thinking a morning wedding with a waffle bar brunch. That way it could be all over with by noon or a little after. Logan says we're going on a cruise out of Galveston for our honeymoon. We could drive quite a ways before dark and then get there the next morning to board the ship. Have you ever been on a cruise, Seth?"

He shook his head. "Never actually been outside the state of Texas since I came home from Germany. I did go over there and come back on a military ship, but I expect that's far different than a big fancy cruise ship."

"Okay, enough about the wedding." Emmy Jo shut the book and pushed it away from him. "We're going to make a bucket list for you."

"A what?" he asked.

"It's a list of things you need to do before you die. You are not poor and you aren't getting any younger, so what do you want to do with the rest of your life?" she asked. "When that hip is healed, you need to do something other than sit here and grow mold."

"Maybe that's what I want to do," he grumbled.

She rolled her eyes toward the ceiling—just like Nora used to do when their mother wasn't looking. Then she wrote at the top of a clean page in big letters:

Seth's Bucket List.

Then she started writing without even looking up.

Number 1: Get a television and watch *The Bucket List.*

Number 2: Go to the Grand Ole Opry in Nashville, Tennessee, and visit the Ryman Auditorium and the Country Music Hall of Fame.

Number 3: Go on a senior cruise.

"Hey." He tapped a bony finger on the paper. "What is this damn bucket list, anyway?"

Had the girl lost her mind? He was not getting on a boat and going anywhere. He'd had his share of that when they shipped him home from Germany on a troop ship. It stormed so bad that he didn't hold down a bite of food for four days.

"I told you," she said as she wrote down number four.

And why would he go to Nashville and fight the crowds when he could hear the Opry on the radio any time he wanted to listen to it?

"A bucket list sounds a lot like something you crazy kids would think up," he said.

"Actually, it was two old guys who made it popular with a movie," she said.

"Why do I need to watch it? And do I have to have people in my house hooking up all kinds of shit to see it? I've only seen a few movies in my time. I was too busy for such things, and I liked books better anyway," he asked.

She laid a hand on his forearm. "No, you just need a television or a computer with a DVD player. I can rent a television and take it back after a week if you don't want one in your house."

"Can't we watch it on your computer?"

"We can, but the screen is pretty small," she said.

"Well, go get one of the damned things. Buy it. If I don't like it, I'll store it in one of the upstairs bedrooms. You'll have to watch it with me tomorrow night."

Of all the asinine things on the list, that one seemed the least invasive of his privacy.

"Are you serious?" she stammered.

"I'll see to it Nora pays you extra for your day since you'll be assisting on your day off."

"I don't need extra pay. You sure you want to buy it? We can lease it for a week or even for a month."

"Buy the damn thing." He stabbed a finger on number three. "Cruise, my ass!"

"Well, I suppose if you get on the ship and sail around the world in a fancy hotel on the water, then your ass will go with you," she told him.

He chuckled. "You are just full of sass, aren't you? I like movies, but I haven't been to one in more than forty years. Last thing I saw on the big screen was *The Great Gatsby*."

"Which one?"

"The one that came out forty years ago with Robert Redford."

She put the pen to the paper and wrote after her number four:

See lots of movies.

"And yes, I'm sassy but you knew that on the first day I came to work in my red scrubs."

"I hate red," he growled.

"And I hate orange. Good thing we aren't Okies, ain't it?"

"Good thing." He picked up the pen and wrote:

Number 5: Get this smart-ass kid out of my house.

She broke into laughter. "Now you are getting the idea."

CHAPTER SIXTEEN

Oma Lynn brought blueberry muffins and coffee to the office that Thursday afternoon and set them on the table in front of the sofa. Seth had a leg propped on a hassock.

"I'm expecting Logan Grady in a few minutes. Just send him in when he arrives," Seth said.

"Logan? Why?"

"Need to talk to him," Seth said.

"All right. Does Emmy Jo know this?"

"No, and I don't want you to tell her, either," Seth said.

"Too damn many secrets," Oma Lynn muttered as she left the room.

Thirty minutes later Oma Lynn showed Logan into the office and quietly shut the door behind her as she left.

"Have a seat. Would you like something to drink?" Seth asked.

"No, sir, I'm good," Logan answered. "I got to admit, I'm a little nervous about why I'm here, though."

"Well, I guess I'd have to get right to the point and tell you something that might be hard for you to hear," Seth said. "But I need to know that it'll stay between us at least for a little while longer."

"You don't want me to tell Emmy Jo?" Logan took a deep breath and let it out slowly.

"Just for a few days. She needs to talk to Tandy first," Seth said.

"About?"

"Something that happened a long time ago. I'm not really the one to tell you, but I don't think Jesse ever will," Seth said.

"Okay," Logan said slowly.

Seth told him the story of how he'd fallen in love with Tandy when they were in high school. Telling him the whole thing about Jesse disrespecting Mary Thomas wasn't necessary, but Logan had to know about the triangle between him and Tandy and Jesse. When he finished, he said, "I'm pretty sure that she was only messing around with me and Jesse, and I've figured out by blood type that the baby Tandy had did not belong to Jesse. That means she was mine, and I would have done right by her if I'd known, which also means that Emmy Jo is my great-granddaughter."

Logan looked as if he'd just been slapped in the face with an iceberg. "Why are you telling me this?"

"Do you love Emmy Jo?" Seth asked.

Logan looked him right in the eye and did not blink. "More than anything in the world."

"And it's not going to matter to you that I'm related to her? You are young, but you know very well what people think of me and why. I won't have her hurt, Logan."

"God, no! I don't care who she's related to. I love her, not her family tree," Logan answered.

"Okay, then. I have not told her anything, beyond that she had to talk to Tandy. So give it a couple of days and then we'll talk again. That okay with you?" Seth asked.

"Yes, sir, it is," Logan said. "And thanks for telling me. I can let myself out."

"You ever play Scrabble?" Seth asked.

"Lots of times."

"How about a game before you leave? I've got Emmy Jo up in Wichita Falls lookin' for a television and some crazy movie about a bucket list."

"Would love to. Mind if I take off my tie?"

"Not a bit." Seth smiled. "And open the door. I'll tell Oma Lynn to bring us some more muffins and sweet tea."

"Okay, are you ready?" Emmy Jo carried a remote control to the sofa and handed it to Seth.

"You stayin', Oma Lynn?" she asked.

"Hell, no! Ain't no way you could get me to watch that again. I cried when I saw it ten years ago, and I still get weepy when I think of it even yet," she said.

"Have you got a bucket list?" Seth asked.

"Yes, I do, and it does not include flying all

over the world in an airplane. I'll keep one foot on the ground, thank you very much," she said as she closed the door to the office.

"Hit that 'Play' button when you are ready to start," Emmy Jo said. "It lasts a little more than an hour and a half, so it will be over before supper time."

He hit the red button and was totally mesmerized from the beginning of the movie. Tears rolled down his cheeks at the end of the movie, and he truly understood what Emmy Jo was telling him, not only with her words but her sass. He hadn't been living these past twenty years. He'd only been existing—waiting to die. Two questions were asked in the movie: Have you had joy in your life? Did you bring joy to others in your life?

To both he would have to answer no. The lump in his throat was the size of a grapefruit, and no matter how many times he swallowed, it wouldn't go away. He owed Emmy Jo more than he could ever repay. She was his blood kin, his friend, and, more than that, his savior. She'd awakened him from a dead sleep and brought him back to life.

At the end of the movie, he handed the remote to Emmy Jo. "I need a yellow notepad. It's time to make my real bucket list."

"Do I get to see it?" she asked.

"No, you do not, but I'm changing one of my earlier points. I'm not kicking the smart-ass kid out of my house," he answered. "She's a genius, and I'll keep her around as long as I can. After we eat I'm going to watch this again. I can pause it when supper's ready. You can join me or not. Your decision."

"I think I'll pass and work on our story." She pulled a tissue from the box on the desk and blew her nose. "I fell in love with those two old guys the first time I saw this."

Will you ever love this old great-grandfather? Or will you think he's a son of a bitch for not figuring out things and making your life easier from day one?

"When did you watch it the first time?" he asked.

"Last year. Granny rented it, and we watched it together."

Seth rewrote the first three things she'd put on his bucket list the day before and crossed out the first one. "One thing done. So many left and so little time."

"You ain't dead or dying," she scolded. "Remember that and don't let your age hold you back." He tapped his upper leg. "It's getting better every day, and when it's strong, you'll be able to do anything you want. Drive. Go on that cruise."

"But I need someone to go with me. It wouldn't be fun to do it alone," he said.

"Ask Nora," she said.

*Like I'd want to spend months with her fussin'
at me over every little thing.*

He eyed the one about the cruise. Maybe he'd
do that one first after the doctor cleared him to
drive. Then he wrote down another one:

**Ride a motorcycle, even if it's just to
Graham and back.**

Emmy Jo settled into a chair on the patio after
supper that evening. It had been a busy day. She'd
spent the whole morning buying the television
and going to three stores before she found a copy
of *The Bucket List* and then watched it with Seth
in the middle of the afternoon. The rest of the
time she'd spent writing, and now she was caught
up with what Seth had told her. "I thought you'd
be in the office finishing watching that movie for
the second time."

"It's paused. I'll go back to it later," Seth said.

"Did you add anything else to your list?"

"Oh, yes, it's half a page long."

"Did you talk to Nora about going on the cruise
with you?"

He shivered. "I did not, and don't you ever say
a word to her. She'll try to talk me out of doing a
third of the things on the list, and I definitely do
not want her to go with me on a single trip. I love
her. I appreciate what she did for the family, but
I'd rather jerk all my hair out one strand at a time

than go on a vacation with her. She's even more OCD than I am."

"My lips are sealed," Emmy Jo said. "So are you going to work on the list or talk to me? What happened when you came home from the army? Did you go to the cabin?"

"Don't get your underbritches in a twist," he said and then laughed so hard that he grabbed his chest and wheezed. "God, that felt good."

"So which one are you going to do, Mr. Smarty Pants?" She grinned. "And have you found joy and given joy in your life today?"

"No, but life ain't over yet. Now let's get down to your story. I came home in 1957, the same week that Jesse did."

"So you stayed at the cabin?"

"About thirty minutes. Too many memories and ghosts. I picked up my duffel bag and walked back to town, booked a room at the hotel. I hadn't even gotten my bag unzipped when Clifford O'Dell showed up at the door and offered me a job in his real estate agency. He'd been a resident of Hickory his whole life so he knew all about my mama and the family, so I was a little surprised. But hey, I wasn't going to look a gift horse in the mouth, as the old saying goes. He said he needed an assistant and that he had a two-room apartment upstairs that I could use free of charge."

Emmy Jo laid her pen down and frowned.

"Why? After the way you'd been treated before, why would he do that?"

"I didn't know then, and I didn't question him. Part of me wondered if Clifford wasn't one of the men who visited the cabin late at night and he felt guilty about it. At the time, he offered a job and I said thank you and told him I'd give him an honest day's work for my paycheck. I got a refund from the hotel and moved my duffel bag to the apartment."

"What did the apartment look like?" she asked.

"It was furnished." He grinned. "In those days, that meant it had a small refrigerator, a two-burner stove, a broken-down sofa in the living room, and a bed and dresser in the bedroom. I took the refund money and bought a set of sheets and a week's worth of groceries and went to work the next morning. From sleeping in a room with dozens of soldiers to having my very own space, it looked damned fine," Seth said.

He took his yellow paper out of his pocket and wrote something on it, but she couldn't see and didn't question. Evidently, something about that apartment made him think of another item for his bucket list.

"They had a parade the next week when Jesse came home. Jesse rode in the fire engine with the high school band marching behind that, and then there were a few floats and lots of loud music. And afterward the mayor gave a speech in the high school auditorium about how proud the town was of Jesse for doing his duty, and the church had a reception with cookies and punch. I did not go," he said.

"How did Jesse react to you?" she asked.

"He came in a few weeks later and wanted to buy a house next to the church. He didn't even recognize me. I'd gained about thirty pounds in the service and didn't look like that tall, lanky kid who'd been the butt of the jokes anymore. Yet once Clifford introduced us, he studied me for a long time." Seth paused and his eyes drew down. "Finally he asked if I was stayin' in Hickory. I just nodded without answering and went back to work."

"Did you sell the house to him?"

"I did," Seth answered. "I made one dollar and twenty-five cents an hour that first six months. That amounted to fifty dollars a week, and I saved forty of it. I didn't need a car, didn't go out except to the movies on Sunday afternoons, and ate very well," he said.

"And after six months?" she asked.

"Alfred Conroy died," he said. Seth pulled out his paper and wrote on it again.

"What was that? Get away with murder?" she teased.

"No." He smiled. "If I was going to try that, I'd have killed Jesse years ago. Alfred had gone to Clifford while I was in Germany and told him, if

I came back to Hickory, to give me a job. Alfred owned the building and the business, and Clifford just managed things for him."

"Guilt?" Emmy Jo asked.

"Maybe some of that, and maybe just insanity. He had good eyesight and could see me very well the whole time I was growing up. I am the image of Sam Thomas, my father," Seth said. "But then, Alfred was tall and had dark hair, so maybe he got the crazy notion in his head. What he saw in the mirror every morning was different than what I saw."

Emmy Jo wiggled in her chair. "He thought you belonged to him, didn't he?" Her heart raced, and her palms went sweaty. The man must have gone through hell with the guilt eating away at his soul all those years.

Seth exhaled loudly. "Yes, he did. Maybe it was because his only child died and he had no one, or maybe the brain cancer messed with his mind, but he left his entire estate to me. Overnight I was a rich man, with more money than Midas."

So that's where the money came from. Seth had inherited it, plain and simple. Who Tandy's child belonged to would sure take a backseat to that well-kept secret. She held her breath and waited, then remembered that for the first time he'd initiated the conversation, so maybe by the time he finished, she'd know everything.

"I bought a new sofa and a new bed and a

bookcase," he said. "After that, if I wanted a property, I bought it, until I owned half the town."

Emmy Jo let that sink in for several minutes before she asked, "Did you ever buy your family land back from the Gradys?"

His chin lowered to his chest, and he looked up at her from under a furrowed brow. "Took twenty years, but Jesse's dad was retiring and Jesse didn't want the place. He was into the preachin' business by then, so I bought it through one of my corporations and he didn't know that I was the buyer until after the deal was signed and sealed," Seth said. "You do realize that no one else in the world knows this, Emmy Jo?"

Are you telling me about your finances because I'm your great-granddaughter or because I'm your friend? Or because I helped you make a bucket list?

"What did you do with the land?" she asked instead of voicing her true questions.

"I tried to get my sister to come back here and live on the farm, but she liked city life, so I've leased it for years," he said. "You and Logan want the house? I'll give it to you as a wedding present."

"Your ancestral home? Don't tease me, Seth."

"I'm not teasing. One of the things on my bucket list is to do something big and something nice for a pesky, smart-ass kid." He grinned. "It's

281

not as big as this place. Tell you what—you can have your choice. This one or that one."

"No, no, and no!" she said.

"Why? I'll end up giving it all to charity when I'm dead anyway." He removed the paper and wrote on it.

"You are going to have to live to be a hundred to do all the things you are putting on that list," she said, her mind spinning in circles at his offer.

"If I did, I couldn't spend all the money I have made over the years," he told her. "Know what I wrote just now? I'm going to buy my own jet airplane so I don't have to fly commercial. I'm too damned old to drive to Galveston to get on a cruise ship or to Nashville to go to the Opry."

"That'll mean hiring a pilot, or are flying lessons on your list?"

"Oh, no! I'm eighty-two, and I am going to learn to live," he told her with conviction. "I'm thinking that I might spend everything I've got before I die."

Emmy Jo laid her notebook aside and applauded. "Now, that should be at the top of your list."

CHAPTER SEVENTEEN

A nice breeze ruffled the new spring leaves on the trees in the cemetery. Bright sunshine warmed the day without making it hot. Birds chirped away as they flitted around, keeping the cemetery cleared of gnats and bugs. Baby squirrels used the tombstones for an obstacle course, romping and playing on them like a jungle gym.

It didn't hurt as badly that day when Seth bent to remove the old bouquet and put a new one on his mother's grave. He settled into his chair and motioned for Emmy Jo to go on and visit with Tandy, who waited on down the road a hundred yards. When she was out of hearing distance, he sighed.

"Mama, Emmy Jo has changed my life. There's a chance after the doctor clears me that I won't be here every single Sunday. I've made a bucket list. You would laugh at the idea." He held his face up to the sun and enjoyed the warmth.

"What goes on in heaven, Mama? On some level do you know that I'm here?" He chuckled, looked down, and laid a hand on the quilt that had covered his mother's bed the whole time he was growing up. "Did you use Nora to send Emmy Jo to me? Right now I don't even care how it all happened. I'm just glad she came into my life even at this late date, because she's opened my eyes."

A tiny sparrow lit on the lilacs and cocked its head one way and then the other at him before it flew away. Three squirrels played chase over his mother's tombstone and then used it for a game of king of the mountain. Life was going on all around him, and Seth was finally ready to embrace it.

"But it's scary. I've done nothing for so long that I'm not sure I know how to step out into the crazy world," he whispered. "I think maybe I'll go on a cruise. That doesn't sound quite as daunting as riding a motorcycle. And Mama, what do you think of me offering to let Emmy Jo have her wedding at my house?"

The little sparrow returned, perched on the bouquet, and then pulled a silk petal from one of the flowers and flew straight up with it. Seth followed it to a tree limb above his head, where the bird wove that bit of purple into its nest. He smiled and nodded. "It don't get much plainer than that, Mama. It's never too late to build a nest, is it?"

I want to be a grandfather even if she never sees fit to call me Grandpa. I want to be something more than a friend to her, Mama. If she's willin', I'd even let her live in the big house with me. She and Logan could have the whole upper floor.

284

Wouldn't it be something if I lived long enough to see their children and hear laughter in that big old place?

With the car windows down, Tandy lurked behind the wheel when Emmy Jo bent at the waist and peeked in through the passenger side. "Want to talk inside the car or get out and sit on the grass?"

"Inside is fine, unless you've got folding chairs for us like Seth has."

Emmy Jo left the door open to get more air in the car. "You didn't bring me a brownie?"

"Well, you didn't bring me a million dollars, so we're even," Tandy said.

"No, we're not. Who is my great-grandfather?"

Tandy sputtered and stammered and finally threw up both hands. "Dammit, Emmy Jo, I've told you that's in the past and I'm not talking about it. You know that I was not a little Goody Two-shoes, and you also know that I got right with the Lord." She wiped her brow with the back of her hand and stared straight ahead.

"Is it Jesse Grady? Is that why you've always hated Logan?" Emmy Jo blurted out. Emmy Jo knew the answer, but she wanted to hear her grandmother's side of the story.

Tandy set her mouth in a firm line and looked out the side window. "Seth has been talking to you, hasn't he? What has he told you about me?"

"He didn't tell me anything. When I pressured

him to tell me about you, he said I should talk to you. I've been spending a lot of time at the library looking up things about you and Seth and Jesse, as well as Rose. Did Rose belong to Jesse?" She had to push her grandmother or they'd never move forward.

Tandy pointed down the road. "What is he saying? Has he lost his mind in his old age? People do that when they shut themselves up in the house and do nothing for twenty years. They completely lose sight of reality and begin to think the dead can hear them. And what's that in his lap?"

"You're changing the subject."

Tandy didn't say a word for several moments. "He has lost his mind, hasn't he? Do you have to feed him? Does he wear a drooling bib?"

"I do not have to feed him. He reads about half a dozen newspapers every morning from front to back, and he loves the old classic country music, just like you do. And it's not insane if he talks to his mama once a week; it's therapy. And that is a quilt in his lap. It holds a memory of his mother, I'm sure, but I haven't asked," Emmy Jo said tersely.

Tandy's head jerked around so she could glare at Emmy Jo. "Whose side are you on? I'm your grandmother. I raised you and did right by you. All Seth has done is tell you stuff to confuse you and give you a big paycheck."

"Well, since you brought it up, why don't you want me to marry Logan? And I'd like an honest answer. Is it because we share a bloodline all the way back to Jesse? Did you sleep with him?" Emmy Jo pushed again.

"Humph." Tandy snorted. "I will not answer those damn fool questions. And if this is the way you're going to treat me, then get out of my car."

"You have always answered every question I asked, Granny," Emmy Jo said softly as she got out and slammed the door shut. "But for your information, I'm not kin to Jesse in any way, so if that's why you hate Logan, it can end."

"How do you know that?" Tandy's voice was little more than a stunned whisper.

"We both have things we aren't going to talk about, but I know beyond a shadow of a doubt that Rose was not Jesse's daughter. With all of our blood types, it's not possible."

"Well, shit!" Tandy groaned. "I ain't sayin' nothin' more."

"See you Tuesday morning for breakfast at Libby's. Be thinking about telling me just who else could be my great-grandfather," Emmy Jo said and walked away.

As she neared Seth, he looked up and smiled. "I'm ready to go for ice cream. I think I'll have chocolate today."

"Really? I thought vanilla was your favorite."

She started toward the car for his walker.

"And I don't need that thing today. Just let me rest my hand on your shoulder. Those exercises the doctor made me do have been working. I think I'm ready to give up the walker. That's two things off my bucket list."

"Good for you! Two big changes in one day." She folded his chair, took his quilt, and put them away and then came back to lend a shoulder for support. "So chocolate, huh? If you are going out on a limb, maybe I'll try one of those lemon chillers."

"Change is in the air. Must be summer on the way." He got comfortable and fastened his seat belt.

He opted for a chocolate malt, and she got a lemon chiller. They carried them to the porch, his left hand on her shoulder until he could grip the porch post for support to get up the steps. Then he went to the rocking chair and eased down into it. She sat down in her regular spot and used a post for a back brace.

"This is really good, but I like vanilla ice cream better," she said.

"I'm with you. Vanilla ice cream is better," he agreed. "Did you miss Logan on Thursday?"

"Yes, I did. I thought when he went away to college, it would be terrible, but I got to see him every weekend. I can't remember a time when we had to live on text messages and phone calls this long. But it's only for a few more weeks. Do you realize that tomorrow I'll be your assistant a whole month?"

Seth kicked off the rocking motion with his good leg. "What are we going to do to celebrate? Got another movie in mind that we could watch?"

"Nothing comes to mind, but when we leave here we could go to the movie store in Graham and see what they've got to sell or to rent. How would you like to watch *The Sacketts*? They made a television miniseries about them."

His old eyes glittered. "Are you serious? Can I buy it?"

"I'm serious," she said.

"Does either of those two actors we saw in *The Bucket List* play in it?"

"No, but Sam Elliott does. You kind of remind me of him, with your hair and mustache," she answered.

Seth's chest seemed to puff out a bit. "Really? You think I look a little like a movie star?"

"Wait until you see him," Emmy Jo answered. "It's like looking at your doppelgänger. You even sound like him."

"Well, what are we waiting for? Let's go buy movies."

She finished her lemon chiller and tugged her bright-blue T-shirt down when she stood up. "You have to tell me more about your years in the real estate business while we drive, okay?

But I need to tell you that Granny wouldn't own up to anything today. I told her that Jesse was not Rose's father, but I'm going to have to wait until Tuesday to make her talk to me."

"No hurry," he said. "But there's not much to tell there. Clifford died and everyone thought I'd saved enough money to buy the business and life went on."

But there is a hurry, because I want to know for absolute sure.

Emmy Jo whipped her red hair up into a ponytail before she started the engine. "Did they begin to understand that you could buy the whole town, plow it under, and plant turnips on it if you wanted?"

"No, I was still that Thomas kid who'd finally gotten a business in town. They came to me to sell their property, to buy property, and to take care of surveying for them," he said. "Some of the old diehards didn't like dealing with me, but they were afraid to say too much. After all, I knew every single man who walked under that red light on our porch."

She giggled as she put the car in gear and backed out onto the road. "And then you went to visit Nora and fell in love, right?"

"We'll talk about that another day," he said. "Right now I'm interested in watching *The Sacketts*."

"You might like *Lonesome Dove*, too. It was

made into a miniseries that is still available to buy," she suggested as they left Hickory behind them.

"Oh, I do want that one, too." His voice reminded her of a little kid's on Christmas morning.

"Granny got on a kick and watched Westerns for a whole summer when I was about thirteen," she said.

"One of the things on my bucket list is to watch a movie at least once a week. I might buy enough to last all summer."

"Or two weeks if you watch one every day."

He slapped his good leg and grinned. "You know what the nice thing about actually owning movies is? I can watch them over and over and study the characters." He pulled his yellow paper from his shirt pocket and crossed off something.

Look at us now. Seth Thomas is my friend. I wonder if I could convince him to walk me down the aisle at my wedding. Then I'd show the whole town that not only am I breaking the Massey curse, but that Seth Thomas is a good man.

Graham was not a busy town at three o'clock on a Sunday afternoon. Very few cars were on the streets and most of the stores were closed, but the movie store out on the edge of town was open until five, so they had plenty of time.

"You are going to use your walker. It's not an option," she said.

He unfastened his seat belt and swung the door open. "I don't need it."

"Trust me and don't argue. You are going to take it inside and use the seat part to sit on, because this is not going to be a five-minute trip. It will take you a while to figure out what you want to buy or rent," she told him.

"It will take me three minutes. I want everything they have about the Sacketts and whatever movies any of Larry McMurtry's books have been made into."

"What about *Hatfields and McCoys*? I was thinking maybe that would be our celebration movie, since it's about six hours long. We could spend the whole afternoon with it and maybe even have supper in the office if it's not finished."

"Get the walker out," he said.

He truly felt like a kid let loose in a candy store with ten dollars in his pocket. He kept handing Emmy Jo movies until the basket was full. She took it to the front of the store and brought it back empty, and he started all over again.

"Why didn't you do this years ago?" she asked.

"Like I said, I preferred a book, but I'm going to make up for lost time now," he answered as he handed her a copy of *Quigley Down Under*. "This one looks good, too. It's got a Sackett in it, even if he's not a Sackett."

"Don't you want some of the newer movies?" she asked.

"Maybe after I watch all these a few times, we'll come back for more."

"Seth, it's going to take you months to watch all these movies. I'll only be with you another four weeks," she said.

"What if I paid you double what you make now to quit your other job and be my assistant full time?" He put one more DVD in the basket and stood up.

"Don't tease me," she said.

"Who says that I'm jokin'? We can discuss it later. Right now, let's pay for this and go home. We can stop by the Dairy Queen and have a burger for supper. When we get home maybe we can watch one of the Sackett movies together."

"Wow! You are getting daring. No dumplings for supper?" She carried the basket to the front of the store.

He whipped a credit card from his pocket and signed the receipt. She carried two bags to the car and got everything loaded in. "You serious about a burger? Ever tried a bacon cheeseburger?"

"No, but it sounds good. And there's something I really want to talk to you about on the way." He took a deep breath. "How much is the rent on the trailer that Logan is looking at?"

She shrugged. "I have no idea."

"When we get parked, call him and ask him."

"Why?"

"I'm about to make you an offer you can't refuse."

She giggled. "I read *The Godfather* and saw the movie. If I refuse will I find a dead horse head in my bed?"

"You are too young to have read that book. It's almost fifty years old."

"Had to read it for psychology class, but I liked it, so I rented the movie and watched it, too," she said. "Dead horse?"

"No, I'd be afraid of what you'd do to get back at me." He laughed.

She pulled into a parking place right in front of the café and fished her phone from her purse. Her thumbs worked double time over a tiny keyboard, and then she hit an icon on the screen. In only a few seconds the response came back and she sent back a smiley face.

"The trailer will be six hundred fifty a month," she said.

Seth shut his eyes and swallowed hard. "My farmhouse is empty right now. You can have it as part of the package if you will agree to be my assistant. I'll give you the month of June off for your honeymoon and wedding, pay your insurance, and match every dollar that you put into retirement. When I'm home, you will work for me Monday through Friday from nine to five with Friday afternoons off. If I'm not home, then all you have to do is check on the house every few days and call me once a day. Think about it."

"Are you crazy? Did that doctor tell you that you were dying of bone cancer or something?" she asked.

"He says I'm healthy as a horse, have the vital signs of a fifty-year-old man, and, once the hip is healed, I can do anything I want," Seth said. "Don't give me an answer today. Talk to Logan about it on Tuesday. The downside is that it is three miles out of town. The upside is that you won't be in a trailer court with Tandy."

"I'll think about it," she said. "But right now let's go have a burger."

"Sounds good to me," Seth said.

She hadn't said no. That was a good sign. He made a mental note to call the contractors he used from Wichita Falls and have them come to Hickory next week to do some cosmetic work on the old farmhouse. New paint inside and out, put in a central air-conditioning unit, tear up the old carpet and lay new, and put new appliances in the kitchen. Update the upstairs bathroom and make sure that the wiring and plumbing were all in good order. Maybe even plant a few flowers in the front yard. That should help sell her on the idea.

CHAPTER EIGHTEEN

The gray skies were pouring down rain so hard that Emmy Jo drove into town at fifteen miles an hour. Even with the windshield wipers at full blast, she could only see a few feet ahead of the car at any time. She'd already parked in front of Libby's when she remembered that she'd forgotten her umbrella, so she pulled up the hood of her zippered sweatshirt and jogged through the puddles.

Her insides were quivering when she threw back the hood and looked over the café for Tandy. There was going to be no going back this Tuesday. Tandy was going to tell her what she wanted to know—period. Her hands shook. She bit at her lower lip in nervousness. Her stomach was twisted up like a pretzel.

"You look like a drowned rat," Tandy said from the first booth to the left.

"I feel like one." Emmy Jo removed her sweatshirt and hung it on the coatrack and kicked off her wet sandals. "Sorry, Libby, I know the sign says I need shoes and a shirt, but my feet are cold and wet."

"Need some socks?" Libby asked from behind the counter.

"Got some in my purse, but thank you. Has Granny ordered?"

"I'm waiting on you, but I want the Tuesday morning special with two extra pancakes," Tandy said. "And a bowl of stewed prunes on the side."

"Make that two, only with a big glass of orange juice instead of the prunes," Emmy Jo said.

Tandy was sporting a new haircut and she wore her lucky bingo pants again, so maybe she was in a good mood even if it was raining hard enough to flood the whole state of Texas. She was a force to be reckoned with when she was pissed, so Emmy Jo didn't jump right into the deep waters of the ancestry question.

In the sleepless night before, she'd formed a strategy where she would ease into the conversation and simply chat. Maybe Tandy would give her a name before she even realized it had come out of her mouth.

"So how did you do at bingo this week?" Emmy Jo asked.

"Came away with twenty more than I went in there with, and I'm not telling you jack shit about my past," Tandy said. "I've got two new recipes that I wrote down for you. They're similar to that Texas sheet cake you like so well—lemon sheet cake and vanilla coconut sheet cake. Here, I brought you a piece." She set a plastic container on the table with two note cards on top.

297

"Go on and eat it while you wait on breakfast."

"Thank you." Might as well enjoy the cake while she tried to wait her grandmother out. She shoved the recipes into her purse and removed the lid from the container. "Oh. My. God," she muttered when she took the first bite. "This is amazing, Granny."

"Thought you'd like it, the way you love lemon so much. They'd both be good recipes for some of the cupcakes at your wedding," Tandy said.

Emmy Jo swallowed fast to keep from choking. She pinched her leg to be sure she wasn't dreaming. *What in the . . . oh . . . now that she knew Jesse wasn't Rose's father, Tandy was coming around.*

"So you are ready to look at my wedding book and help me make decisions?"

Tandy's bony hands toyed with her coffee cup. "Maybe, but that don't mean I'm going to be nice to Jesse at the wedding."

"Fine, I'll bring it by the house on Thursday morning. You think you could make another one of these cakes? I could use a bigger piece than this little taste you brought to tease me with. And I'd still like to use your mama's ring in my bouquet."

"I'll make half a lemon and half of the coconut so you can taste them. I could even make them up in cupcakes so we can see how they hold up when the paper is peeled off." She sipped at her coffee. "And if you want to use the ring, I'm okay with that."

"That would be wonderful, Granny," Emmy Jo said. Baby steps. Just like with Seth, she had to take tiny little steps. First it was getting him to smile and then to trust her as a friend. She'd get Tandy excited about the wedding and then she'd work around the elephant in the room called whoever the hell had really gotten Tandy pregnant more than sixty years ago.

"My colors are shades of purple, and I'm going to carry a lilac bouquet. Will you go shopping with me and get a pretty dress in a shade to match your lilac corsage?"

"I look better in red, but I guess I could wear a deep, dark purple."

"You'll be the belle of the ball." Emmy Jo beamed.

"No, honey, you are the one who's supposed to be the center of attention. I'm just there for pictures with you. Promise me that you won't make me take one with Jesse or make me stand beside Logan."

Emmy Jo held up her pinky finger and Tandy locked hers into it. "I pinky promise that you won't have to do anything at my wedding that you don't want to do. But you have to promise me that you won't create a scene with Seth or Jesse. I doubt that Jesse will even come, but we're holding out hope that he will."

Tandy jerked her hand away. "Why would Seth come to your wedding?"

"He's my friend," Emmy Jo snapped. Nice hadn't lasted very long, but at least she'd made a little progress.

"Well, I'm damn sure not promising anything."

A smart-ass remark leaped to Emmy Jo's tongue, but she bit it back and silently thanked God that Libby brought their food right then. "I saved one bite for you, Libby." Emmy Jo pushed the container to the edge of the table. "You might want to start making this to sell in here."

Libby forked the last piece into her mouth and groaned. "I've got to have that recipe, Tandy."

"It's right here. You can write it off while we are eating breakfast." Emmy Jo handed it to her. "So what do you think, Granny? Lemon, coconut, red velvet, and maybe your famous Hawaiian wedding cake?"

"And an assortment of mini cheesecakes on the groom's table," she said as she poured maple syrup on her pancakes.

Food. Cooking. Wedding. Three safe topics for the morning. Next week maybe she'll be ready to tell me something.

When Emmy Jo arrived at noon, only one booth was left in the whole Dairy Queen. It was across the room from where she and Logan usually sat, but at least it was beside a window. She kept her eyes on the parking lot outside. Something didn't feel quite right. She figured that the crazy feeling was right when Logan got out of the truck, his eyes on the ground. He looked as if he was bearing the weight of the world on his shoulders. Good Lord! Had someone died or had he gotten bad news? Instead of meeting him, she waited at the booth. He kissed her on the cheek and slid in across from her instead of beside her.

"It's been a hell of a week," he said.

"Family? Work?" she asked.

"Both." He took her hands in his. "Just seeing you even for an hour helps. I'm planning a surprise on Thursday, so please don't get sick or let anything happen."

"Do my best." She wanted to tell him about Seth's offer, but this wasn't the time or the place. Maybe they'd discuss it on Thursday in the hotel. A picture of a nice hotel room with lit candles and rose petals on the bed flashed through her mind. "Want to talk about it or just sit here and soak up the fact that we are finally getting to be together?"

"I don't want to talk." He picked up her hand and kissed each knuckle. "Did you order for us?"

She nodded. "I sure did. Six tacos. Two chocolate malts and two large fries."

"Fantastic." He dropped her hand and fidgeted with the salt-and-pepper shakers.

The waitress brought their food, and Emmy

Jo was in the process of taking the paper off the first taco when she looked up to see Jesse Grady entering through the door. She caught his eye. He scowled and set his mouth so tight that a gnat couldn't have wiggled its way between those thin lips.

"Well, hello, Preacher Grady." She waved. "Come on over here and sit with us."

"What are you doing?" Logan whispered.

"Making peace, not war." She grinned.

"No, thank you," Jesse said as he walked past their booth.

"Ah, come on," she said sweetly. "There's no place else to sit, and besides, I want to talk to you about performing the ceremony at our wedding."

"No, thank you, again," he growled.

"You are still a preacher, right?" she asked.

"I am, but—"

She held up a palm and butted in before he could say another word. "And you can marry people, right?"

"Yes, but—"

Her other palm shot up. "Sit down and let's visit, or the whole town will think that you've got something in your past concerning me that you don't want the world to find out."

You are chasin' ghosts, the voice in her head said. *That's the best-kept secret in all of Texas, not just Hickory.*

"Don't you threaten me, young lady," Jesse hissed as he sat.

"Don't you be such a jackass," she shot back.

"What exactly are you accusing me of, anyway?" he asked.

"Why don't you tell me what you think it might be?" Emmy Jo smiled sweetly, enjoying every second of his squirming.

"Most likely that my father didn't want Tandy in his church because she was pregnant and unmarried," he said. "I was gone when my dad told her to find another church. That's not on me." He pulled up a chair from a nearby table and sat down at the end of the booth.

"Did you ever commit a sin, or have you been perfect your whole life?" Emmy Jo handed him one of her tacos.

He instinctively took it and then dropped it on the table.

"Hey, I did not spit on it. It's just a taco," she said.

Logan chuckled, and Jesse shot a dirty look over his shoulder. "What's so funny?"

"Emmy Jo does not bite. She's kind and sweet and she's trying to get to know you. She's right. You *are* being a jackass. Jesus wouldn't act like this," Logan said.

"She don't want to know me. She wants to humiliate me. I might be a jackass, but she's a smart-ass, just like her grandmother," Jesse snapped.

"Yes, I am like her and proud of it. She raised me to speak my mind. So here goes: I will marry your grandson. If you want to be a part of our lives, then be nice. If you don't, then we won't bother you with our presence. Now, are you going to perform our wedding or not?"

"Not," he said. "Not in a million years will I condone this marriage."

"Why?" she asked with another smile. "You seem so set on that point."

He glared at her, pushed the taco back her way, stood up, and left without another word to her or Logan.

Emmy Jo removed the paper from the taco and bit into it. "Well, that went well, didn't it?"

A chuckle started down deep in Logan's chest, built into laughter, and then went to a full-fledged guffaw. Before Logan got control of it, he had the hiccups and tears poured down his cheeks, dripping on his pretty blue shirt and leaving water circles. "That was horrible. How can you even think it went well?"

"He didn't try to suffocate me with a fistful of paper napkins or nail me to a cross," she answered. "So it went very well. I'm alive and you are laughing, which is better than that sadness you brought in here with you."

"Emmy Jo Massey, I love you," Logan said.

"Well, I'm damn sure glad you do." She stirred her malt with the straw and then sucked up part of it, her focus never leaving his face. "Our love will be tested."

"I believe it's strong enough," he answered.

"Good! Now tell me about this surprise on Thursday. And why were you so mopey when I first got here?"

"I can't tell you right now, but believe me, darlin', I will pretty soon. The surprise has something to do with water. That's the only hint that you get."

When the hour had passed and they said good-bye, she thought about going to the library, but there was nothing she could look up. Edith likely wouldn't know who Tandy had been seeing, with one of her two relationships having been a secret. Seth's story was almost told, but for the part when Clifford died and Seth took over the business.

Deciding on Seth's house, absent other options, she found Oma Lynn putting a roast in the oven for supper. Emmy Jo handed her the two new recipes, and Oma Lynn immediately went to the pantry to see if she had everything to make the lemon cake. She clapped her hands together several times when she found the can of lemon pie filling.

"Seth is in the office watching that show y'all watched yesterday. He said that there were parts of it he needed to study," she said as she turned the oven on. "I don't imagine he'd mind if you joined him."

"No, thank you. One five-hour session with the Hatfields and the McCoys is enough for me. Besides, I've got my own feud to worry about," she said.

Oma Lynn clucked like an old hen gathering in her chicks. "It's time for Seth and Jesse to let whatever it was go before they have to face off with God over all that bitterness in their hearts."

"Ain't it the truth," Emmy Jo said as she left the kitchen. She was going to succeed in putting an end to the Grady-Thomas-Massey feud. She could feel it in her soul. Squeezing her great-grandfather's identity out of her great-grandmother had to be part of the way forward.

CHAPTER NINETEEN

S everal strands of Emmy Jo's hair had escaped her ponytail, and she wore very little makeup. Cutoff jean shorts showed off muscular legs. A cute plaid, pearl-snap shirt was tied at the waist. Watching her eyes light up when she saw Logan took a little of the weight from his chest.

"I smell burgers," she said as she got into the truck. "And I brought cupcakes from Granny's house. She has new recipes we might use for the wedding and I want you to taste them."

He leaned across the console, cupped her face in his, and kissed her with enough heat to fog the windows. "I just picked up the burgers at the Dairy Queen, and there's a quilt back there. The surprise is that we're having a picnic at the creek today. And you know how much I love cake, so I'd love to sample the cupcakes."

"Oh, I thought we were going to the hotel. It's been forever." Her tone left no doubt she was disappointed.

"If we're in a hotel, we'll shut the door and forget words until five minutes before it's time to leave. I want us to talk," he said.

Her quick intake of air and the way her eyes opened wide said the words before she whispered, "Are you breaking up with me?"

"No, but you might be telling me to hit the road. We'll wait until we are under our favorite willow tree to start this conversation. Until then I love you with my heart and soul," Logan said.

He needed five more minutes to collect his thoughts and get the story outlined in his mind. And he wanted to be where he could hold her hand while he told her. He turned right after they crossed the bridge over Hickory Creek, then made another quick right and parked the truck off the road. She got out and opened the back door, picked up the quilt, and, without a word or even a nod, headed toward the willow tree down the sandbar about fifty yards. She had the quilt spread out and was sitting right in the middle when he reached her with the food. He dropped the cooler in front of her, removed his tie, and sat down. Taking her hand in his, he took a deep breath.

She jerked her hand away. "Did you cheat on me, Logan Grady?"

"How could you even ask that?" he blurted out.

"You've been acting weird for more than a week, and the creek? Come on, Logan, you never missed a chance at spending an afternoon in bed with me before now," she said.

"I did not cheat on you. I wouldn't, Emmy Jo. I couldn't, because I love you too much, but I did keep something from you, and it's been eating at me, so that's what you sensed," he answered.

"We don't keep secrets." A sharp shot of guilt pierced her heart.

"We never have, and that's been driving me crazy. I went to see Seth while you were buying a television."

"Why?" she asked.

"Because he asked me to and because something was buggin' me about this Jesse-Tandy-Seth thing, too. Have you talked to Tandy?"

"Of course, just a couple of days ago. I was waiting to tell you until we were together."

"Thank goodness. I'm not breaking Seth's confidence, then."

"What are you talking about?"

"Keepin' things from you was killin' me. I'm so excited that we can talk about this. It's great news," he said. "I had no idea about my grandpa and Tandy. That really is a pretty big secret. To think it never surfaced all these years. When Seth told me about bein' in love with Tandy and she was pregnant and thought it was Gramps's baby but it wasn't because he and his doctor figured it out with blood types"—he stopped and took a deep breath before he went on—"I was blown away. I couldn't hardly believe it, but it sure made sense as to why they'd all three carry a grudge all these years."

"I don't know why I didn't think of our blood

types and go back to the charts," she said.

"Do you think you need to do a DNA for sure?" he asked.

She shook her head. "I want Granny to own up to it, and I want to hear it from Seth's mouth. So I'm waiting them both out."

Logan heaved a breath of relief. "God, I'm glad that's over. Hamburgers are probably cold. Do you want to toss them into the creek to feed the fish and go get something else to eat?"

She shook her head. "Cold burgers, soggy fries, and even warm beer won't be nearly as bad as not telling you about this whole thing without breaking the privacy rules at work."

He brought her hand to his lips. "What else haven't you told me?"

"Classified." She giggled. "But Logan, the past has to surface, not for our sakes but for theirs. Granny, Jesse, and Seth need to get over themselves and grow up."

"At eighty-two years old and with a grudge that's been going on for the better parts of their lives, I don't see that happening, but I do see a wedding in our future."

"And possibly a new job." She told him about Seth's offer. "We'd have a house and the money would be fantastic."

He opened the bag and removed the food. "That's your decision, Emmy Jo. Do you like working with one elderly client as much as you do with all your patients? If you decide to do this, would you be able to go back to the health place if it doesn't work out? I think it's a wonderful opportunity and if I was in your shoes I'd do it, but I'll support you in whatever you decide. Now let's talk about the wedding. I'm so ready to be with you all the time instead of just an hour here and there."

At that moment, Emmy Jo didn't care if they were on a creek bank or in a five-star hotel—she was with Logan. Divine intervention or fate or destiny, whatever it was called, had put her in Seth Thomas's pathway a few weeks ago, she was sure of it. Maybe it was so that nothing would shake her marriage to Logan.

"I can't wait, either, darling." She wrapped her arms around him, shut her eyes, and let her heart do double time when their lips met. After several minutes she pulled away. "What's wrong?"

"Gramps had a fling with Tandy. That your grandmother was not the result doesn't change the fact that he thought she was all these years. My grandfather left your great-grandmother high and dry. Are you going to hold that against me?"

"No, I am not," she said with conviction. "Are you going to hold it against me that the town recluse is my great-grandfather and that his mother was a prostitute?"

"No, ma'am."

"Then we're even, I suppose. Now let's eat. I'm starving," Emmy Jo said.

"Since you aren't going to break up with me for keeping secrets, we need to use some of that time before the wedding to go to the courthouse to get our passports started for the honeymoon," he said.

"Then let's get with it. I'm so excited that we're really going on a cruise," she said.

"But first the cupcakes."

She pushed him over on his back and snuggled up against his side. "You can take the cupcakes home with you. I want to make out before we go to the courthouse. I miss being in your arms so much."

"Have I told you that you are the most beautiful woman on the earth?" He got lost in her eyes. "That sounds corny, but it's the truth."

"And the truth will prevail." She grinned as she brought his lips to hers.

That evening Emmy Jo worked with the story, staring off into space every few minutes. "Oh, what tangled webs." She recited part of a quote that Tandy came up with often. "If this was really fiction, no one would believe it," she said. "There's too much sadness and too little happiness and up until now there is no happy ending. But I'm writing it for Seth, so I'm going to tell it like I feel it."

Taking a short break, she worked the kinks from her neck and checked the time. It couldn't be midnight, and yet the clock on the nightstand beside her bed said that it was exactly 12:34. She and her grandmother had always played a game when those numbers came up on the clock. Whoever saw them first got to make a wish. She figured Tandy had been asleep for hours, so she shut her eyes tightly.

Emmy Jo closed the laptop and put it away, turned down the covers on her bed, and slid in between them. Forgetting all about her heritage, she thought about the house where Mary had raised her children. On Sunday she would finally get to see the inside of Seth's cabin, and she could better describe what had happened in that living room where Mary had died. And on Tuesday, Tandy was going to say the words. And then Seth was going to do the same thing. Procrastination was over.

CHAPTER TWENTY

"Oma Lynn, how old are you?" Emmy Jo asked as she stirred sausage gravy for breakfast.

"That's a rude question. I'm fifty-seven years old, and I've been working right here for Seth since I was forty-three. I didn't plan to work this long when I took the job, and I've told him that in another year at the most, he'd better find someone else. He said that he offered you a job. Will you be taking this over as well as being his assistant? I think he should hire a cook and housekeeper in my place."

"I agree with you," Emmy Jo said. "So you knew Rose, my grandmother?"

"I knew her very well. We were friends."

Emmy Jo stopped stirring. "Really? Why didn't you mention that before now?"

"You didn't ask until now, and if that gravy burns, you'll be in big trouble, because the biscuits are almost done."

Emmy Jo went back to doing her job. "What was she like?"

"She was a beautiful person, inside and out. Had a sweet nature about her. Tall and slim, blue eyes like yours." Oma Lynn checked the oven. "Pour the gravy in a bowl and fill the skillet with water so it won't be so hard to clean."

Emmy Jo followed orders. "Who fathered Crystal?"

Oma Lynn pulled the biscuits out. "A boy who came through Hickory working in the oil well business. Give me a minute and I'll think of his name. Didn't Tandy tell you all this?"

"She's pretty tight-lipped about the past," Emmy Jo answered.

"Newton. That was his name. Johnny Newton. He rode into town on a motorcycle, and she was working at Libby's place in those days. They hit it off right away and when the job was finished, they were, too. I never knew why she didn't marry him. They seemed crazy about each other. Then she found a job over in Graham as a secretary in a real estate place and had Crystal."

"Then Rose got killed in a car wreck, right?" Emmy Jo said. "But I want to hear about things y'all did as friends. Did you talk boyfriends, or did she tell you when she found out she was pregnant?"

"Honey, that was more than forty years ago and a lot of water has run under the Hickory Creek Bridge since then. We didn't tell each other every detail of our daily lives. We were friends, but not close enough that she was a bridesmaid at my wedding."

Emmy Jo pressed on. "Who do you think Rose's father was?"

"That part is something you'll have to ask Tandy. Far as I know, she never told a living soul who Rose belonged to. Not to speak ill of your great-grandmother, but it could be that she didn't know. She was pretty wild in those days," Oma Lynn said. "Now let's get this breakfast on the table so you and Seth can get about the business of reading the morning newspapers."

"One more question." Emmy Jo whispered, "What happened to that woman he was going to marry? The one he built this house for?"

"I never asked," Oma Lynn said.

They'd barely finished breakfast when the whirring noise of a helicopter sounded overhead, getting louder and louder until it finally settled down on the roof. Seth got up from the table and left his walker behind. The elevator doors opened, and Seth motioned for the doctor to follow him into the office.

"Well, look at you!" The doctor smiled.

"Gettin' better. Got to get a release from you if I'm to get serious about my bucket list."

The doctor winked at Emmy Jo. "So you've made a list. What's first? To drive?"

"That would be nice, but I have an assistant who can do that. I was thinking maybe a trip to the Grand Ole Opry or else a cruise. You comin' or not, Emmy Jo?" Seth looked over his shoulder.

"Slow your horses, old man. I want to hear what the doctor has to say," she said.

Dr. Everson glanced over his shoulder at her.

She shrugged. "He's liable to tell me that you said he could drive now."

"Well, crap! A man can't get away with nothing around here," Seth grumbled.

Emmy Jo helped pull Seth's pants down so the doctor could check the incision and was amazed at how well Seth had healed. Maybe that strict schedule was therapeutic after all.

"Well, it's looking really good, and you are moving around very well. I'd say you are ahead of where you'd be in therapy. I'll see you in a couple of weeks."

"Thanks." Seth smiled.

"How's those allergies?" the doctor asked.

"All better. Whatever was tossing around pollen must have gotten done. Thank you for asking," Emmy Jo said.

The doctor took time to listen to Seth's heart and lungs and take his blood pressure. "I've got forty-year-old men who'd trade places with you any day with these vital signs."

"With a broken hip?" Seth asked.

"Hips heal," Dr. Everson said as he pulled up Seth's pants. "Y'all have a good day. See you next time." And he was gone.

"That was great news," Emmy Jo said.

"I was hoping he'd say I could drive now."

"Maybe next time." She rolled his walker over to him. He tried to wave it away, but she shook her head.

"I can do without it," he said.

"Probably, but just use it as a brace to get up and down."

"As my assistant I want you to make some phone calls and book two places on a cruise leaving the Sunday after you get married." That surprised her more than him not arguing about the walker.

"Two?"

"You heard me." He took two steps toward the door.

"I'll need the name of the person going with you and his or her passport number."

"Well, shit!" He stopped and frowned. "It's a surprise. How do we get around that?"

"I'll have to see what I can do." She smiled. "Whoever it is will need either passports or a valid birth certificate. You'll have to spring the surprise on them in time for them to get that taken care of before it's time to leave."

"How long does that take?" he asked.

"Logan and I went to Graham to the courthouse yesterday and got ours started. They said we could have it in three weeks if we paid extra, so we did," she said.

"Okay, then, I want to leave three weeks

after your wedding," he said. "I don't have a passport, either, so we'll go to the courthouse together the Monday after you and Logan are married."

"But you were in Germany with the army," she said.

"Yep, went over there and came back without one. Army is one thing. Civilian travel is something different," he said.

"Better make it four weeks to give them time to get here," she said. "We're getting married on June 10." She pulled out her phone to check dates. "So how about the second of July? That way you can see fireworks from the ship on the Fourth. What are you thinking about? A five- or seven-day Caribbean?"

"Hell, no, I want one of them long things that takes us around the world. If we're going to do this thing, I want to do it up right. What good is a bucket list if you're only going to commit to seven days?"

"Seth!" she said hoarsely. "You are talking sixty to ninety days. You wouldn't be back on US soil until mid-October."

"Then you wouldn't have a lot to do as my assistant until then, would you? Give you and Logan plenty of time to get adjusted to married life," he said.

"I'll see what I can get arranged. You are sure that the other person will go with you?"

"No, but someone will." He grinned. "Now let's go read our newspapers."

He read through two newspapers before he spoke again. "Are you giving my offer some serious consideration?"

"I am," she said. "Do you think Logan and I could look at that farmhouse on Tuesday at noon?"

"Sure you can, but it's getting a face-lift. Last folks that lived there left it in a bit of a mess, so my contractors are working on making it livable again. And speaking of that . . ." He paused.

She was as smart as she was sassy and was figuring out things way too fast, so he had to approach the next subject carefully. His hands went clammy, and his chest tightened.

"Speaking of what?" She laid her paper aside.

"Your wedding and that book. You don't have a place yet, do you? Time is getting real short and you still have to get your dress. Why don't you have the wedding here? I can call a caterer to do the waffle brunch that you mentioned and set up some chairs. Maybe call a landscaping company to come plant purple flowers everywhere. We can have an arch hanging with lilacs and daisies and cut flowers everywhere there is a place, maybe even put some of that filmy stuff up over the aisle for you to walk under. It could be real romantic." He stopped to take a breath.

"You've given this a lot of thought, Martha Stewart. Why would you do that?" Emmy Jo asked. "And besides I don't have the money for all that stuff you just said."

"I can't take money with me when I'm dead. You've helped me, Emmy Jo. I can't ever repay you, but I can finance part of this wedding," he said. "You buy the dress and the cake. I'll do the rest if you'll let me."

"Seth, do you realize that would mean people in and out of your home? And where would the reception be?"

He felt as if he'd awakened from a deep sleep to find his mother still alive. There were problems, yes. But there was also peace and happiness in his life. It had come about gradually, but helping Emmy Jo meant more to him than anything. She'd lifted the burden of sadness from his heart, which was something that money and power couldn't do. He wanted to lift the financial burden of a huge wedding from her heart and give her a wonderful day that she'd remember forever.

He took another deep breath before he went on. "I was thinking we could send my cars over to Willard's for a couple of days. Then the designer people could turn the garage into a reception hall. It's air-conditioned, and we could have tables set up there and on the patio, maybe move the furniture out of the living room for more tables and give the kitchen to the caterers for a couple of days."

"Sweet Lord! Have you lost your mind? That's thousands of dollars. Do you know how many people would come to the wedding just to get a glimpse of this place? It's been a mystery for so long that everyone would swarm up here," she whispered.

He couldn't keep the grin from spreading. "And that way everyone in Hickory will know that you've broken the Massey curse, right? What better way to get them to come to your wedding? Say the word and I will put it in motion."

"Thank you," she whispered.

"That's what I like to hear." He nodded. "Go get that book and show me some more pictures. Can I keep it to show the wedding planner?"

She raced off and was back in a flash. She laid the book in his lap, pulling her chair up close to his side. He reached for the notepad and pen he kept by his chair.

"Seth, I can't do this," she said, withdrawing a little.

"Why?" His heart fell to his toes, aching all the way down.

"The money," she said. "I'd always feel that I was taking advantage of our friendship, and I would never do that. It means too much to me."

"If it means anything to you, let me do this," he

said. "You said we're friends. Please." He wanted so badly to be her grandfather in every sense of the word. *Dammit!* If Tandy didn't say the words soon, he was going to, and to the devil with what Tandy thought of it. "I can make one phone call and the planner I talk to will then visit with you. If you don't like anything I've suggested then do it your way, but have it here. And we'll need to get the invitations sent within the next week if we're going to be right according to etiquette."

She giggled. "Masseys and Thomases don't exactly get things done the Emily Post way."

"So what do you want to do different than what I said?" he asked.

"Not one thing. It sounds like a fairy tale," she said.

"It should. Do you want any sort of horse-drawn carriage bringing you from Tandy's to the wedding?"

She held up a palm with a giggle. "That's going too far. I'll get dressed right here in my bedroom upstairs. I'm only doing this on one condition, you realize. That's if you'll walk me down the aisle and give me away."

Seth thought his poor old heart would stop beating right then and there. "I would be honored, but I want to leave this open. If you change your mind later, then I will understand and there'll be no hard feelings."

He was going to get to play the role of a grandfather. He'd never known such joy in his whole life. She had no idea about the gift she'd just given him.

"Why would I change my mind?" She eyed him carefully.

"We are both caught up in the fun and excitement, but between now and then you could have a change of heart. I'd understand," he said.

"I won't," she said, putting a warm hand on his shoulder. "I never thought I'd say this, but I truly do value our friendship so much and I appreciate everything you are offering and doing for me. Now tell me, exactly how is this worded on your bucket list? 'Do a good deed for a kid who doesn't have a father'?"

"No, it's not like that at all. If I had to write it out, it might say that I would love to have a true friend who'd trust me enough to put her wedding in my hands," he said.

"Are you sure it don't say that you're going to throw a big wedding to have an excuse for the town to see that you don't live in a haunted house?" she asked.

"Yep, that's it." He grinned. "Now let's look at this book and decide exactly what else we want for this shindig."

No matter what it was called, he was getting to do the first thing ever for his great-granddaughter, and it felt damn fine.

He opened it to the first page. "White tablecloths?"

"How about light purple with lilac bouquets in the middle? Nothing big—maybe in Mason jars?" she said.

He wrote that down. "Mama used to put her lilac bouquets in Mason jars. I like that idea. Now for the food. You sure you want a waffle brunch?"

She nodded.

"With fried chicken, sausage patties, bacon and ham, and all kinds of fancy syrup plus whipped honey butter, and then we'll need the juices, coffee, sweet tea, and milk." He kept writing without looking at her. "If you think of anything else, just tell me and we'll add it in."

Just like that decisions were being made. Whoever said money talked sure knew what they were saying.

"Is this kind of what you'd like the driveway to look like?" He pointed to a gorgeous wedding that was probably held by royalty. Yards and yards of chiffon and illusion were draped everywhere, and they must've stripped every red rosebush in the whole world to find that many blooms. "Only not with red, right?"

"Purple," she said. "As in lilacs, hydrangea." She pointed to the pictures as she named several varieties. "And instead of scattering rose petals,

I've always thought it would be neat to have lilac petals."

He sighed and made more notes. "My mama would have loved this, Emmy Jo, but don't use purple for my sake. This is your wedding. We all know Tandy loves red."

"I'm not doing it to spare your feelings," she said, pretending not to notice his line for now. "Look at those pictures. I've been making this book for three years. Your mama and I would have gotten along very well, Seth. Sometimes I feel like I knew her in another lifetime and that we were close."

"I think you would have," he agreed. "So purple and white all tangled up together. What about your bouquet?"

"That is for Logan to take care of. So I've already given him a picture of what I want. It'll have lilacs, purple calla lilies, and white baby's breath scattered in it. I'm supposed to take care of his boutonnière," she said. "It will have a calla lily with a little bit of fluffy stuff around it."

She imagined Seth serving as her escort. She had a grandfather, a privilege to be sure, since she'd never had a male role model in her life, and it made her want to sing and dance around like a little girl.

He turned a page. "Are you wearing pearls like this?"

She shrugged. "Granny has a string that I want

326

to wear. And she might let me tie her mother's wedding ring into my bouquet for good luck. You'll have to find a shiny penny to put into my shoe for good luck."

"You want one from the year you were born or one from this year?" Seth asked without looking up from his notes. "Or should I get a real sixpence and then we could have it made into a necklace for you later? They quit issuing them more than thirty years ago, but I bet I can find one."

"Oh. My. Gosh!" she exclaimed. "You'd do that?"

Was this what it felt like to have a father or even a grandfather? If so, she hoped that Seth lived to be a hundred so that her children could grow up with him in their lives.

"It's not a big deal. The bank probably has a few." He smiled.

"I'd love a pence and a necklace," she said.

By noon he had a page full of notes and she had a headache. Could she really, truly let him do this for her? They ate and he excused himself by saying he was going to watch one of his movies. She had an hour and a half to work on her story or to go through the wedding book and make any changes to the plans. She raced upstairs and called Diana first to spill all the details.

"Well?" she said when she finished.

"Do you realize that you just went from a

hundred people, tops, to maybe a thousand?" Diana asked.

"I wanted to do my wedding on my own. Tell me what to do," Emmy Jo said.

"You don't argue with Mama Fate." Diana laughed. "It's exactly what you wanted and couldn't ever afford. A wedding with the whole town invited and a gorgeous place to have it. You have to do this. Don't you even think of turning him down. Besides, like he said, you've helped him come out of being a recluse."

"Now I'm getting jitters. I have to tell Granny," Emmy Jo said.

"Is this the sassy, brassy friend I've had my whole life? The one that wouldn't back down from a Texas rattlesnake?"

Emmy Jo smiled. "Granny is meaner than a snake, and I really want her to be at the wedding. But I'm not sure even the angels and Jesus could talk her into coming to Seth's house."

"She'll bitch and moan, but she wouldn't miss your wedding for the world. After all, you are breaking a curse," Diana said. "You have to call Logan. You think it's going to be hard to convince Tandy to go to Seth's place, think of how hard it'll be to talk Jesse into it."

"I've been so hung up on the Tandy issue, I hadn't even put that together. Holy crap!" Emmy Jo whispered.

"You got that right—since only God is going to

know how mad he gets when Logan tells him."

"Amen." Emmy Jo sighed.

She hit the "End" button and called Logan, talked even faster than she had with Diana, and then waited for his response.

"Great! That's another step toward the wedding. Oh, man, that means I have to tell my grandpa." He groaned loudly.

"I don't envy you that job at all. Make sure he's sittin' down, because his blood pressure is going to raise the roof," she said.

"I'll do it, but you could invite me to dinner on Sunday as a reward for doing a hard job."

"Yes," she said. "That would be great. Dinner is at noon, so sneak out of church a few minutes early."

"Are you serious?" Logan asked.

"I am very serious. If he's going to deal with the whole town, then one extra person for dumplings on Sunday shouldn't be a problem. Do you think you can get Jesse up to this house for our wedding? Or even your folks, for that matter?"

"Hey, if you can get Tandy there, then I'll do my part. There's always duct tape and rope if any of them get testy."

"Come on, Logan, get serious," she said. "I'm worried. It wouldn't be fair if your folks weren't here. I didn't even think of that when I agreed to this."

"All a wedding needs is a bride, a groom, and a preacher," he said. "And that's as serious as I can get, darlin'."

"I love you," she told him.

"That's what we take to the wedding—a whole heart full of love. I will see you Sunday."

"Lookin' forward to it," she said.

CHAPTER TWENTY-ONE

Logan had been in the garage once before, but he'd been too nervous to pay much attention to the vehicles. On Sunday he really got a look at them. He was careful not to drool on the old pickup truck or to leave fingerprints on the vintage convertible. He jumped away from the car when he heard a noise and turned to find what he'd thought was a storage door opening to an elevator. Emmy Jo stepped out looking like a picture in a pale-blue dress that hugged her tiny waist and skimmed her knees. He forgot all about the vehicles as he quickly crossed the garage floor to hug her.

"I was just lookin' at these vehicles and about to climb up the stairs. I didn't know there was an elevator," he said. "You are gorgeous."

"You clean up pretty good yourself." Her eyes started at the toes of his shined cowboy boots and traveled up starched and creased jeans to his plaid shirt. Then she rolled up on her toes and brushed a kiss across his lips. "Seth is waiting and dinner is on the table." She took his hand and led him into the elevator.

"And how did he take the news of me coming to dinner?"

"He didn't fire me or threaten to shoot you."

She grinned as she pushed the button to take them to the first floor.

He wasn't expecting Seth to be right in front of the doors when they slid open, but there he was, looking much taller than he did from a distance in the cemetery or sitting in the office. Logan stuck out a hand. "Thank you for inviting me to Sunday dinner."

Seth's shake was firm. "Emmy Jo has the food on the table. You can say grace."

Logan seated Emmy Jo first and then circled around the long table to sit at the only other place setting, which was directly across from her and to Seth's left. He bowed his head and said a quick grace.

"I like a short prayer," Seth said.

"I learned by example." Logan smiled.

"Jesse says short prayers?" Seth asked.

"No, sir. He prays forever. Being thankful doesn't have to mean letting a little boy starve plumb to death."

Seth laughed. "Example of what not to do."

Emmy Jo pushed back her chair. "I'll ladle out the dumplings, since this bowl is too hot to pass. Seth, will you hand Logan the basket of hot rolls? Save room for dessert. We have apple pie and ice cream."

"She's as fine a cook as she is an assistant," Seth said. "You are getting a good woman, Logan."

"Yes, sir, I am, and thank you for letting us have the wedding here."

"Jesse coming?" Seth asked.

"I hope so," Logan said. "We've asked him to do the service."

Not that I hold out a bit of hope. He can't even say Emmy Jo's name without having steam come out his ears.

Seth turned slightly toward Emmy Jo. "And Tandy?"

"I'm going to talk to her on Tuesday. I don't want to discuss this on the phone. She might not like it, but she'll be here," Emmy Jo said.

And I don't even want to be within hearing distance when that happens. She's got a shotgun and a temper.

The dinner table wasn't as uncomfortable as the tension in the parsonage when they all gathered around the table; still, Logan felt the need to fill in the quietness with conversation. Yet he drew a blank.

"Tell me about the banking business. You like it?" Seth asked.

"I do like it, but I have to admit that it's not exactly what I thought it would be. With my business degree, it's one of the things I could get into in this area. I don't want to live in a big city . . . I'm rambling," he said.

"No need to be nervous," Seth said. "Emmy Jo never was."

"I just bluffed my way through it." She grinned. "But I was nervous."

"She did some fine bluffing, then," Seth said. "What else would you like to get into?"

"I don't know. Maybe real estate someday or a mortgage company. I hear they do really well. I'm happy where I am and have no problem working there the rest of my life, but it's something to think about if we have a house full of kids who all are as smart as Emmy Jo and want to go to college," he answered.

"Well." Seth nodded slowly. "A man does need to think on those things."

"Logan, you never told me any of that," Emmy Jo said.

"It just came to me these last few days when this wedding started getting set in stone. I want us to have a big family." His eyes met hers across the table. "And I want them to be well provided for."

"I was thinking," Seth said, "that maybe Tuesday evening when you get off work you might come up here and the three of us will ride out to the farmhouse together. I'd like to see how the remodeling is coming along, and y'all could look at the place," Seth said. "Maybe we'll get the convertible out."

"I could be here soon as I get off work." Logan nodded, his eyes never leaving Emmy Jo's.

"I'd love it if just the three of us could go

the first time we see the house," she said.

There was something special in her smile and her eyes that day. He couldn't put his finger on it for a while, but finally he realized that it was newfound confidence. She had a grandfather, and it didn't matter to her if he was a recluse or if he came from a less than stellar background. He was hers, and she was proud of him.

Come on, Tandy, own up to it, and you, too, Seth! I love the look in her eye right now.

"Have I told you today that I love you?" She shifted positions until she was sitting in his lap with her head on his chest that Sunday afternoon in the cemetery. His heartbeat thumped in her ear, matching the speed of hers. Together, they'd overcome all the adversity. Love could conquer anything; she believed that with her whole heart.

"No, but then I'm not sure I've said the words today, either. Let's make a vow to never let a day go by that we don't tell each other."

She sighed. "I promise to always tell you. Even when I'm mad at you, I'll still love you."

"Me, too." Logan's lips met hers.

"What does he talk about when he's looking at his mother's grave for a whole hour?" Logan asked. "Why don't you ever go visit your grandmother Rose's grave, or even your mother's?"

"I did a couple of times when I was younger.

Granny would take me to her mother's and then to Rose's and Crystal's. I would stand there and look at the tombstones, read the writing on them and want so bad to feel something. Granny cried as she'd put flowers out, but I didn't. Sometimes I'd even look at the other tombstones just to see if any of them made me sad. Does that make me a bad person?"

"No, it does not." He hugged her even closer. "It makes you an honest person."

"Thank you, because I've felt guilty about that. And to answer your earlier question about what he's talking about, whatever it is, it's like therapy. If it was me, I'd tell her everything that happened that week, ask her advice on problems and maybe remember the good times I'd had with her before she died. Seth is a complicated man, though, so I have no idea what he's saying to her."

Logan kissed her on the tip of her nose. "It wasn't awkward at dinner like I thought it might be. He's a nice old guy."

"Yes, he is, letting us have the wedding there when he's been such a recluse all these years. I can't get over that he's suggesting giving us a house rent-free and me a job. Have you thought about any of that?" She wiggled backward so she could look at him.

"It's a really good opportunity. We can buy furniture if we don't have to pay rent," he said.

"And if we do go with the trailer?"

"We will buy a bed. And then we will save up to buy a table for the kitchen and a sofa for the living room."

She flashed a wide grin. "I'm thinking about one of those big recliners where I can snuggle up next to you while we watch movies in the evenings."

He wiggled his dark brows. "I had something else in mind to do in the recliner."

"Then we'd better buy a heavy-duty one."

Later that day Seth held two butterscotch milk shakes in his hands while Emmy Jo drove to the cabin. He handed them off to her while he maneuvered his way out of the car. It was slow going to the porch and his hip ached, but he made it without the walker, and that made him feel less like a cripple and more like a man. He settled into the rocking chair and she handed him the malt.

"It's really good," she said. "Still not as good as vanilla, but it's a close second."

He tasted and nodded. "Better than chocolate, but vanilla is still the best. On our birthdays, Mama made vanilla ice cream and whatever flavor cake we wanted. I always asked for lemon."

"But you like chocolate?" she asked. "We're having lemon cupcakes at the wedding and chocolate ones, so you can have both."

"Well, I will be sure to sample everything," he said. "And I always chose lemon because Matthew had a birthday the very next week. His favorite was chocolate. So I got both with that choice." He grinned.

"What did Nora want?" Emmy Jo leaned against a post.

"Blackberry cobbler, and the berries were usually pretty much available at the end of May, but just in case they weren't ready, Mama made sure to hold back a few jars from her cannin' to make Nora's cobbler. We had an old crank freezer, and Mama had to pay for an extra block of ice so we could have the ice cream."

Emmy Jo cocked her head to one side. "Block of ice?"

"We didn't have electricity. We had an icebox, not a refrigerator, so in the summertime we had to buy ice."

"Does it have electricity now?" Emmy Jo asked.

"Yes, I had it wired years ago. It's not air-conditioned, but I wanted a security system put in, and that required power. Today, we'll walk through it and make sure everything is in place." He dreaded the Sundays when he had to do that chore and was glad that Emmy Jo was there. Always, without fail, he visualized his mother lying in a pool of blood and the life ebbing out of her eyes.

"I worked on our story some more," she said. "It was as if I could feel Mary talking to me when I wrote about her."

"I like that," he said. "I had the feeling that Mama was talking to me when I broke up with Rachel."

"Who's Rachel? You never mentioned her. Was she the high school sweetheart?"

"No, she was the one that everyone thought ditched me a week before the wedding. The lady from Amarillo that I told you about. By the time the house was built, the wedding was off. People assumed that she broke it off with me because she found out that my mother put a red light on the porch post. I didn't tell them any different."

"Why did the wedding get called off?" Emmy Jo asked.

"Bottom line is that we wanted different things. She was the one who wanted the big house, and she didn't want to get married until it was finished. So I had it built. Mama told me that I was doing it for the wrong reasons." Seth could well remember arguing with himself about the mansion. "Did you ever hear a song called 'The Old, Old House' by George Jones?"

"No, but I can call it up." She whipped her phone out and poked a few buttons and cocked her head to one side as she listened to it. When the song ended, she put the phone back in her pocket. "But that says that her love withered, and you are telling me that yours did."

"True." Seth nodded. "I was in love with the idea of being in love. She was in love with the idea of having a place in society. It all withered when we finally had a big fight about children. I wanted enough to fill the big house. I could hear little boys arguing and little girls giggling. I could visualize them sliding down the banister and me putting a swing set up in the backyard. I was thirty years old and I wanted to get started right away on the family."

"And she didn't?" Emmy Jo asked.

"One week before the wedding, she told me that she was never having children. She didn't like kids and they would ruin her body. That ended it right there." Seth paused. "So she threw the engagement ring at me and stormed out. She went back to Amarillo, and the next year she married a man who was in some kind of high-powered corporation that sent him all over the world on business trips. They're both dead now, but I hope she was happy."

"Why didn't you sell the house? That's a lot of room for one person."

He sighed and went on. "When a person dies, their memory lives on. It's not Rachel that I'm thinking about in the fall when I kick the dead leaves out of the way. It's Mama. That's when I tell her she was right. That having the biggest house in Hickory, and setting it on a hill, does not bring a man peace or happiness. I live there to remind myself of that."

"What are you going to do with it when you die?" she asked.

A wide grin split his face. "You are one blunt piece of work."

"That's old news. What's on the front page today?" she joked.

"I'm considering a few options. One is that while I'm gone on the cruise, I have this place remodeled. It could be like one of those tiny houses I read about in the newspaper. The room where all three of us kids slept could be my bedroom and office. The other one could be a combination living room and kitchen like it is now. But I'd have Mama's bed taken out and some comfortable chairs and a television put in," he said.

Emmy Jo whipped around so quickly that it made her dizzy. "You'd move from the big house to this?"

"Depends on how I feel when I go through that door today," he said. "It's an option, and at my age, I don't need to prove anything to any-one."

"What about the big house?" What about it? He'd been thinking some, but as usual, seeing Emmy Jo seemed to put his thoughts into shape.

"More options. I'm thinking about donating it

to charity. Maybe to a place that would turn it into an unwed mothers' home. There would be counselors and nurses to help run the place," he said.

Tears welled up in Emmy Jo's blue eyes. "That is so sweet and so beautiful, Seth."

"It's all ideas right now. You ready to go look inside?" he asked.

She nodded and popped up from a sitting position so fast that he was instantly jealous. To be young and agile again instead of old and fragile. He punched in the right buttons to get into the house and disabled the alarm system. With Emmy Jo right beside him, he waited for the horrible vision of his mother dying right there beside the kitchen table to appear, but it didn't.

Seeing this place through her eyes put a whole new spin on the place. She turned around a dozen times, taking in every single thing. "It's so cozy. I can see a little galley kitchen right here and a nice big comfortable sofa with recliners on the end where the bed is located. And you will need to have a bathroom installed. Make sure it's got a walk-in shower. We don't want you slipping and falling and breaking your other hip." She stopped to suck in air. "And you could have a dog walk out this back door to a garage where your cars could go."

She chattered on as they went to the bedroom

next; instead of sorrow, he felt pure joy at really being home.

"Oh. My. Goodness. This room is huge. Take out these twin beds and you'd have a lovely office and bedroom combo." She went to the window facing the back. "Seth, there is a deer. Look, it's right there by the trees."

"The place butts up to a wildlife refuge. There is a barbed-wire fence beyond those trees about twenty yards. The deer probably hopped over the fence to get a drink from the little creek between my place and the refuge."

She waved her arms. "Knock out this little bitty window and put in sliding doors with a patio out here. Maybe not as big as the one at home, but a place where you could read your papers and watch the animals."

"Good ideas, every one of them." He turned around in the doorway, expecting to see his mother dying again. But the picture that flashed through his head was of the family sitting around the table as she read a story from the Bible to them on Sunday morning.

Emmy Jo looped her arm in his. "I feel peace in this place."

"So do I," Seth said.

CHAPTER TWENTY-TWO

"Good mornin', Granny!" Emmy Jo waved from the front of Libby's Café. "Did you order the special for us?"

Tandy smiled and waved back with a nod. It could easily be the last time that Emmy Jo would see that sweet smile for a long time, so she stopped, shut her eyes, and memorized it. She sat down across the booth from her grandmother, and in seconds, Libby brought out two huge plates of food and an extra one piled high with pancakes.

"So what did you think of the cupcakes?" Tandy asked. "Are we making them for the wedding?"

"Yes, the caterer is going to use your recipes for all of them."

"Caterer?" Tandy rolled her eyes and fluttered a hand. "La-di-da!"

"I want you to be there with me and enjoy the day, not cook for days before and be frazzled at the reception. The wedding is going to be held at Seth's house with the ceremony outside on the huge driveway. The reception will be in the garage, but the rest of the house will be open with tables set up." Emmy Jo reached for the saltshaker.

Tandy slapped her hand. "Stop right there."

"I can't have salt?"

"No, if you want me at the wedding, then it's not going to be out at that house," Tandy answered. "What has gotten into you, girl?"

"Seth is my friend, and I've asked him to walk me down the aisle," Emmy Jo said. "And it's time for you to tell me the truth, Granny. Is Seth my biological great-grandfather? If not, who is? I know it's not Jesse because of the blood types."

From the look in Tandy's eyes, Emmy Jo half expected to see smoke coming from her ears. The steps for resuscitation went through her mind as she salted her scrambled eggs. "I've tried everything short of coming right out and asking, but it's time you told me, Granny. I'm not judging you. I just want to know."

Tandy put her hands together and clapped. "Well, ain't you the smarty-pants, figuring that out all by yourself? Now you see why I'm not going up to that house."

Emmy Jo leaned across the table. "You have to go. If you don't, then everyone is going to figure out the secret that you have kept for all these years. His old eyes still light up when he talks about you, you know. What he said to you about you not being as good as his mama, that's why you've hated him all these years. And you've hated Jesse because he ran away and wouldn't marry you. People won't get all of that, but they'll

345

start to put things together," she whispered.

"Maybe at my age I don't give a shit if everyone knows," she said.

"Good, then when Seth gives me away, I'll have him say, 'Her grandmother and grandfather, who is me.'"

"You wouldn't dare!" Tandy said.

"Who cares at this late date, Granny?"

"You aren't upset that you are kin to a man whose mother whored for a living?" Tandy seethed.

"No, ma'am. I kind of like Mary." Emmy Jo went back to eating.

"You never even met her." Tandy stabbed her fork in Emmy Jo's direction.

"Seth told me about her and now I understand why . . ." She paused. "Now I realize why her spirit called to me. I'm her great-great-granddaughter, and I needed to hear her story. I know it's crazy, but sometimes I think of all she had to endure because of the way the town treated her. It's like I'm feeling what she did."

"I'll think about coming to the wedding," Tandy said.

Emmy Jo could have jumped up on the table and done a tap dance to celebrate things going even that smoothly. Next week, she'd spring the idea of working for Seth permanently on her granny. Baby steps. One tiny little bit forward at a time.

• • •

Emmy Jo went right to Seth's house after she'd had breakfast with Tandy, marched out to the patio, and picked up a newspaper. How on earth did she begin the conversation, and how was Seth going to react?

She stole glances at him as she read and tried to see some of his features in the pictures she'd seen of Rose or Crystal, but nothing came through. Then she remembered the picture of his grandmother on the mantel. Yes, that's who Rose looked like.

"You talked to Tandy, didn't you?" Seth said from behind the newspaper.

"Why didn't you tell me when you found out?" she asked.

Seth folded the paper and laid it in his lap. "Wasn't my place. Tandy needed to be the one. Is she mad?"

"Not so much. She still don't like you," Emmy Jo answered.

"Feelin's mutual, because we could have had sixty good years together by now, but I'm workin' on it," he said.

Emmy Jo laid her paper to the side, amazed that knowing the big secret hadn't changed things so very much after all.

"So are you mad at me?"

"Why should I be? You thought Rose belonged to Jesse. He's the one I'm mad at for not doing right by Granny, and yet, if he had, he would have been raising your daughter. It's true that we weave tangled webs when we tell lies, isn't it? Only you didn't lie and you didn't know about Rose, so it's not your fault."

He folded his newspaper and put it aside. "That means we still get to have the wedding here? I'm going to need my assistant to oversee a lot of remodeling on my little house while I'm on the cruise. It'll be a full-time job doing that and getting this place in order to host unwed mothers. Lots of paperwork, lots of decisions."

Emmy Jo inhaled deeply and let it out very slowly. "I don't know if I'll ever feel like you are my grandfather, Seth, but I will always know you are my friend. Maybe it is because of your mother and what we both feel when we think of her, or maybe we are just both full of the same spit and vinegar," Emmy Jo said. "It's a relief to understand why things are the way they are. I doubt much will change where my granny and Jesse are concerned, but miracles do happen."

"Amen," he said. "I kind of like knowing that I'm not going to leave this world with no one behind to miss me. Knowing that you are my granddaughter, well, it . . . I can't explain how I feel."

Emmy Jo laid a hand on his arm, and the warmth went all the way to the depths of his soul. "I know you would have, because you loved her."

"Yes, I did," Seth said. "Now what do we do?"

"We have snacks and this evening we have supper with Logan. And even before we go see the farmhouse, I'm saying yes to your offer for the job. I'll call the health care agency tomorrow and give them notice."

"Hot damn!" Seth grinned. "I guess blood is thicker than water."

Emmy Jo felt kinship to the farmhouse the second that she and Logan followed Seth inside that evening. She tried to take it all in with a first glance. This was where Seth's father, Samuel, had grown up. *How would his life have been different if he hadn't thrown that rock at those horses in a fit of anger?* As they went from room to room on the ground floor, she thought of things she should add to the story that she was writing.

"I love this house," she said as she and Logan climbed the stairs. "It's huge by trailer standards, but it's still cozy."

"Three bedrooms and a bathroom. Got to limit it to two kids," Logan teased.

She wrapped her arms around his waist and laid her head on his shoulder. "Oh, no! Girls in this room. Boys in that one. And no yelling about the bathroom in the mornings. With two sets of bunk beds in each room, I'm figuring eight would be the limit."

He kissed the top of her head. "So we're

really doing this? I still can't believe that the big mystery of why our grandparents all hate one another has been solved."

"I love Seth. Please tell me that I'm not taking advantage," she whispered.

"He offered and you thought about it for a long time. I'm sure he doesn't feel like you are using him, darlin'," Logan drawled. "Do you realize we are standing in our bedroom, right in the middle of where our bed will be?" Logan wrapped his arms around Emmy Jo's waist and drew her to him. "And when we get home from the honeymoon, we will sleep in this bed for the next fifty years." His arms tightened around her. "In this room, but most likely not in the same bed. I'm planning on wearing out at least half a dozen beds in that length of time."

A soft giggle escaped her lips. "Now that's the most romantic thing you've said in a long time." She took a step back. "We'd better go back downstairs before we start trying out this pretend bed."

"I don't mind a few splinters on my butt if you don't." He grinned.

"Oh, darlin'," she whispered, "it's been so long that this floor would seem like a feather bed right now."

With Logan's arm around her shoulders, they walked slowly down the staircase to the living room where her grandfather waited.

CHAPTER TWENTY-THREE

Logan stopped on the porch of his grandfather's house and said a silent prayer. He rang the doorbell and immediately felt heavy footsteps as Jesse crossed the hardwood floor. The door opened, and Jesse frowned. "Why did you make me get up out of my chair? The door's never locked in the daytime. You know that. What do you want, anyway?"

"Let's sit on the porch," Logan said.

"No, thank you. Last night I was out there and got bit twice by mosquitoes. You got something to say, then come on in here where it's nice and cool."

"Okay, then." Logan opened the screen door and followed Jesse.

He'd spent lots of nights in the spare bedroom when his grandmother was living, and there were good memories there. Two bedrooms, living room, kitchen, and a tiny little study where Jesse could prepare his sermons when he was asked to be a guest speaker. Jesse went back to his recliner and pulled the lever on the side to prop up his feet. As always, he was dressed in dark slacks and a white shirt open at the neck, but it would take only a few seconds to put on a conservative tie if he was needed at a hospital or had to go over to the church to perform a quick marriage. No one could ever say that Jesse Grady wasn't ready for anything that popped up.

At least not until that day, Logan thought as he sat down on the end of the sofa and wished he knew exactly how best to start the conversation. "Gramps, I've got something to tell you. It's not easy for me to say, and it sure won't be easy for you to hear, since you've carried around this weight on your shoulders for most of your life."

"Spit it out, Logan," Jesse said.

"Rose was not your daughter. Emmy Jo and I have figured out this whole thing between you and Seth and Tandy. You've punished yourself all these years. You weren't the person who got Tandy pregnant," Logan said.

Jesse sucked in a lungful of air and let it out slowly. His old eyes narrowed, and Logan could almost feel the heat of his anger filling the room. "She said I was the father and that we'd go to college together. Why would she lie?"

"I don't think she did. She wanted you to be the father, so she convinced herself that you were. Was the fact that Emmy Jo and I might be distantly related the reason that you've been so against this marriage?"

Jesse shook his head. "No. I don't like that girl. She comes from bad blood."

"Get over it, Gramps," Logan said. "Or you'll

stand before God with a nasty spirit that won't get through the pearly gates."

If looks could kill, Logan would have stopped breathing on the spot.

"Do you believe that she really thought I was the father?"

"Yes, she did, but after you deserted her, she must've decided that she didn't want anything to do with you," Logan said.

"But who?" Jesse whispered.

"Seth Thomas," Logan answered.

Jesse's hands knotted into fists, and he pounded the arms of his recliner. "That man has ruined my life since we weren't anything but kids."

"You want to tell me about what else went wrong between you? More than the fact that you were both having a teenage fling with Tandy?" Logan asked.

Jesse clammed up, his mouth a firm line and his jaws working like he was chewing gum.

"You were the popular kid and Seth was the outcast. What happened between y'all?"

"I'm not talking about it," Jesse said through clenched teeth. "I hate that man and I'll never forgive him for the misery he has caused me."

"Do you think he'll forgive you?"

"For what?" Jesse turned a cold glare on Logan.

"Whatever you did to start this problem between y'all. I was like Seth in high school, remember? Kids picked on me all through elementary and junior high because I was a preacher's kid. Then Jack and I became friends the summer before high school and he took up for me. So what did you do?"

"I stated the obvious. His mother was a whore, and I said as much in class one day."

Logan sighed. "Seth was the one who beat you up and knocked you out of playing football, wasn't he? It wasn't a gang at all, but one boy who was taking up for his mother."

"And he's been destroying my life ever since," Jesse said.

"From where I stand, it looks to me like you're both guilty. You started that fight and got what you deserved for it. Then you were the reason that Tandy wouldn't marry him, since you were the better catch. Then you had to carry the burden of guilt for not doing the right thing," Logan said. "You do realize that it's time for this to end, don't you?"

Jesse shook his head. "It'll end when I'm dead."

"Okay, then have it your way. What about my and Emmy Jo's wedding?" Logan asked.

"Before I didn't want you to marry her because she might be distant kin. Now I'm against it even more because she has Seth Thomas's blood in her veins. Go away," Jesse said. "Just get up and walk out of here and know this—I'll never forgive Seth."

"Then I doubt if God will have much compassion on you when you get to Judgment Day. Have a great day, Gramps. I'm going out to Seth's house for supper this evening. The wedding is going to be at his place. Dad will perform the ceremony if you are too stubborn, but if you change your mind, just show up wearing a purple tie and you can do it for us," Logan said and then began to walk out of the house. "One more thing." He stopped and glanced back. "Seth has given us the old farmhouse that his dad lost in a poker game to your father. We will live in it as part of Emmy Jo's new job as his permanent assistant. We'd love for you to visit us."

"Get out of my sight," Jesse seethed.

Diana propped the picture of her and Emmy Jo in their wedding dresses up on the dashboard of her car for them to look at while they drove home that afternoon. "We're going to get you back before dark, but it was sure nice of Seth to tell you to take all the time you needed."

"I got a text from Logan while you were in the dressing room taking off that gorgeous ball gown back there. He and Seth already had supper, and they are playing checkers. Logan talked to Jesse today," Emmy Jo said.

"And?"

"It did not go well. I feel sorry for him, Diana. Seth loved my granny so much that he was willing to marry her, but she wanted Jesse, and he ran away to the navy to get out of marrying her. What a mess. Let's stop at that burger place in Graham and get something to eat before we go home."

"I'm still in total shock about all that." Diana caught the next right and drove right to the place. "No wonder they've hated one another all these years. I still think Tandy will come to the wedding, but if Jesse shows up, I'll probably faint."

Emmy Jo shook her finger at Diana. "You better not! You are my bridesmaid, and you have to keep me standing up straight that day."

Diana flashed a lopsided grin. "With your sass, you'll be bossing everyone around. I also can't believe I get to go inside that big house today and meet Seth Thomas."

Emmy Jo sighed. "I wish those three could see that the past isn't as important as the future."

Diana laid a hand on her shoulder. "Don't press your luck."

They made it home by eight o'clock to find Seth, Logan, and Jack deep into a poker game. Seth looked up and grinned when the ladies stepped off the elevator. "Did y'all have any luck?"

"We did. Seth, I want you to meet my friend Diana," Emmy Jo said. "And Diana, this is Seth, the man I've been talking about all month." She crossed the room and dropped a kiss on Logan's forehead. "And this is the man who'd better not be losing at poker."

"Oh, he's not. He's won a dollar and twenty-nine cents," Seth said. "He's way ahead of me and Jack here."

"Okay, then. Is it okay if I give Diana a tour of the place and tell her all about what we're doing for the wedding?" Emmy Jo asked.

"It's your house as much as mine until we turn it over to the charity fund, so go do whatever you like and let us finish this hand," Seth said.

When they were upstairs in Emmy Jo's bedroom, Diana let out the giggle that she'd been holding in. "Is that really the mean old recluse that we've all been scared of?"

"Oh, yes, but the old coot is a great-grandfather now. I've heard that having a child or a grandchild changes people," Emmy Jo said.

"I hope he lives long enough to see your kids. He's never had a little kid in the house. You came to him full grown," Diana said. "Wonder how he'd be around little kids?"

"Who knows? A month ago I wouldn't have thought he'd even smile or be nice. Miracles do happen." Emmy Jo flopped down on the bed.

"And you think if one can happen here, then it just might wake Tandy and Jesse up."

"One can only hope," Emmy Jo said. "Now let's go down to the garage and bring my dress up here so we can stare at it until they finish playing cards."

Chapter Twenty-Four

*E*mmy Jo should be able to attend church with her grandmother on Mother's Day, right? Seth checked his reflection in the mirror. He hadn't worn it in twenty years, but the suit still fit and his boots were shined. He'd even gone to his favorite barber in Graham and gotten a haircut the day before. It was the first time he and Tandy would be in the same building since they went to school together. He'd seen her from his office window on Main Street a few times, but to actually be in the same place—it was a scary thought. But he wanted to see her, especially now that they shared a great-granddaughter.

But now he was having second thoughts about going with her that morning. He hadn't been inside a church house since he was sixteen, the week that the ladies thought it best if his mama didn't come to their place of worship any-more.

Lightning isn't going to strike you dead. His mama's soft voice was inside his head again. *Times are changing and you might be an old dog, but you are still kicking. Square up those shoulders and walk in like you are used to entering through those doors every Sunday morning.*

"First sign of a dark cloud and I'm outta there," he said seriously.

He fidgeted the whole way to the church and really wanted to tell Emmy Jo that he'd changed his mind. He could sit in the car and wait for her, maybe listen to the radio to pass the hour or even take a little walk around the parking lot to exercise the hip. But she was just so darned excited about the day that he couldn't do it.

"I've got a table reserved for all five of us at Libby's soon as church is over, and then we'll go to the cemetery and to the old house. I want to go through it again with you and talk about the changes. And Libby does make dumplings on Sunday, but most people like her chicken and dressing special better." She hopped from one subject to the other. "I'm so excited that you are coming to church with me, Seth. You'll never know what it means."

"Are you absolutely sure that Tandy left her shotgun at home?" Seth asked.

"Yes, I am. She can't get it in her purse."

Seth opened the car door. "Okay, then let's go hear some hellfire and damnation."

The clouds didn't part. No great, booming voice welcomed him into the building. But then lightning didn't shoot out of the clear-blue summer sky and strike him dead right there inside the doors, either. Tandy did give him a go-to-hell look, but he'd expected much worse.

He settled in at the end of the pew, the old codger trailing along with the young folks. At least Emmy Jo was sitting beside him, and that brought comfort. They sang a couple of congregational hymns, and sure enough, the preacher talked about a few of the mothers. Seth listened for a few minutes; then his mind wandered as he checked out the old building.

The windows needed replacing, and the air-conditioning was barely keeping up with the crowd that morning. It would really have trouble in July and August. The piano was out of tune, and the choir robes were shabby. He would add a little upkeep to the place to his bucket list when he got home that evening—if no one said a word about his mother or his attending services that morning. If anybody did, then he might throw a stick of dynamite up under the foundation and blow the whole thing to smithereens.

Seth William Thomas. His mother's voice was back. *Don't even think thoughts like that. You've found a long-lost great-granddaughter, which means you are not dying without anyone to remember you. Rejoice in that and stop thinking about dynamite.*

"And now we will sing 'The Lilac Bouquet' in closing," the preacher said.

Every word in the old hymn came straight from heaven that morning as Seth sang along with the rest of the congregation. If he'd been a songwriter, he could have penned every one of those lyrics and dedicated them to Mary Thomas. When she died he'd found a faded blue ribbon in her Bible, a leftover from one he'd gotten from Nora on Mother's Day to wrap around a bouquet of lilacs he'd picked from the bush in the yard. And he'd sure enough found tearstains on the pages, no doubt from wishing that she had the privilege of sitting in church like he'd done that morning. At the end of the song, the words said that someday he would pick his mother another lilac bouquet from the Garden of Eden.

But before he died, he had a bucket list that he needed to fulfill. And today he was adding to it, rather than crossing something off. When the hymn finished, he followed the young folks toward the back, where everyone shook hands with the preacher as they filed out.

"Mr. Thomas, we are so glad you could join us. We'd be honored to have you here every Sunday," the preacher said as he pumped Seth's hand up and down. "Please come back and make this your home church."

"Thank you," Seth said, surprised at his own seriousness.

They were outside in the bright sunshine when Emmy Jo turned around and waved. "Granny! Happy Mother's Day!" She let go of Logan's hand and ran back to greet her grandmother.

Leaning on the front fender of the car, Seth watched Emmy Jo hug Tandy and tug at her hand to lead her toward the car. Although she was gray haired now, Tandy's eyes still flickered with excitement—and anger when she saw Seth. She stopped thirty feet away and shook her head. Emmy Jo said something to her and set her pretty mouth firmly in a tight line. Seth recognized that gesture and grinned.

It must have been the smile, because Tandy tilted her chin up, locked gazes with him, and marched straight to the car. He couldn't run, not yet, and he wasn't sure he wanted to. He'd known the time would come when they'd face off again, but he hadn't expected it to be in the middle of the church parking lot.

"Tandy." He nodded when she was three feet away.

"Seth," she said curtly.

"I'm taking these kids to Libby's for Sunday dinner. Would you like to join us?"

"Hell, no!" Tandy said.

He chuckled. "You'd best fluff up that gray hair. Bad time for your horns to be showing, right after that sermon about good mothers."

"Your hair is as gray as mine, so I'd say that's the pot callin' the kettle black," she snapped.

"After all these years, you are still afraid to be seen in public with me, aren't you?" Seth wanted to reach out and brush a hand down her cheek, but he was afraid he'd come back with nothing but a bloody nub.

"I'm not afraid of the devil and you should know that, but then maybe your memory is failing."

The grin on his face widened. "I have the memory of an elephant. I can recall every word you ever said."

"Granny, I wanted to give you this for Mother's Day and to tell you that I love you." Emmy Jo handed Tandy a small velvet box. "I'm hoping that you will wear it to my wedding."

Tandy flipped the lid open to reveal a lovely gold brooch that looked like a tiny bunch of lilacs tied with a ribbon encrusted with sparkling crystals. Her face softened, and her eyes glimmered with tears. "It's so pretty, Emmy Jo. I love it."

Emmy Jo tiptoed and kissed her on the cheek. "Thank you for being such a good mother. Won't you please join us for dinner? It would mean a lot to me."

Tandy looked over Emmy Jo's shoulder and met Seth's gaze again. He could read her mind just like he could more than sixty years ago.

It was hard for him to deny Emmy Jo anything and even more difficult to keep from trying to spoil her rotten. Seth had only known about her being his grandchild for a little while; he couldn't imagine having had her in his life for more than twenty years.

"It's Mother's Day, Emmy Jo," he said, but his eyes didn't leave Tandy's. "Drive me home and she'll go with you. You should spend this day with her."

"I'm not afraid of you or to sit at the same table with you, Seth Thomas. Emmy Jo, you can ride with me so we can visit, and Logan, you can drive Seth to the diner." Tandy issued orders before she looped her arm in Emmy Jo's and turned her back on Seth.

"Well, that went well," Logan whispered.

"I'm still breathing, so I guess it did," Seth said. "Lord, that woman has always been able to push my buttons. That's one of the reasons I stayed on my hill and away from Hickory after I retired. I flat out didn't want to run into her."

"You mean," Logan opened the door for Seth, "that you haven't seen her in twenty years?"

"I mean I've managed to avoid her for more than sixty years," Seth said. "I might have seen her walking down the street or even caught a glimpse of her once a year as I drove to work or home, but I have not spoken to Tandy since the night my mother died."

"But that's crazy in a town as small as Hickory," Logan said.

"Yep!" Seth fastened his seat belt and shut the car door.

Dinner could have been awkward, but bless his heart, Seth tried to fix things when he pointed to the chairs. "Why don't you sit right there with Emmy Jo beside you, Tandy, and Logan can sit beside her? I'll take this seat and Jack can sit beside me with Diana across from Tandy. That'll put you lovely ladies together and us old ugly guys down on the other end."

"Don't you bark orders to me," Tandy said.

"Tandy, darlin', would you please sit right here beside Emmy Jo?" Seth grinned.

"Don't call me *darlin',* either." She glared.

"Okay, then, sweet—"

"Hush! If you call me that in front of these kids, I'll kill you with the sugar bowl."

"What?" Emmy Jo asked. Were Tandy and Seth flirting or fighting? It was hard to tell.

"Nothing that you need to know." Tandy sat down in the chair where Seth had told her to sit in the beginning. "More than sixty years of raisin' kids should get me a seat at the head of the table."

The bell above the door jingled, and Emmy Jo glanced up to see Wyatt, Paula, and Jesse entering Libby's. Jesse's expression left no doubt that he'd rather be eating his Sunday dinner in a pigsty as in the same café with them. Emmy Jo wanted to slap the meanness out of him and had to remind herself that he was a bitter old man.

"Excuse me, darlin'." Logan pushed his chair back. "I want to say happy Mother's Day to Mama." He went to the table where his family was sitting, kissed his mother on the cheek, and talked to them for a few minutes before he returned. "I'm having Mother's Day with them tonight. Mama wants to go to the Dairy Queen for banana splits before Sunday night services at the church," he said. "She's of the opinion that nothing is fattening on Mother's Day."

"Smart woman," Tandy said. "Are they staying in Hickory?"

"Yes, they are," Logan said.

"I have an idea for after we have dinner," Seth announced to the whole table. "Why don't you take me home, Logan? Jack and Diana can follow us and pick you up there, and Emmy Jo can ride with Tandy out to the farmhouse. That way y'all can show it to your friends and to Tandy."

"What about the cemetery?" Emmy Jo asked.

"We'll go after Tandy drops you off at the house. I've got a bouquet of real lilacs to go on her grave today, since this is Mother's Day. Do you realize that the anniversary of her death is coming up real soon? She was born a hundred years ago this fall."

"We'll have to do something special that day," Emmy Jo said.

"I always put fresh lilacs on her grave on this

day and her birthday." Seth smiled. "It's a ritual that I won't stop as long as I'm alive."

"And one I'll keep up after you are gone," Emmy Jo said seriously.

Tandy shot one of her sideways looks toward Emmy Jo.

"Hey, I'm her great-great-granddaughter, so don't give me that evil eye," Emmy Jo said.

"I swear, she looks like Nora and acts like you, Tandy," Seth said. "And Emmy Jo, thank you for doing that for me. It brings an old great-grandpa comfort to know that you will take care of things. Here comes our waitress. I'm having the chicken and dressing special."

The baby steps were turning into giant steps where Seth was concerned, but the way Jesse kept shooting dirty looks their way said that his feet were firmly glued to the ground.

Diana disappeared into the kitchen for a little while to wish Libby a happy day and returned with two plates of fried green tomatoes and three kinds of dipping sauce on each. She set one on each end of the table along with smaller plates for individual servings. "Mama says that this is on the house. She knows how much Tandy and Seth both love her fried green tomatoes."

"Well, thank you, Diana," Tandy said as she loaded her small plate and spooned out the white sauce on the side. "I do love these. My mother

367

made them every spring when we were growing up."

"So did my mother," Seth said as he did the same. "We could hardly wait for the tomatoes to get big enough to slice so my mama could fry up a bunch for us. That and when we busted the first watermelon of the season were big days for us."

"Or when the new potatoes got big enough to dig a few to go in a pot of fresh green beans with some salt pork to season them. Add a pan of corn bread and we had a meal," Tandy said. "Kids these days don't know anything about gardening."

They're talking! It might not be about anything but food, but neither of them is acting like Jesse. I bet his heart is so hard that a jackhammer couldn't break it up.

Logan parked the car in the garage and rode the elevator up to the first floor with Seth. Emmy Jo had given him orders to see that Seth was settled in front of a movie or else in his chaise lounge on the patio with his stack of Sunday papers before he left him alone. Logan would have done that without being told, because he could see that Seth's stamina was wearing thin before they even left the café. It had been a big day for the old guy.

"I'm going to watch that Sackett DVD while I wait on Emmy Jo," he said when he stepped out of the elevator. "And Logan, I'm so glad that y'all are going to live in the farmhouse. That means the world to me."

Logan clamped a hand on Seth's shoulder. "Thank you for everything."

Seth waved him away. "Get on out of here and go enjoy showing it to your friends and Tandy. She's just as bossy and sassy as ever, isn't she?"

A soft chuckle escaped from Logan's chest. "That's where Emmy Jo gets it, I'm sure. Her sass from Tandy and her intelligence from you."

"She got that from my sister, Nora, which reminds me . . . I need to call her and invite her to the wedding. And maybe fill her in on a few things. I'll do that while y'all take a look at the house with Tandy. You don't think Emmy Jo will mind, do you?"

"The more the merrier," Logan told him. "And I'd love to meet the rest of your family."

Seth pushed the "Play" button, and Logan slipped out of the room. He took the stairs rather than the elevator and hopped into his truck, where Jack and Diana waited.

Tandy and Emmy Jo were in the house when they arrived. Jack and Logan went through it quickly, then sat on the steps while the ladies moved through each room discussing details. A touch of jealousy shot through Logan as he listened to Emmy Jo, Diana, and Tandy talking about the place. Seth's name kept coming up every other sentence, and Tandy wasn't even cussing when it did. He wished that they could talk about Jesse like that, too.

"I am not going to grow up and be like Gramps," he muttered.

"Me neither," Jack said.

"Your grandpa died before you were born," Logan said.

"That's right. I'm not going to die young. I want to be married to Diana for a long, long time and sit on a porch like this one and watch my great-grandkids chase fireflies on a spring night. And I don't never want a bunch of secrets between me and them," Jack said seriously.

"We'll make it happen, won't we?"

Jack smiled. "Damn straight we will, partner."

Chapter Twenty-Five

"Happy wedding day," Seth called out from behind her bedroom door that morning.

The past weeks had gone by in a blur. There were wedding plans from daylight to dark every single day, seeing Logan, Jack, and Diana when they got off work, and talking to her grandmother at night before Emmy Jo went to sleep. Tandy had agreed to come to the wedding as long as no one expected her to talk to either Seth or Jesse. And yes, she would be there for the whole morning to help Emmy Jo get dressed.

She and Diana both sat straight up in bed. Emmy Jo squealed when she saw that the sun was shining. She bounded out of bed, swung the door open, and hugged Seth.

"Oma Lynn sent breakfast." He rolled a cart into the room. "She says you aren't to come down until it's time for me to walk you out to the wedding, because Jack and Logan are already here and us guys will be dressing in the office. If you want to see the final touches, take a peek out the bedrooms on the other side of the hallway."

"Tandy?" Emmy Jo asked.

"Not here yet, but—"

Tandy yelled from the hallway. "Yes, I am, and thank God for that elevator. I was dreading hauling all my stuff up here by the stairs."

"I'll leave you ladies alone. Oma Lynn figured Tandy might be joining you, so she sent plenty." Seth took two steps back and let Tandy bring her things into the room. "I'll leave the door open. Anyone else that tries to get up here will have to go through Oma Lynn."

"I'm so glad you are here, Granny. You'll never know what it means to me." Emmy Jo beamed.

"This is a helluva house. Lord, one man living here seems like such a waste," Tandy fussed. "Oh, cranberry orange muffins. And coffee. I didn't take time for breakfast. Let's eat first, and then Diana can start on your makeup and hair."

Emmy Jo picked up a piece of bacon with her fingers. "You've got to try this. Oma Lynn makes a paste of brown sugar and Jack Daniel's whiskey, paints it on the bacon, and cooks it real slow until it's crispy. It's amazing. Seth and I call it bacon candy."

Tandy added a piece to her saucer and tasted it. "Now that's the way to use whiskey. I've got to remember to ask her for the recipe. How are you doing your hair, Emmy Jo?"

"I'm fixin' Diana's first. We've got three hours, so we don't have to hurry. And Granny, Seth is only going to live in this place a few more months," Emmy Jo said. "When his cabin in town is ready for him, he's turning this into a place for unwed mothers. If they decide to give the baby up for adoption, the counselors will work with a reputable agency to place the baby in a good home. If they decide to keep it, then they will help them find a job and a good day care and get on their feet."

"You mean that little shack he grew up in? He's moving from this back into that?" The wrinkles in Tandy's forehead deepened when she frowned.

"Well, it won't look so much like a shack when the remodeling is done. The location is beautiful and there's going to be a lot of changes, but yes, he is moving into it this fall," Emmy Jo answered. "I can't believe it's finally my wedding day. And tonight we'll be in a hotel in Galveston and tomorrow we'll be on a cruise ship. And we don't have to drive any farther than Dallas this afternoon. Our plane departs at three."

"You know my dreams are coming true today, too." Tandy wiped a tear from her cheek.

Emmy Jo kissed her granny on the tearstain. "I know, and that makes it double special. I just wish Jesse would be here and that his absence doesn't make Logan sad."

"He's always been a stubborn brat," Tandy said. "Now hand me another piece of bacon and then let's get started. Lord, that dress is beautiful." She pointed to the wedding dress hanging on a hook on the back of the door. "And I expect that bossy bitch that's running this show will be up here soon to tell you what to do and think and when to put the dress on, right?"

"You got it!" Diana giggled. "It takes a bossy hussy to make something this big go together without a hitch. I wish I could afford her for my wedding."

"Honey, you got the bossiest women in the state of Texas working for you when you got me and your mama," Tandy told her.

Emmy Jo raised her hand. "And don't forget me. I'll be in on everything, too."

"It's a beautiful day for a wedding. Not too hot and no rain," Wyatt said as he joined Logan, Seth, and Jack in the office. "You have a beautiful place for this event, Seth. Thank you for hosting it for these kids. Logan has told us about the past problems, and I want you to know that—" He stopped midsentence and stuck out his hand.

Seth shook hands with him, then shrugged. "That's over and done with. Let sleepin' dogs alone and all that. Havin' the wedding here seemed like the right thing to do. It's a big place and there'll be lots of people here, I hope."

"They are already filling up the chairs. I expect many will end up standing. The pasture is full of cars, and the two valets are transporting folks as fast as they can," Wyatt said.

"It will be the only wedding probably ever held

here," Logan said and glanced over at Seth, who gave him a nod.

"Oh?" Wyatt asked.

"Seth is turning the place into a home for unwed mothers this fall or winter, depending on when his little house gets remodeled. The business part is already in the works," Logan said.

"That is very generous of you. If you need a counselor at any time, I've had some training and experience in that line," Wyatt said.

"Jesse?" Seth said.

"My dad and I don't always agree on things. The offer stands if you ever need me," Wyatt said.

"Thank you." Seth nodded.

A big smile deepening the wrinkles on Nora's face, she crossed the floor and hugged Seth. "Admit it. I gave you the best birthday present ever."

"Okay, you gave me a great present," he said softly. "Thank you for that."

"Does that mean you won't get even?" She stepped back and looked up into his face.

"It does not," he laughed. "Have you seen Emmy Jo?"

"Oh, yes, and she's breathtaking. How are you holdin' up, Logan?" Nora turned her attention away from Seth.

"I've waited for this day. I've prayed for it to go well, and now it's here and my prayers have been answered. So why am I as jittery as a sugared-up kid?" Logan asked.

"Because this is the biggest day of your life to this moment. There will be bigger days, like the day your firstborn is laid in your arms, but right now this is the best day of your life, like that song says. So enjoy it and don't be nervous." Wyatt hugged his son. "And know that your mother and I are very proud of you."

"Thanks, Dad."

The wedding planner knocked and then stuck her head in the door. "Time to put on your boutonnières. Everyone needs to be seated." She glanced at Nora.

"I'll see you there, Seth." Nora straightened his tie and kissed him on the cheek. "This is a glorious day."

The wedding planner stood to one side to let her pass. "Now, I need you at the elevator in exactly fifteen minutes. We are seating the mother and grandmother right now. Then you will slowly go to the front and stand under the archway, just like we practiced last night. And by the way, that was a lovely rehearsal dinner, Mr. Grady, and thank you again for inviting me."

She deftly pinned each of the men with a small lilac-and-baby's breath boutonnière and stood them side by side to be sure that they were all perfect. "Ten minutes. Meet me at the elevator doors. All but you, Mr. Thomas. You will wait at the foot of the stairs for Emmy Jo."

"Yes, ma'am." His drawl seemed even deeper than before.

Following the planner's orders, Emmy Jo looped her arm in Seth's and stepped into the elevator. There was only room for the two of them, so the planner said that she would take the stairs.

"You are the most gorgeous thing I've ever laid eyes on. I'm glad for this little time we have alone," Seth said. "I want you to know that I'm glad we are friends, and—"

She squeezed his arm. "I know, but we are more than friends. We're kinfolks and I love you."

"I love you, too, and I expect every week that passes, I will love you more. I might not have gotten the privilege of raising you or Rose or Crystal, but that doesn't mean I can't enjoy all the time we have left."

"Amen," she said as the doors opened.

Diana was standing there in a lovely lilac dress, her bouquet in her hands. "Seth, you look so handsome," she said.

"And you are beautiful," Seth said.

"Thank you," Diana said. "But this is Emmy Jo's day, and she is stunning."

Seth straightened his back, and pure joy swept over his face. "Yes, ma'am, she surely is."

The wedding planner put a lilac bouquet in

377

Emmy Jo's hand and motioned for Diana to follow her. "There's the music, right on time. Go, darlin', walk just like I told you to last night."

"It's time," Seth said. "Got any last words for a stubborn old man?"

"No, except that I love you, Poppa. That word fits you better than Grandpa or Gramps to me," she said.

"Sweetest words in the whole world," he said as he slowly crossed the floor with her toward the open garage door.

They were halfway down the long aisle, walking on a gorgeous pale-lilac carpet that had been laid out for her, when Seth hesitated for a split second. "I'll be damned."

"What?" Emmy Jo asked.

Everything had gone so perfectly well all day that she could hardly believe something could go wrong this late in the wedding. Everything looked like it came out of a fairy tale. The place was crowded with people standing with smiles on their faces as she and Seth made their way down the aisle, so why had he paused?

Emmy Jo looked down the aisle to see the bright sun reflected off the bald head of the preacher standing below the fresh lilacs hanging on the archway. She blinked twice and then a third time, but Jesse Grady didn't disappear. She glanced over to the right and there was Logan, grinning like he'd just won the lottery. Wyatt was standing beside Jack with an equally big smile on his face.

"Darlin' granddaughter, I believe that you could part the clouds with your sass and determination," Seth whispered.

"Not really. That old coot just doesn't intend to let you get ahead of him," she said out the corner of her mouth.

When they were in place, Jesse made a motion for the crowd to sit and opened his Bible. "Dearly beloved, we are here today to join together my grandson, Logan Grady, and his lovely bride, Emmy Jo Massey. Who gives this bride to be married to this man?"

Seth bent and kissed Emmy Jo on the cheek. "Her great-grandmother and I do." Then he put her hand in Logan's. "Son, you'd better treat her right, or you'll face the wrath of me and Tandy Massey combined."

A few giggles lightened the mood, and Jesse, wearing a deep-purple tie, went on with the ceremony. Emmy Jo handed off her bouquet to Diana and took each of Logan's hands in hers to say her vows. Jesse finally pronounced them man and wife and told Logan he could kiss the bride. She was expecting a sweet little kiss, but he bent her backward in true Hollywood fashion. Everyone in the place whooped and clapped when the long, passionate kiss ended.

"And now, darlin', no one will ever doubt

that the Massey curse has been erased," Logan whispered as he scooped her up into his arms and carried her down the aisle and into the reception hall.

The kids had left in a limo that would take them from Hickory to the Dallas airport. They would be in a five-star hotel in only a few hours, and the next morning they would begin their honeymoon cruise. All the guests had left, and the wedding planner was barking orders to the folks about getting things cleaned up when Seth headed toward the balcony. Two and a half months ago he'd been reading his morning papers when Emmy Jo showed up in those hideous red scrubs, and from that moment his life had been turned upside down.

"But that's what kids do when they come into a person's life, whether they arrive as babies, teenagers, or full-grown adults," he muttered as he sat down in his favorite lounge chair.

"And that is?" Tandy asked from the shadows, where she was having a beer.

"They make you see things different," Seth said.

"Oh, I didn't know you were here," Jesse said at the doorway. "I came to see the view one more time, but I'll leave."

"Might as well come on out here and join us," Seth said.

Jesse leaned on the doorjamb as if he couldn't make up his mind what to do.

"Jesse, how many of the graduating class of 1953 are still living? You got any idea?" Seth asked.

"No, but I do know the only three left still living in Hickory are me, you, and Tandy," he answered gruffly. "I came today and did my duty, but I'm not stayin' any longer."

"While we are alive, we have time to do the things we want, whether it's as simple as enjoying the wedding of our grandchildren or something bigger. Both of y'all have a seat. Tandy, kick off your shoes, and Jesse, take off your tie. I lost mine a while ago." Seth pointed to extra chaise lounge chairs.

Jesse unfastened the top button on his shirt, removed his tie, and tucked it into his pocket. "It was a nice wedding, but I have no desire to sit here and talk to either of you." He disappeared through the doors back into the house.

"Well, that's his loss if he can't forgive and forget. The wedding really was everything and more that Emmy Jo ever dreamed of," Tandy said.

"Those two kids have their heads on straight. They will be fine." Seth nodded.

Tandy sighed. "You are right. I want to apologize to you, Seth, for saying ugly things about your mother and for not marrying you."

"You were the only woman I ever truly loved, and I wanted to marry you so badly that my heart ached. I'm glad that we can talk to each other now. I've missed having you in my life. Tell me, Tandy, have you ever been on a round-the-world cruise?"

EPILOGUE

The first Sunday in October

Twilight was setting in when the big black limousine drove down Main Street in Hickory. Seth gave directions, and the man finally maneuvered the vehicle onto a side street and parked in the circular driveway in front of a newly remodeled house.

Tandy laid a hand on Seth's arm before he slid across the seat. "Thank you for all this. I can't begin to repay you . . ."

Seth covered her hand with his. "I should be thanking you. Having a friend on this trip made it amazing."

"We had such a good time. I hate that we missed all those years together," Tandy said.

"All goes to show that miracles do happen. Why don't you come over to dinner after church next Sunday? I'll have Oma Lynn make up some chicken and dumplin's for us."

"Poppa and Granny!" Emmy Jo squealed as she and Logan ran from the porch.

"Kids." Seth grinned as he hurried out of the backseat and opened his arms to the two.

"Welcome home! We know y'all are tired, but we wanted to see you for a few minutes. We'll talk tomorrow at dinner to celebrate your new house. Oma Lynn says she won't abide anyone being late." Emmy Jo left Seth to slide into the limo and wrap her arms around Tandy.

"That would be great," Tandy said. "I'll bring all the pictures of the cruise. It was amazing. But now back out of here and let Logan have a turn," Tandy said.

Emmy Jo looped her arm into Seth's and walked with him to the front porch. "I finished our story while you were gone. And you'll never believe it, but Logan's folks invited us to Sunday dinner. And Jesse was pretty nice. And I put fresh lilacs on your mama's grave for her hundredth birthday. We'll go to the cemetery tomorrow and you can see them."

Seth patted her hand. "Thank you for taking care of that for me. And there's hope for Jesse as long as he's got breath, but it's up to him what he does with it. He's missin' out on two great kids if he doesn't shape up. About the story, I'm glad that you did, but I don't even want to read it, Emmy Jo. You do whatever you want with it after I'm dead. Keep it for your kids or delete it, but I don't want anything done with it while I'm still alive. I've let go of the past, and I'm living for today and the future with my family. It's a wonderful new life."

Tears welled up in Emmy Jo's eyes and ran down her cheeks. "That makes me so happy. But

I'm glad you told me the story, because it's my past, too. And it's what brought . . ."

He pulled a clean white hankie from his pocket and gently wiped her eyes. "I know, darlin' girl. Would you look at this cabin," he added, changing the subject. "It hardly looks like the same place. You sent pictures over the phone, but it's so much better seeing it now. It's hard to believe you got it all done in time for me to come home to after the cruise. We can't hardly call it a cabin anymore, can we?"

"We've been calling it Seth's place," she said.

"I like that a lot." He paused and then chuckled. "But I still hate red."

She giggled through the tears. "And I'll never like orange."

"So some things never change." He smiled.

"Thank goodness. See you tomorrow." She hugged him one more time.

The limo driver brought his luggage to the porch of Seth's new place.

New life. New future. New family. New friend.

Seth Thomas had come home, and it felt right.

"Hey, Tandy," he called out across the yard before opening the door to go inside. "You ever been to the Grand Ole Opry? I hear it's something to behold at the holidays."

ᴀCKNOWLEDGMENTS

Dear readers,

Many, many years ago when Mr. B. and I were first married and he was going to college, we didn't have money for entertainment, so we started telling each other a story. It all started with an old country song called "The Son of Hickory Holler's Tramp" by Merle Haggard and evolved from there. When we took short trips to visit my parents for the weekends or long road trips to see his parents in the summertime, we added to the story.

I started writing it down on paper when our third child was born and would not sleep at night. In those days all I had was a spiral notebook and a few sharpened pencils. When Mr. B. found an old Underwood typewriter at a garage sale and bought it for five dollars, I was ecstatic.

Seth was a young man in that original edition, but the manuscript had too many problems to ever make it to market, so it got put away for twenty years. I dragged it out again when he was a middle-aged man, and it still had too many problems to be published. Now more than forty years after that first draft, Seth is past eighty years old and the time is right. I hope *The Lilac Bouquet* touches your emotions so much that you fall in love with him and with Emmy Jo.

As always, there are so many people who helped take this book from that story that Mr. B and I talked about all those years ago to the book you hold in your hand. Big Texas-size hugs to the whole team at Montlake Romance for all their hard work. Special thanks to my editor, Anh Schluep, for continuing to believe in me, and to Krista Stroever, my developmental editor, for all her hard work in helping me turn this from a forty-year-old idea into finished work. Thanks to my agent, Erin Niumata, and my agency, Folio Management, for everything you do. Y'all are all amazing!

Thanks to Mr. B, the man I've been married to for half a century. He's my support system and my best friend, as well as the guy who listened to me talk about this story for all those years. And thanks again for buying me that first typewriter . . . which is still sitting in my closet.

What would an author be without readers? I'll answer that. We'd be at the top of the endangered species list, a place I would never want to be for sure. So thank you to each and every one of you who buy my books, talk about them, and consider them as possibilities for your book clubs. And a special thanks to the ones who leave reviews!

Happy reading,

Carolyn Brown

ABOUT THE AUTHOR

Carolyn Brown is a *New York Times, USA Today*, and *Wall Street Journal* bestselling author and a RITA finalist. *The Lilac Bouquet* is her eighty-fourth published book. Her books include romantic women's fiction, historical romance, contemporary romance, cowboy romance, and country music mass-market paperbacks. She and her husband live in the small town of Davis, Oklahoma, where everyone knows what everyone else is doing—and reads the local newspaper on Wednesdays to see who got caught. They have three grown children and enough grandchildren to keep them young. When she's not writing, Carolyn likes to sit in her gorgeous backyard with her two cats, Chester Fat Boy and Boots Randolph Terminator Outlaw, and watch them protect their territory from all kinds of wicked varmints like crickets, locusts, and spiders. Visit her online at www.carolynbrownbooks.com.

Books are produced in the United States using U.S.-based materials	Books are printed using a revolutionary new process called THINKtech™ that lowers energy usage by 70% and increases overall quality	Books are durable and flexible because of smythe-sewing	Paper is sourced using environmentally responsible foresting methods and the paper is acid-free

Center Point Large Print
600 Brooks Road / PO Box 1
Thorndike, ME 04986-0001 USA

(207) 568-3717

US & Canada:
1 800 929-9108
www.centerpointlargeprint.com